A DEATH AT THE ROOKERY

This book is dedicated to the Galveston Island Nature Tourism Council staff, members, and suporters.

A DEATH AT THE ROOKERY

PAT JAKOBI

Copyright © 2025 by Pat Jakobi
All rights reserved. No part of this book may be reproduced in any manner whatsoever without written permission except in the case of brief quotations embodied in critical articles and reviews.
First Printing, 2025

CONTENTS

Dedication ii

1 Monday 1
2 Tuesday 14
3 Wednesday 37
4 Thursday Morning 61
5 Thursday Afternoon 78
6 Friday 97
7 Saturday 120
8 Sunday 144
9 The Second Monday 171
10 The Second Tuesday & Wednesday Morning 201
11 Two Weeks Later 218

Acknowledgments 224

CHAPTER 1

Monday

Evelyn Baldwin used the back of her hand to wipe the perspiration from her forehead. She remembered the old saying, "It's not the heat, it's the humidity," but she blamed both the heat and the humidity for the damp sheen on her exposed skin. Not that much of her skin was exposed. She wished she could have dressed lighter. Shorts and sleeveless top would have been nice, but the swarm of mosquitoes, only barely kept at a distance by copious amounts of insect repellent, made trousers and long-sleeved shirts mandatory.

It was mid-June, nesting birds at the rookery were still active, but the Texas summer weather kept many visitors away. She had promised the trip a few months back to her friend Trudi Olson, but what with one thing and another they had set the excursion back a couple of times. They now found themselves on a path winding through a forest of oaks and volunteer shrubs, heading towards an island rookery located in the middle of an old dredge pond. It was Evelyn's favorite bird-watching site. The woman at the ticket booth near the parking area had given them a map showing some newly constructed observation platforms, and Evelyn was eager to scout them out after they visited her usual spots.

"What is that smell?" Trudi asked as she followed Evelyn up the path.

"Ammonia," Evelyn answered. "There have been hundreds, maybe thousands, of birds here. You can imagine how much defecation has gone on over that time."

"And those honking, croaking sounds? Certainly, they can't all be bullfrogs."

Evelyn laughed. "The rookery birds are not known for their lilting calls. The raspy squawks are probably egrets, the grunts most likely spoonbills, but there are certainly a fair share of bullfrogs and other amphibians."

"Do you think we'll see alligators?" Trudi asked with some excitement.

"There's a good chance we may see a few. They serve as a safety patrol against predators who would otherwise dine on birds nesting on the island rookery and their eggs. Some of the alligators are huge, eight or nine feet long. I imagine that they eat well on eggs that roll out of the nests and careless birds that wander too close to the shore. Not to mention fish, frogs, snakes, and nutria." She thought to herself that she knew the standard spiel so well that she could apply for a job as a tour guide.

"I know that alligators have to eat," Trudi said with a small shudder, trying to disregard the image that her mind kept conjuring up. "But the idea of eating a beautiful bird is rather upsetting."

The footpath ended at a wooden staircase that took them up to yet another path that followed the periphery of the pond. As they stood at the top of the stairs, Trudi looked around and gasped. "Oh, my heavens!" she said. "This is so wonderful!" An egret glided by not far from where she stood, and she followed its flight until it landed at a nest on the island located in the middle of the pond. "I know you told me I would be amazed, but I never pictured so many birds. And they fly by so close."

Evelyn looked around. She could see a couple of people further along on the path, but that was all. For some reason, the birds seemed more uneasy than usual. A few egrets were circling above the island, landing, and then taking off again. As she had anticipated, there weren't many visitors at the rookery now that the weather had become so hot and muggy. She led Trudi to a small platform that had been constructed between the path and a steep drop-off to the pond some eight or ten feet below. They stood at the railing, silently taking in the activity before them. There were still a few nests with birds roosting, indicating that not all eggs had yet hatched. Most of the nests, however, looked like they had chicks in them and both parents were busy feeding their young.

"Use your binoculars for an even better view," Evelyn said. "There are a few baby spoonbills in the nest over on your far right. They're in their pink powder puff stage, not yet fledged. I think we can get a better look if we go a little farther along. There are at least a half-dozen viewing platforms all along this path, and there are some new ones that have been built since I was last here. We might be able to find a better spot that will not only give us a view of the spoonbill nest but also the entire end of the island."

They walked carefully along the path, avoiding encroaching branches and plants. Evelyn thought how vegetation would narrow the walkway even more over the next couple of months. The path around the large pond and its island would be increasingly less hospitable to visitors as the year went on. And then, sometime near the beginning of the new year, members of the Egret Bay Bird Society, owners of the rookery and much of the woods surrounding it, would once again clear the path for the next year's viewing.

She stopped suddenly and put her arm out to make sure Trudi stopped as well. She pointed to a spot about ten feet in front of them where a dark-colored snake was slithering across the path, traveling from the pond on their left to the trees and brush on their right.

"Oh my," Trudi exclaimed. "Is that a water moccasin?"

"I don't think so," Evelyn said. "I think it's just a common water snake, but I'm not going to get closer to find out."

They waited until the snake disappeared into the brush and then carefully walked forward, making sure the snake didn't decide to turn around and come back.

"This is quite a wild place, isn't it?" Trudi said. "I guess I had not thought of it being so, well, natural, given that it's only about twenty miles from Egret Bay."

"Yes, it's very wild in spite of all the visitors," Evelyn said, putting on her tour guide persona again. "I imagine the woods here are full of squirrel, opossum, raccoon, and other small animals hiding in the brush and wishing we would go away."

They had reached her favorite viewing area. There was a bench on a platform that jutted a few feet over the drop-off to the pond below. The entire platform was surrounded by a waist-high wooden railing. They sat and watched birds as they flew back and forth to and from their nests. There were still a few birds circling over the island and Evelyn wondered what was bothering them. She pointed out the different species to Trudi as they flew by. "Great Egret, Snowy Egret, cormorant–probably a Neotropic, but not sure–Cattle Egret, Roseate Spoonbill." She explained to Trudi that the tall wooden structures on the island with small platforms on the top had been constructed as nesting platforms after the last hurricane tore up many of the island's trees. The manmade platforms were now covered with new nests. A male spoonbill still in breeding plumage flew by flashing his electric orange tail feathers.

"Oh, look, Trudi," Evelyn said, pointing toward a small open area on the island, surrounded by bushes and short plants. "There's one of your alligators. It's basking in the sun over there, next to...." She stopped talking and stared at the island.

"Next to where?" Trudi asked.

Evelyn lifted her binoculars and focused on the area around the alligator.

"Next to what looks like a khaki shirt."

"But what's a shirt doing there?" Trudi asked.

They both stood up and adjusted their binoculars. Evelyn moved to the corner of the platform to get a better view. She then put her binoculars down and turned to look at Trudi. "What does it look like to you?"

"It's hard to tell at this distance," Trudi said, "but whatever it is it's bobbing up and down in the water. And the alligator is just lying quietly in the sand next to it."

"It could just be an old waterlogged cardboard box. They are about that color. Or maybe a backpack," Evelyn said. "If it were just a shirt, it wouldn't keep its shape like that. I wish I could get a better look, but the bushes over there are in the way. Maybe if we go back where we were, we can get a better view."

They retraced the path back to the first observation platform. Once there, Evelyn raised her binoculars again. "I still can't figure it out. My concern is that it may be a person."

"Oh," Trudi exclaimed with a rapid intake of breath. "You don't think that the alligators...." She couldn't finish the sentence.

"No, Trudi, I don't think so. It's probably nothing. Probably just something that's remained snagged there for days and no one wanted to disturb the nesting birds by removing it. Nevertheless, I think I'll go talk to the lady in the ticket booth and see if anyone else has reported this. Why don't you sit here and wait, and I'll be right back."

"That sounds like a good idea. I'll keep watch," Trudi replied. She held up her cellphone. "I'll call you if anything changes."

Evelyn returned about ten minutes later with the woman from the ticket booth and two bottles of water that she had gotten from their car. "I'm Doris Gibson," the woman said to Trudi. "I see you both have binoculars, but I brought mine in case you didn't." Evelyn pointed towards the area where the alligator was basking. Doris nodded and said, "Yeah, it's a little tricky getting a good view from these old viewing platforms. The shrubbery has grown enough to block a clear view. I think we can get a better angle from one of the new platforms farther down the way. If you'll follow me, we'll take a look. It's probably just something that blew into the water. We get that all the time—hats, vests carelessly slung on the railing when it gets hot—but never hurts to check."

Doris continued to talk as they retraced their steps back past the stairs they had come up on and continued on a path that Evelyn had not been on before. "When it's this hot, the alligators are mostly nocturnal, spending their days like the big guy you saw down there," Doris told them. "Their mating season is coming to an end, so they don't provoke as easily as they do in the spring, and they certainly don't want for food. There's plenty for them in the water and around the island. I wouldn't be super concerned about whatever you saw over there."

When they reached the new platform, Evelyn had to admit that it was a major improvement over the older ones. There were three tiers. The one at the bottom ended at a sturdy railing just before the drop-off to the pond. It was built three stair steps down from the second tier and was obviously designed for photographers, including those with tripods. Anyone standing at the bottom tier would probably not be in the way of those seated on the middle tier. The top tier included an open area large enough for two wheelchairs.

"How do people in wheelchairs get up here?" Evelyn asked.

"You came up the old stairs," Doris answered. "There is another path farther on that leads to a newly constructed ramp."

Doris stepped down to the bottom tier. "We should be able to get a good view from here." She lifted her binoculars and, with a few quick adjustments, focused on the area of interest.

"Can you see it?" Evelyn asked.

Doris didn't immediately answer. She just let her binoculars down gently. "I think," she said, "that I need to call our manager." The other two women stood there, looking at her. "Here, if you want to, you can take a look. My binocs are a bit stronger than yours," she said as she handed her binoculars to Evelyn and then reached for her phone.

Evelyn lifted the binoculars and looked at the island. "Wow, these are sure sharp," she said. She searched along the shore of the island, passing over the area where the alligator was and then coming back to that site. There was no doubt. What they had seen was not just a shirt, but a khaki-clad body. The person was lying next to the alligator on his stomach, headfirst, with his feet and calves in the water. It was the bobbing of his legs that had initially caught their attention.

"Oh, my God. Trudi, do you want to look?"

Trudi shook her head, "No, thank you."

Trudi and Evelyn stood there, not knowing what to do or say while Doris placed her call. After a few "yes" and "no" responses, Doris said, "I'm on platform five and you can see it clearly from here." Then a pause, and "No, it looks intact." At that, Trudi abruptly sat down. Evelyn paused and then sat down beside her.

"Not again," Trudi said with some dismay.

Evelyn didn't know whether to console her friend or try and make a weak joke out of the fact that this was the second time in just over a year that Trudi had been present when a body was found. The last time, at the Egret Bay Art League's gallery, Trudi had been alone when she found a dead man on the gallery's mezzanine. And now this.

She decided to go with consolation.

"Just pure bad luck, Trudi. Someone would have discovered this, and it just happened to be us. Or me, actually. And it's probably good that it was me–us–because some other person might have just shrugged the whole thing off as a piece of debris."

Doris interrupted them when she finished her phone call. "Lainey, the rookery manager, is going to call 911 and have them send an ambulance just in case that person on the island is alive and in need of assistance. It will take them about twenty minutes to get out here. She also called the sheriff and asked to have someone from his office come out here to tell us what to do next in case the individual there is…," she hesitated, "…deceased."

Her phone buzzed again. "Yes," they heard her say. "Thanks." She turned to the other women. "They are sending a couple of deputies who happen to be on the road relatively close to us. They should be here shortly. She's pretty sure whoever comes will want to talk to the two of you. If it's too uncomfortable to stay up here, given the heat and the mosquitoes and all, you're welcome to wait down in the ticket booth where it's cooler. I can take you down there since I need to be at the ticket office to direct the deputies up here. I doubt they've been here before."

"How will the ambulance get over there?" Evelyn asked.

"There's another entrance off of the county maintenance yard for vehicles that need to get to the back of the pond," Doris said.

"Why don't you go down to the ticket booth, Doris, and we will stay up here and wait," Evelyn said. "That way we'll be here in case anyone wants to talk to us or if someone else sees the man on the island and wants to know what's going on." She looked at Trudi. "Do you want to stay here, or would you rather go down to the booth?"

"I'd like to stay with you, if you don't mind."

"No, of course I don't mind. I'd like you to," Evelyn said with a smile.

"Well, that seems like a good plan," Doris said. "I'll get down there right now."

The two women sat on the bench as they waited. They tried to avoid looking in the direction of the body on the island, but it was difficult to keep their gaze away from it.

"I wish that it had turned out that someone just took off their shirt because of the heat and it fell into the water," Trudi said. "How would a person get out there to the island?"

"Well, I suppose it's possible that he climbed over the railing and fell in the water, or that he strayed off the path to get a better view and lost his footing," Evelyn replied.

"And we really don't know if he's dead, do we?"

"No, we don't. But he's not moving."

"Maybe he's staying still because of the alligator," Trudi said. "But how will they get to him, what with the alligators and all? They can't swim over there."

"Oh, heavens, no. I'm assuming they have a boat or boats. I mean, people must go over there all the time. There are those nesting platforms, for example. People had to go over there to build them, take the lumber and supplies over, and all that kind of thing."

Just then they heard voices near the stairs coming up to the path. Doris was in the lead, followed by a man and a woman in khaki uniforms. The man was carrying a pair of binoculars and the woman had a small camera on a strap hanging around her neck.

"These are the ladies who notified me of the possibility of a body on the island," Doris said. "Ladies—I'm sorry, but I guess I forgot your names—these two are from the sheriff's office."

The male nodded at the two women. "I'm Deputy Sheriff Doug Fraser and that is Deputy Sheriff Dana Jefferson," pointing to the woman accompanying him. He then stepped down to the bottom tier of the platform, swatting at the mosquitoes. "Now, let's have a look." He raised his binoculars. After a minute or so, he said, "Well, if it's not a mannequin, it's definitely a body. How does anyone get over there to take a closer look? And can the ambulance get over there?"

"There is a road that goes around to the back," Doris said. "The rookery's manager–her name is Lainey Gomez–probably gave them directions when she called. She is on the way to meet them there."

"How will they get over to the island where the body is?" Deputy Jefferson asked, waving her arms about to deter mosquitoes from landing.

"We keep a boat and other equipment on the other side of the island," Doris said. "Lainey can bring them around here if they don't know how to use the boat." She reached in her pocket and brought out a couple of packages of bug spray tissue. "You'll need these if you're going to be staying around the pond." The deputies quickly unwrapped the tissues and began rubbing them on their faces, necks, ears, and hands.

There was a buzz and Doris reached in her pocket for her phone, checking a message. "Lainey's almost to the back gate. She'll open it to let the ambulance in. She says she can hear sirens in the distance." She turned to the two deputies. "You can get over there by taking this path. It goes all the way around the pond. Otherwise, you have to go back to the parking lot, exit to the street, and then drive around to the other road. This will be much quicker. Just continue along this footpath until you see a boathouse. Lainey should be waiting for you. I'll stay here with the ladies until I receive instructions to do otherwise."

"Give me your cell number," Deputy Fraser said to Doris. "We'll call when we get there if we have questions." He jotted the number down in a small notebook and then the two deputies hurried off down the path.

"What about the ticket booth?" Evelyn asked Doris.

"I posted a sign that says to go ahead with your visit and then stop and pay on exit. I haven't seen anyone come up so far, but I don't want them lingering down there waiting for me."

"I don't mind staying as long as I can be of help," Trudi said, "but I really have to use the restroom. I think I saw one near the ticket booth."

"Do you want one of us to go with you?" Doris asked.

"No, that's fine. Thanks."

Evelyn pulled out her car keys and handed them to Trudi. "While you're down there, bring up a couple more bottles of water." She turned to Doris and asked if she wanted a bottle.

"No thanks, I'm a firm believer in the Boy Scout motto and always go prepared." She turned so that Evelyn could see the clear water container attached to her belt. "I always carry water and a nutrition bar, just in case I get stuck away from the booth."

Trudi returned shortly, bringing four bottles of water. "Just in case," she said. It was another ten minutes before they saw a small metal boat with four passengers appear round the edge of the island. "Looks like Lainey, the two deputies, and what I assume is an EMT from the ambulance are in the boat," Doris said, tracking them with her binoculars. Trudi and Evelyn watched as the woman in the back of the boat skillfully maneuvered the craft until it was within about fifteen feet of where the man and the alligator were located. She lifted a pair of binoculars from her neck and handed them to the EMT. Deputy Jefferson began taking photos. The three women standing on the viewing platform could see the two men with binoculars move their glasses from side to side, staring at whatever they were seeing on the left and then on the right. Gomez then had a short conversation with the others on board before moving the boat a little closer to the scene. They then repeated the binocular examination and the EMT handed the binoculars he had been using back to Gomez. She raised them and took a look and then picked up her phone. A couple of seconds later, Doris's phone buzzed.

"What?" Doris said. "Are you sure? Well, that explains a lot. What next? OK."

Doris turned to Evelyn and Trudi. "The man is almost certainly dead. The alligator, however, is also dead," she said. "Or unconscious. Lainey says that both the man's head and the alligator's head are swarming with flies, and neither is making any effort to fend them off. The clothing on the deceased is all wet and covered with lots of mud and sand. The EMT has called the medical examiner's office for him to come out and bring a crime scene inspector with him." She paused to respond to a second call, said "OK," and disconnected.

"That was Deputy Fraser. He asked that I get your names and phone numbers and any other contact information for both of you. Then you can leave. Someone will be in touch later if they need more from you."

After writing down the two women's phone numbers and email addresses, Doris thanked them both for reporting what they had seen.

"Are you going back to the ticket booth?" Evelyn asked Doris.

"No, I'll stay here for now. We don't seem to be overrun by visitors, and my shift will be over in a little while."

With one more quick look at the activity at the island rookery, the two women started back to the parking lot.

"I'm so sorry," Evelyn said. "I wanted this to be a fun day for both of us and an introduction to a prime birding spot."

"That's fine," Trudi replied. "We can come back some other time."

"Next year."

"Yes, let's say next year."

"For now," Evelyn said, "let's hope that our names are not connected with this. We are, after all, simply bystanders. I don't know about you, but I'm too much on edge to go directly home. Can we stop someplace and get something to eat, or just get an iced tea and talk, so we can unwind a little?"

"That sounds lovely," Trudi said.

"In fact," Evelyn said, "I have an even better idea. You have to go back to my place to get your car, so why don't we go there and put a lunch together with whatever I have at hand. I'll make some iced tea, and then we can talk all we want without any concern of anyone hearing us."

"That sounds even lovelier," Trudi said.

Evelyn pulled a bag with a couple of bagels out of an old-fashioned breadbox on her kitchen counter. "I don't have lox, but I do have cream cheese and I can slice a couple of strawberries to sweeten it up a little." She set a tub of cream cheese and a box half full of strawberries on the counter. "Why don't you slice some strawberries, and I'll toast the bagels and pour some tea. I have some in the fridge that I made yesterday."

Ten minutes later they were sitting at the kitchen table, helping themselves to generous scoops of cream cheese for their bagels. "I am so happy you suggested this," Trudi said. "Why don't we limit our conversation to the food until we finish, and then we can have any conversation we want."

When they had finished their bagels, Evelyn brought two chocolate chip cookies and laid them on the empty bagel plate. "Dessert," she said. "A serious conversation always calls for dessert."

"Well, I'm going to open the conversation because I have a question," Trudi said as she reached for a cookie. "Do you think that poor man fell into the water from one of the viewing platforms? There was no boat that I could see. But the platforms look so sturdy, even the old ones. How could that happen?"

"I don't know," Evelyn said. "I suppose he could have been doing something foolish and fallen in the water. It would be very difficult to climb back up the embankment by the platforms. It's not very high, but it's very steep and there is not much vegetation to grab onto to help you climb."

"And the alligator. What's with the alligator? Did it die of natural causes? I don't suppose it's easy to kill an alligator."

"Well, the situation is weird enough. I doubt it just up and died. That's too much of a coincidence. I wonder if someone shot it. I don't know how you kill an alligator, but I don't imagine it's easy."

"Who would shoot it?" Trudi asked.

"A poacher maybe, although Doris–that's her name, right? Doris–didn't say anything about hearing shots and she must have been there from the time it opened at 7:00."

"Well, we don't know when either the man or the alligator died," Trudi said. "It could have been last night or early this morning, before the rookery opened. Aliens from space, maybe, collecting specimens. I know I shouldn't make fun of it all, but it somehow makes the whole thing less threatening."

"I forgive you," Evelyn said with a smile. "I suppose anything is possible. Heaven knows. When we saw the alligator, it just looked like it was basking, enjoying the morning sun. Nothing unusual. We both thought it was alive, and we were concerned about that, at least I was and I assume you were, because of its proximity to the man, afraid it may have hurt him somehow."

"I suppose there will be more information in the paper tomorrow after the medical examiner has a look. I remember from my previous encounter at the art gallery that they can't move the body until the examiner has confirmed the person is deceased."

"I've always liked alligators," Evelyn said. "They are so magnificently prehistoric."

"I must admit that it was exciting to see one," Trudi said. "I have never seen an alligator before, and then when I finally do, it turns out that it's dead."

CHAPTER 2

Tuesday

It was just after eight the next morning when Evelyn poured herself a cup of coffee and set it on the table next to the local paper. The story about the events that had taken place at the rookery the previous day were on the front page, but it had been pushed to the bottom, "below the fold," Evelyn remembered from her high school journalism class, by a story announcing the discovery of a rat infestation at the city's conference center. Rats, snakes, alligators–she had never encountered so many potentially threatening animals in such a short period of time. She wanted to call Trudi, but thought she'd read the article on the rookery first. Maybe the authorities knew who the dead person was by now. She wondered how they had managed to get him off the island. And what would they do with the alligator?

She was relieved to find out that she and Trudi were referred to as "two visiting birdwatchers." Apparently, the sheriff's office hadn't released their names. That was good. There were no details about how the body was transferred from the island to wherever they took bodies. Nor was there anything about cause of death, outside of being declared "suspicious." Of course it was suspicious. No matter how he died, there was absolutely no reason for a person to be on an island in the middle of a pond patrolled by alligators. Ah, she thought, as she read on. They know who he is, but they're not saying. "Name withheld until notification of next of kin."

The photograph of the rookery that accompanied the article was not the newspaper's best. Their photographers were pretty good, but it was difficult to make out what the picture in the paper was actually trying to portray. The photographer had stood at one of the lookout sites and taken a picture of the island. Mostly it showed trees and the man-made nesting platforms. The bird-built roosts were difficult to make out among all the foliage and the pink beauty of the spoonbills did not show up in the black and white photo. A photo of an alligator would have gotten more attention. She realized that newsprint was not the best type of paper to use for complex photographs. It dawned on her then that she couldn't remember a mention of the alligator in the article. She skimmed back over it. Nope, no alligator. Strange.

Just then, her phone rang. She guessed correctly that it was Trudi.

"I know you've been up long enough to read the paper," Trudi said. "Thank heavens they left our names out of the article."

"I was thinking the same thing. I wonder if anyone will get in touch with us. We really aren't involved except for having raised the alarm."

"I wonder who he is...or was."

"Well, he looked like he was wearing the standard khaki uniform of so many birders and other naturalists. Somehow, I think of people like that as being more careful when they are out in the wilderness. If he fell in, he must have been there by himself. Certainly, if he had a companion, they would have gone for help. And I wonder if he was lying there all night. The sheriff's deputy said that the bodies had attracted flies. How long does that take? Sorry, that's probably a morbid question. We'll find out in the next day or two. It seems as though the authorities know who he is...or was, and that might shed some light on the matter."

"Do you think that it could be anyone you know?" Trudi asked. "You run around with some of the nature people around here, don't you? Birders, butterfliers, turtlers."

"Turtlers?" Evelyn replied with a laugh. "But, no, I don't know that many people outside of a few birders and nature photographers that I've met at various Egret Bay birding festivals."

"Did I just miss something or was the alligator not mentioned in the story?"

"I noticed the same thing. No alligator. Wonder why."

"Well, if you hear anything, keep me posted," Trudi said. "And I'll do the same. And thanks again for the lovely lunch."

After hanging up, Evelyn refilled her coffee cup. She was on her way to her desk to see if there was any interesting email when her cellphone rang again. The caller was identified only as "City of Egret Bay Police." With slight trepidation, she answered.

"Good morning," she said.

"And good morning to you, Ms. Baldwin. This is Detective Sam Pierson from the Egret Bay Homicide Division. I trust I'm not calling too early."

"No, I'm already on my second cup of coffee. I was wondering if I would hear from you and was hoping I wouldn't–no slight intended."

"This should only take a couple of minutes. Just need to clarify a few things. To make it clear, this has not been declared a homicide case, but since it's been sent to the medical examiner's office, I thought I should ask a few questions of the eyewitnesses just in case it should land in our laps. Your name and Ms. Olson's came up on the sheriff's notes that were sent to me for our files, and I thought I'd give you a call."

"I understand and am glad to help. Now's as good a time as any. Are you going to call Trudi as well?"

"Not if I can get what I need from you."

"It would be nice if you don't have to bother her."

"As I understand it, the two of you were the first to notice the deceased over on the island."

"Well," Evelyn said with a little hesitation. "We didn't know that it was a person at first. It just looked strange. We thought–maybe hoped—it was a discarded or lost shirt that had drifted over towards the island and gotten snagged on the bushes near that little beach."

"What made you take a second look?"

"The way it bobbed in the water. It had too much—what would be the best word? Substance, yes, substance, for just a shirt. So then we thought it might be a backpack."

"You could have just shrugged and called it a backpack that someone accidentally dropped into the water and gone on your way."

"Yes, but we were concerned enough and unsure enough that we didn't just leave. There was just the smallest chance that it was not a lost shirt or a backpack. Had we left and then found out later that we were wrong, that we hadn't followed through, or—worst of all—the person might have still been alive, we would have felt really guilty."

"So you told the woman at the ticket booth, a Ms. Gibson."

"Yes, and she was the one who first identified it as probably being a person instead of a backpack and that led her to call the rookery's manager."

"And the manager, a Ms. Gomez according to the notes from the sheriff's office, she called 911 for an ambulance and then called the sheriff's office."

"That's my understanding. A couple of deputy sheriffs showed up not long after Doris—Ms. Gibson—called the manager."

"But you two—you and Ms. Olson—stayed there for a while after you notified Ms. Gomez of your concern?"

"Yes. We thought we should stay just in case anyone had questions, but as soon as they told us we could go, we left."

"And you were glad to get out of there."

"Yes, indeed."

"That's all I need for right now, thank you."

"Before you hang up," Evelyn said, "are you still partnering with Detective Forster? I haven't seen her since she was involved in the death at the gallery."

"Yes, we're still a team and she's fine. She had a lot of personal time and has been off for the last five days. I expect her back on duty tomorrow."

"And you're holding down the fort for now?"

"Nothing's come up so far that I can't handle. Hope that keeps up until she returns."

"Well, tell her hello for us. And can I tell Trudi about this call?"

"Yes. No reason why not. Take care."

Hanging up from talking to Evelyn, Sam gave his partner, Val Forster, a call to let her know that there may be a case waiting for them when she returned. No answer. Probably has her phone off. He left a message saying that the body of a man had been found in a popular birding spot. The medical examiner had questions as to whether it was an accidental death, so there was a possibility that homicide may be back in action in the next day or two. Until then, it was in the sheriff's lap.

As she left the call with Detective Pierson, Evelyn realized that he had not mentioned the alligator either. She thought she should call Trudi and tell her that the homicide detectives knew of their involvement, but her phone rang before she could start dialing. Good heavens, she thought, the lines are sure busy this morning. She glanced to see who was calling: Milly Gonzalez, a young photographer who was a frequent exhibitor at the Art League gallery. What would she be calling about?

"Good morning, Milly, and how are you?"

"Doing great, Evelyn. I just heard that you are somehow involved in that death over at the rookery."

"How on earth did you find that out? I wasn't mentioned in the newspaper."

"Hey, this is at heart a small town, you know. Word gets around. Actually, I heard this from my sister, Angela. Doris Gibson, one of the volunteers at the rookery's ticket booth–you met her yesterday–is Angela's mother-in-law. Doris told Angela about what happened yesterday, and Angela thought your name sounded familiar and asked me if I knew you. You might not remember, but you met Angela at a recent Artwalk.

She's also a photographer and had a few pieces in the exhibit and I introduced you to her. And I told Angela that sure, I know you, and thought I'd give you a call and see if you have anything interesting that you can share. I go to the rookery a lot for photo ops. Do you think there is something dangerous there?"

"You mean besides the snakes and alligators and mosquitoes?"

"Well, actually I was thinking of a human danger."

"No, I don't think so. This seems to be an isolated event. No one, to my knowledge, is currently treating it as anything else." Of course, she thought, all she had to go on was her conversation with Detective Pierson. He hadn't sounded as though he was concerned.

"And you actually saw a dead guy on the island?"

"Well, we weren't sure it was a dead guy. We just alerted your sister's mother-in-law, Doris, that there was something strange in the water over there."

"We?"

Evelyn hesitated, but she knew it would all come out eventually. "Trudi was with me."

"Oh, poor Trudi! This is the second time she's been in involved in finding a dead person."

"Yes, but this was nowhere near as traumatic. We didn't know it was a person for sure until Doris arrived and took a closer look. The sheriff deputies later confirmed it."

"And has anyone said who it was?"

"No. Male. That's all I know."

"Wonder if he fell off one of the viewing platforms. I've seen photographers take some really weird chances to get a good shot. I even saw one standing on the railing with his wife holding on to his belt to keep him from toppling over."

"You've taken some nice shots over there. I remember that Snowy Egret with babies that you entered in an exhibit a few months back. That was darling."

"And I didn't have to stand on the railing to take it either."

"Well, let me know if you hear anything else from your family connections, would you?" Evelyn said. "I'm not really in the loop, by choice, but it would be nice if I could keep Trudi up to date, so the press or police don't surprise her with questions she can't answer."

"Shall do. Thanks."

It seemed even more important that she call Trudi given that word of their involvement might leak out. She anticipated a lengthy conversation with her friend, but the call was briefer than expected. Trudi was pleased that she called and eager to be kept up to date. However, she was baking cookies in an attempt to think about something other than the events of the previous day. Her timer for the present batch went off shortly after she answered the phone.

"Call me when you're free," Evelyn said as she heard the timer in the background.

Evelyn's phone rang again just after 10:00. "Egret Bay Daily News" popped up on the screen. "Oh, good Lord," Evelyn said to herself, "we've been found out." She tapped to open.

"Good morning."

"And good morning to you, Ms. Baldwin. This is Amy Sloan, from the *Daily News*. I understand you were one of the people who first discovered the body at the rookery yesterday."

Evelyn sighed. They had indeed been caught out by the press. "Yes," was all she said.

"I'd like to talk to you more about that, but right now I want to talk to a local nature photographer, and I thought you might suggest one from the Art League. I tried calling the league president, but he didn't answer. So I went to the vice president and that's you."

"Well, yes, I can suggest a few. If you tell me what you're looking for, it will help. I'll give them a call and have anyone who's interested call you back."

"We're in a little hurry here. I need to get some background as soon as possible."

"Background on what?"

"Oh, you haven't heard? The man you found at the bird place yesterday has been identified. His name—no secret because it's already making it into the news—is Lester Burton. Have you ever heard of him?"

"No, doesn't ring a bell."

"Well, he's apparently a very famous nature photographer, famous among photographers at least. When I told a couple of our staff photographers his name, one of them said, 'You don't mean *the* Lester Burton?' She knew his name and had seen some of his work in photo magazines but didn't know much more. So I thought I would see if I could find a nature photographer who might be able to give me more insight and possibly an interesting direct quote."

"OK, I know who I will call. If I can reach her, I'll have her call you right back. If I can't, I'll let you know. Sorry, but gallery policy is that we don't give out phone numbers."

As soon as Evelyn hung up, she searched her recent calls list for Milly's number. Milly answered on the third ring. Evelyn told her why she was calling. The information elicited a gasp and then Milly said, "You mean *the* Lester Burton?"

"Well, it's *a* Lester Burton, so it may well be the one you know about."

"Oh, that news has me quite of two minds."

"Why?" Evelyn asked.

"Oh, he's a fantastic nature photographer, one of the best in, maybe, the world. Well, the Western world at least. But he's also known to be a real jerk. You know how it is, you have a favorite actor, or musician, or such, but you know that he—or she—did something illegal or disgusting. Do you say, 'good riddance' or mourn the wonderful parts of their life that are now sullied?"

"I'd ask you to elaborate, but Amy at the *Daily News* wants to talk to someone as soon as possible. Can you give her a call? Then, if you have the time, call me back and explain to me why you said what you said about Mr. Burton."

"Yes, of course. Give me her number and I'll call her immediately."

Her curiosity building, Evelyn went directly to her computer and googled "Lester Burton." She scrolled down until she found a Wikipedia entry for him. The entry primarily focused on all the awards that Burton had won, with relatively little on his personal life.

There were a couple of examples of his photography in the image samples. They were gorgeous. One was of a Snowy Egret in full breeding plumage, his feathers reflecting the light from a sunrise, or maybe a sunset, in orange and coral colors. The other was a photo of a lake, perfectly still, not a ripple except for the V-shaped wake behind a small waterfowl–looked like a Pied-billed Grebe–that was paddling across the water. That made Evelyn think about the alligator. She tried to remember if Amy had said anything about that. She didn't think so. Maybe the police were keeping it quiet for some reason. She clicked on "Images" for Burton and found herself quickly absorbed, enlarging one after another in order to look at them closer. One of a Barn Owl looked familiar. Of course, she thought, there are probably hundreds of photos of Barn Owls out there, but still she was sure she had previously seen this photo or one very similar to it. Was it in an ad? She wasn't sure.

Milly didn't call back before noon. Evelyn fixed herself a tuna sandwich for lunch, poured a glass of iced tea, and continued her search on Lester Burton. This time she skipped over three pages devoted to his prize-winning photos, coffee-table-sized books filled with gorgeous images, and announcements of speaking engagements. Nothing about his death. On the fourth search page she found a link to a newspaper article headlined "Famous Photographer Banned from City Park." Seems he had commandeered a swing in the children's play area and used it to swing high enough to get a view inside a nest in a hackberry tree next to the swing set. He apparently had swung so high that he lost control of the swing's arc and had almost knocked a kid off the swing next to him. "I just wanted to see if there were eggs in the nest," he was quoted as saying. "I didn't have a ladder."

As she continued, similar stories began to pop up. Complaints of unprofessional conduct, rude encounters with other photographers and birders, paying people to let him in near the front of lines in order to get a quick look at some exotic species that had lost its coordinates and flown somewhere it had never been seen before. She was beginning to understand Milly's ambivalence upon hearing of Burton's death.

She was just finishing lunch when Milly called back. "I hope this isn't inconvenient for you," she said.

"Heavens, no. I've been doing a search on Mr. Burton. I'm beginning to see what you were talking about earlier."

"He's something else, isn't he?" Milly said. "I just wanted to bring you up to date on the latest news. When I talked to Amy, she said that the death is formally being attributed to 'unknown causes' at this point. She said that the medical examiner has told a few people that there are aspects about the death that make him think that there may be foul play involved, although it's too early to say. No official autopsy results yet, but Amy's sources say that the medical examiner's first guess is that, regardless of what led to it, the immediate cause of death is probably a heart attack."

"Did Amy say anything about the alligator?" Evelyn asked.

"What alligator?"

"There was an alligator lying on the sand next to him."

"Amy didn't say anything about an alligator. Next to him? Wow! Do you think the alligator killed him? That doesn't sound like a heart attack."

"No, the alligator was dead."

"Dead? Oh my God. This is getting too weird for me."

"And you're sure that even if Amy didn't mention an alligator, that she didn't say anything strange about Mr. Burton's death? You know, something about unusual circumstances?"

"No, nothing."

"Well, maybe they are keeping that under wraps for now. Perhaps you had better not mention the alligator to anyone until we hear more. Maybe the two are not connected. Maybe the currents swept both of them toward the same location or something like that."

"I doubt there are any currents in that pond," Milly said. "The water is usually as still as glass."

At the Egret Bay Police Department, a lot of talk was making the rounds about a guy found dead on an island in a bird sanctuary. "Sounds like the subject of a mystery novel," one of the uniformed officers said. Initially the in-house consensus seemed to be that the guy had fallen into the water and drowned. A couple of uniformed officers stopped Sam Pierson in the hallway to ask if he was on the case. They seemed disappointed when he replied in the negative. Personally, however, he wondered why no one from the sheriff's office had called him. Then bits of the medical examiner's report filtered out from one of the uniformed officers whose wife worked at the sheriff's office, and they heard Burton had died from a heart attack. So the story shifted. He had a heart attack before he fell into the water and drowned. Now the rumor had altered again, changing the order in which the events–heart attack and drowning–must have taken place. Now he had a heart attack *after* he fell in the water. To top it off, one rumor said he had been shot.

Sam shut the door of the Homicide Division office to avoid being constantly questioned. He sat by himself in the office, clicking and unclicking his pen. The initial autopsy results had just been sent over from the sheriff's office. Thanks to the wallet found in the back pocket of the deceased, he had been identified as one Lester Burton, a photographer, age 58, home was in New Jersey. Cause of death: cardiac arrest. So the rumors around the department were partially correct. Secondary cause: near drowning. Near drowning. Sam had always thought that one drowned or one didn't. If the guy died of a heart attack, then they might be able to file this away as a natural cause or accidental death. Case closed. But it doesn't sound like the M.E. thinks it's so cut and dried. It didn't surprise Sam, therefore, when he got a call from the medical examiner's office shortly before noon.

"I'm recommending that we hand this case over to you. You know the basics, either from my initial report or the newspaper. There is now no doubt that this was not a run-of-the-mill accidental drowning.

Didn't think so yesterday when I went to the scene, rolled the body over and found a bullet hole."

"He was shot?" Sam asked, wondering how that had already hit the rumor mill and he was just now hearing about it officially.

"In the thigh. He was wearing a holster. Nothing unusual about that today. It's no longer an anomaly in Texas. Hell, my wife's hairdresser carries. But we didn't find a gun. If he was wearing a holster, we can assume he was armed at some point. If he was armed, it's quite possible that whatever firearm he was carrying was the source of at least one or more of the three bullets that were discharged that morning."

"Three?" Sam asked.

"Ah, that's right. You don't know the whole story. Two bullets in the alligator…"

"Alligator. What alligator?"

"Ah, you *really* don't have the whole story. There was a dead alligator lying next to the deceased."

"And why haven't we heard about that? There's nothing in the newspaper or the preliminary report you sent over."

"Self-preservation. If we had mentioned the alligator, we would have been overrun by calls to our department, all of them about the alligator. We've seen this before. A short while back a guy on a motorcycle who was carrying his dog in a backpack was badly injured in an accident. We couldn't find an ID, so we put out a story about the guy and his dog, asking people to call us if they know who the guy is. We got one call about the man–thankfully it was the one we needed–and twenty-two calls about the dog, checking to see if it was OK. Two of them wanted to adopt it on the spot. So, not knowing much about the deceased in this case, we thought it smart to neglect to tell the press about the alligator. They'll be mad at me, but they'll get over it. So where was I?"

"Bullets."

"Yes, two bullets in the alligator and one in the deceased. But there is a major inconsistency here. I've been discussing it with my two lab assistants, and we've come up with all sorts of questions for which we have no answers. Answers are your job, but for what it's worth, I'll run some of our questions by you to ponder. If Burton was alone and he shot the alligator, he had to have done that before he went into the water. Even if the gun had avoided getting wet, Burton would never have been able to aim well enough after he pulled himself out of the pond to put a bullet through the alligator's eye and another through the unarmored spot in the back of the alligator's neck. He would have been exhausted, unstable, and confused. But when I did the autopsy, I was able to verify that the gunshot wound in his leg occurred *after* he got out of the water, meaning that the gun that shot him probably didn't go into the water with him. I suppose you could develop a scenario that would explain that. Maybe he wasn't holding the gun when he fell in the water. Then when he got out, he picked it up and then dropped it, and it accidentally discharged and shot him in the leg. Weirder things happen, as you know. By the bullet's trajectory, I can tell you he wasn't holding the gun when he was shot, not unless he's some type of contortionist. It's also possible, of course, that someone else shot him with that gun, or maybe with another gun, after he got out of the water. I've sent the bullets to Forensics to see if they all come from the same gun. That person could also have shot the alligator in fear or self-defense if it suddenly reared up out of the pond onto the beach. That makes sense, but how could one shot come from the front of the alligator and the other from the rear?"

"And no one found the gun," Sam said.

"Well, there's a rather large body of water that it could have been tossed into. Or someone carried it off when they left. And then there's the absence of any kind of watercraft," the M.E. continued. "That was a topic of discussion when I was out at the rookery. It can only be explained by one of two things: we go back to the deceased having accidentally fallen into the pond, rendering the absence of a watercraft moot, or—much more likely given the gunshot wound and other stuff—someone else was there and that person had to use the craft to leave the island. If someone else was there, again that's your business, not mine. So I recommended to the sheriff that his office, already up to its eyebrows in another matter, hand this over to you experts in the various scenarios of death."

"Who's handled it till now?" Sam asked.

"There are two, actually. Deputy Jefferson was the deputy who went out to the island twice, I think, once with me, but I think this is officially in Deputy Doug Fraser's lap."

"Who else was with you when you went to the island?"

"There were four of us. Jefferson, a crime scene investigator, a woman from the rookery who handled the boat–very skillfully, I might note–and me. The crime scene guy took photos of the scene–they should forward those to you–but there wasn't a lot to go on there. The sand near the pond was dry and it had been disturbed by the dying struggles of the deceased, and probably the alligator as well. I'm sure that word is getting around that I didn't help any when I tried to step over the alligator to avoid contaminating what few footprints there were, lost my balance, and disturbed the scene even more."

"Hadn't heard that yet," Sam said.

"Oh, you will. Clumsy of me."

"So the cause of death is officially....?"

"He definitely died of cardiac arrest. The shot in the leg did not contribute to his death. On another note, I also found a lens cap in his pocket, but we couldn't find a camera."

"I've heard that he was a famous photographer, but you didn't find a camera?"

"Professional photographer? No, I hadn't heard that. I just figured that he was a camera buff. No camera. Suppose the camera could have gone wherever the gun went. Famous, huh? Wonder what he was doing there."

"Me too," Sam said. "Find that out and maybe we'll solve the case. No injuries attributable to the alligator?"

"No, none."

"Are you doing an autopsy on the alligator?"

"Good lord, no. They had a hard time getting it off the island and not sure what they did with it. I know that the vet at animal control took the head so he could salvage the bullets they sent over to me, but that's it as far as I'm concerned. It must have weighted at least three or four hundred pounds."

"And you say it was shot twice."

"Yes, remarkable accuracy. One bullet going through the eye and the other from the back of the head directly into the brain cavity. I really didn't know much about shooting alligators until now. Might be valuable if I'm ever attacked by one."

"And the time of death?" Sam asked.

"Of the deceased or the alligator?"

"Well, either or both."

"That's another thing. I'm almost positive that the deceased died sometime yesterday morning between 5:00 and 7:00. When I was leaving, I noticed that the place doesn't open until 7:00, so if my timing is correct, the death occurred before the place was open. So they broke in. As for the alligator, the wounds looked fresh, so my guess is also sometime early yesterday morning. Otherwise I'm all done here except for lab reports. I'm waiting on one to confirm my diagnosis, and I want to make sure he was not under the influence of alcohol or drugs. I took some fingernail scrapings and sent them over too. I'll send all this over to you, but you might want to write my findings down in case you need them before I finish my paperwork."

Sam wrote down what the M.E. told him, double-checking to make sure he got it right: "An examination of the heart revealed smooth-muscle contraction banding in the major coronary arteries. This suggests antemortem coronary arterial spasm." In English, the M.E. explained, "The subject did not die of drowning, but of a storm of cardiac events that followed the near drowning. He must have managed to get from the water to the land before experiencing the spasms that killed him. There are a couple of small things that I noted but can't explain. During the autopsy I found a large bruise–recent–on the front of the deceased's right knee. I didn't see anything on the island that would explain that. I looked back over the photographs and couldn't find any foliage that looked damaged. No rocks or large tree trunks in the vicinity. It is possible, I suppose, that it occurred when he was in the water."

"But before death?" Sam asked.

"Yes, I think so, or very shortly after. I've added those observations to the report."

"And you say you've retrieved the bullet from the deceased?"

"Yes, and I've sent it to Forensics."

"And the vet sent you those from the alligator?"

"Yes, and I've sent those to Forensics. Any other questions about bullets, refer them there."

After hanging up, Sam thought about what the M.E. had told him. Did someone shoot the deceased? If Burton was shot accidentally after getting out of the pond, he may have been, as the M.E. said, very addled and accidently caused the gun to discharge. There is also the question, of course, as to who shot the alligator. Who else could have shot it besides the deceased or someone else who was with him on the island? And if there was someone else, as the M.E. believes, who was it? Is it legal to kill an alligator in Fillmore County? Is there such a thing as an alligator license, like a duck license? And he could see why they had delayed announcing the presence of an alligator. That would probably be the primary item in the news: 'Man found dead next to dead alligator.' Might have made national news. Might still do that once it leaks out.

And the deceased was a photographer, just as the M.E. had suspected when he had found a lens cap in the deceased's pocket. So what was a photographer doing on the island? What could he have taken photos of? Sam decided to wait and see if the request for a transfer of the case was sent over from the sheriff and approved by the chief. It didn't surprise him that the sheriff's office would want a transfer of the case given its many unknowns. For over a month, the sheriff had been assigning deputies to a task force formed by federal drug enforcement agents working with local law enforcement to investigate the possibility a drug smuggling operation in the greater Houston area. Nevertheless, the county–the sheriff, M.E., CSI, Forensics–seems to be handling most of the initial Burton investigation to date. He assumed they had done all the upfront paperwork. He wondered if they had searched for the next of kin.

He was trying to figure out what to do next when Val called.

"So how are things in Homicide?" she asked.

"What you really mean is how is the investigation going into the death at the bird rookery that I mentioned in my message yesterday afternoon? And I can't tell you much more than I told you then except the M.E. is almost positive that he died of a heart attack that occurred as a result of–that is, after–a near drowning. And he had also been shot in the leg. No one can figure out how he ended up on the island unless he fell into the water from the observation area, or someone took him out there and left him."

"Well, I've still got a half day to play, but will be, as promised, in the office tomorrow morning. Maybe we'll have more information by then. It would be nice if this turned out to be an accidental death, so we can hit some of those cold cases that the chief keeps reminding us about. Let me know if anything major comes later today."

He had no sooner hung up than the office phone rang.

"Detective Pierson, Homicide," he answered.

"Good morning, Detective," the caller said. "This is Officer Perez. I'm working intake today and I have a woman on the line who wants to talk to someone about the death at the birding spot. Has that been assigned to you, or should I send her elsewhere?"

"It hasn't been assigned, but I'm being kept up to date with what's going on, so transfer her to me. If it seems pertinent, I'll forward it to the sheriff's office."

"Shall do. Thanks."

"Hello?" a woman said in a rather questioning voice.

"Detective Pierson, Homicide. How can I help you?"

"Well, I wanted to talk to someone about the photographer that died over at the rookery."

"I may be able to help you. The case is still listed as a death from unknown causes, but I'll be glad to help you if I can."

"Well, if it's not a homicide, my call may be unnecessary, so perhaps I'll wait until you know more about it."

"Whatever you have to say may help us to move forward. If you have information that could affect the case in any way, please share it with us."

The caller hesitated for a moment and Sam was afraid she was going to hang up.

"It's only rumor," she finally said. "I don't want to get someone in trouble unnecessarily if there is no need. It's secondhand information, and I was not going to call, but my husband convinced me that I had a civic duty to do so. I probably shouldn't have let him talk me into it. Now I feel embarrassed and somewhat stupid about the whole thing."

"No reason to feel that way. Your husband is correct in saying that if you heard anything that might have a bearing on the case, you should tell us. If it turns out to be unnecessary, we will just shelve the information. But if matters change and it turns out to be important, we need to know everything we can, even the smallest thing."

Sam thought to himself that he wished Val was there so she could hear his eloquent little speech.

"Very well. If you think I'm doing the right thing, where do we go from here?"

"We can continue with our conversation now and I'll make notes, and then if it seems that we need more information, we will contact you and you can come in and we'll have a longer conversation."

"Can I call you back in an hour or so? I'm baking a cake, and I don't want to get involved in a lengthy discussion."

Baking a cake, he thought. That was a new excuse for hanging up, one he'd never thought of before. Why would you place a call, especially one that might be lengthy, in the middle of baking a cake? "That's fine," he said in the most neutral tone he could find. "I should be here, Ms....?"

"Kellogg, like the cereal, although we're not related."

"And your phone number?"

She hesitated and then gave him her number. "But I'll call you, right?"

"Yes, ma'am. I'll give you my direct line, so you don't have to go through intake."

As soon as he hung up, he started an online search for "Kellogg" and "Egret Bay" to see if he could find any background on his caller. There wasn't much. A Kellogg, listed as "woman aged 60+, married," lived in one of the newer developments west of the city, so they were probably financially well off. The only image of her online was as one person among a small group, all of them with binoculars. So she was probably also a bird watcher. That was good, given that the recently-deceased was found in a rookery. It meant that she might not be just another version of the woman who called a few weeks back. That woman had overheard a man in the grocery store talking on his cellphone. She thought she should report it because he had an accent, sounded like a criminal, and talked about his new gun. Turned out the guy was a U.S. citizen born in Italy, had excellent English although with an accent, and was going to go hunting with his brother the next day.

Sam got up to make another coffee run before Ms. Kellogg called back. When he returned, he resumed looking through one of the cold case files. This one, from three years previous, involved the death of a visiting conventioneer where all the leads had dried up.

An hour later, he thought Ms. Kellogg must have taken the time to not only cook the cake but frost it as well. Put candles on it. Sing "Happy Birthday." Val had told him that people who called the station were more at ease in telling their story than people who received a call from someone affiliated with the police, even a call they were anticipating. Just as he was about to ignore Val's advice and call Ms. Kellogg, the phone rang.

"Detective Pierson, Homicide," he answered.

"This is Wilhelmina, Willy, Kellogg. I'm sorry I didn't call back sooner, but something came up."

"That's OK," Sam said, trying to be patient and polite. "Thank you for calling."

"It's just that I've never talked to a detective before. I'm a little nervous."

"Just start at the beginning. What did you hear that impressed you so much that you talked it over with your husband before calling?"

"I told you, I think, that this was secondhand. I have a friend who, when she heard that Lester Burton had died, said that he might have had it coming. That shocked me. It was so out of character of her to say that. She immediately apologized and said she didn't really mean that, but that she had a friend whose whole career as a bird photographer was almost destroyed by Burton. Her friend had been here visiting her earlier this year and they had gone out birding. He told her that he never went anywhere where he might bump into Burton, because if he—my friend's friend—ever saw him—that is, Burton—he still had enough antipathy toward him—I think that's the word she used, 'antipathy'—that he didn't know how he would react."

"You say this friend of a friend was here in Egret Bay earlier this year?"

"Yes, but he was back again last week."

"He was in Egret Bay last week?"

"Yes, because when I saw the article in the newspaper, I immediately called my friend and told her that her friend would not have the chance to do anything to this Burton fellow because someone else beat him to it. And she said that she was worried about him—that is, her friend—because he was in here, in Egret Bay, over last weekend and that he was supposed to have lunch with her on Monday, but he called and left a message late Sunday night that he was leaving early Monday morning to go home."

"And home is where?"

"New Mexico. Santa Fe."

"Did you tell your friend that you were going to call us?"

"I told her I might, and she poo-pooed the idea that her friend really meant what he said as a threat. But then she called me back and said she was concerned because another person had asked her if she thought her friend was behind Burton's death. Apparently, he had said similar things to other people and some local birders are all abuzz about it. It really upset her. I mean, no one seems to like Burton, but murdering him is a little extreme."

"Well, we're still not sure that we're talking murder here. It's still, as I said earlier, officially labeled 'unknown cause,' just as the newspapers have reported. What that means is that we're not sure."

"Well, I hope this was a wasted phone call and you find out that it was all due to natural causes. In which case, please ignore what I've said."

"I need his name, the name of the friend of your friend, just in case."

"Yes, of course you do. His name is Anders MacPherson. That's 'mac,' with an 'a.'"

"And your friend's name?"

"I was hoping you wouldn't ask that. She is very upset about his whole thing. All these rumors and such."

"We won't contact her unless there is cause to pursue this."

"I would really appreciate that. Her name is Phyllis Collins. She lives here, in Egret Bay."

"Full time?"

"Full time? Oh, you mean, is this a second home? Yes, she lives here full-time. I do too."

"I really appreciate this call. I know this is a hard thing to do. Let's hope I don't have to talk to you again about this."

"I do too. Thank you for listening to me."

Sam thought about calling Val but decided against it. It's possible more information might come through from the M.E.'s office or from the CSI unit before then. In the meantime he could write up the information from the phone call, but he had no idea what to do with it once it had been written. Then he could spend more time with the cold case about the conventioneer.

Hours later, Sam was thinking about heading home. It was past 5:30 and he was at a good stopping place with the conventioneer's case. He needed to do his laundry, and things might get busier because of the unusual circumstances of the photographer's death. A call from the chief's office stopped him as he was heading out the door.

"This case with the death at the bird place, the sheriff is calling this one a possible homicide," the chief said. "Tell me what you know."

"Cause of death hasn't really changed," Sam said. "He had a heart attack. But there are too many open questions. We don't know how he got to the island. We couldn't find any kind of watercraft. He may have fallen into the water, but the M.E. is sure that his bullet wound occurred after he got out of the water, so it's possible someone else shot him. He was wearing a holster, but we never found a firearm. Both the absence of a boat and the timing of the bullet wound suggest someone was there with him. If so, that person could be directly or indirectly responsible for his death."

"I think I followed that. You make as much sense as the M.E. OK. Take a couple of days, unless something else comes up, and see what you can find. Is there someone with enough motive to do him harm? Is Detective Forster coming back tomorrow?"

"Yes, sir."

"Good, put your heads together and let's close this one as quickly as possible."

Sam sat back down and turned his computer back on. Might as well see if he could get more info on Mr. Burton so he'd have something to share with Val besides the M.E.'s report and the phone call from Ms. Kellogg. He looked for Burton on Facebook, but no luck. Twitter, Linked In, same thing. The guy didn't seem to fool around on social media. YouTube, however, was full of videos featuring the recently deceased Mr. Burton, too many to start digging in right now. The most recent one was dated the previous month and had to do with a kettle of hawks. That didn't sound very appetizing.

He Googled "Lester Burton" and came up with hundreds of hits, even with the quotes. So he tried "Lester Burton" and photographer and limited the search to the last month. That helped narrow things. "Famous Bird Photographer Dead," from *The New York Times* led the list. According to the article, Burton had been married and divorced three times, not currently married, no kids, home listed as Medford, New Jersey. That checks with the information from the license. Sam wondered what there was in Medford that attracted a famous photographer. Burton was the author of four books featuring his wildlife photography, one how-to book on outdoor photography, and–according to the *Times* obit–over a hundred articles in popular, wildlife, and photography magazines. He had at one time led tours to "exotic birding spots around the globe." Sam wondered what he was doing in Egret Bay. It was uncomfortably hot by this time of year, not a good time for outdoor excursions. But these were birdwatchers, people he always found a little strange, running around hunting birds so they could check them off a list. He doubted a little heat could force them inside.

Armed with a little more information and with a few questions he could suggest to Val when they got together the next day, he signed off and went home.

CHAPTER 3

Wednesday

Val took a deep breath as she got out of her car at the police department parking lot. Back to work. She wasn't sure whether that was good or bad. It had been fun being at home and catching up on a life outside of the department, but she missed the challenges. Sam was on the phone when she opened the door to their office. He gave her a wave and continued with his conversation. When he hung up, he swiveled around toward her and said, "Guess what I found out in an article on the internet. Lester Burton, the great photographer and world explorer who was found on an island in the middle of a pond, didn't know how to swim!"

"And that's important because…?" Val asked.

"Because he nearly drowned, and the near drowning seems to be what led to his death."

"Whoa, boy, whoa. I'm still half asleep and you are much too chipper for me. Let me get another cup of coffee and then maybe you can start at the beginning. The beginning being: is this now our case?"

"As of last evening unless something more pressing comes up. The chief said to 'take a couple of days,' as though he expects that's all it will take."

"And you don't?"

"There is something about this case that reminds me of the death at the Art League gallery last year, not the least being that a couple of the women involved in that case are on the periphery of this one as well."

"Trudi? Is Trudi Olson one of them? She's such a sweet woman."

"Sweet she may be, but trouble seems to find her. She and the woman who was the art historian were the ones that discovered the deceased."

When Val returned with her coffee and a half of a donut that had somehow escaped the onslaught of the employees who had arrived earlier. She wondered at people who eat only half a donut, or–even more confounding–a quarter of a donut. "Nibblers," her husband Deke called them. Eating only a bite or two only makes you want to eat another bite or two. It seems as though it would be much easier to just forego the donut entirely.

"OK," she said as she sat down. "What I know so far is just what you told me in our phone conversations. A man was found on an island in the middle of a lake..."

Sam interrupted, "Everyone calls it a pond, even though I would call it a lake, but..."

"Yes, OK, he's found on an island in the middle of a pond, and no one knows how he got there or what he was doing there. And now we find out that he probably didn't swim out there because he can't swim. Anything else?"

"Did I mention the alligator?"

"Oh, good Lord. Don't tell me we also have an alligator to deal with."

"The deceased was found lying next to a dead alligator. The alligator had been shot, close range, but no firearm found. Also, he–the deceased human–was a photographer. He probably had a camera with him because the M.E. found a lens cap in his pocket. However, no camera has been found. Still haven't located any type of boat, so it looks like he could have been intentionally stranded there, ergo the suspected homicide label and the call to us from the chief last evening telling us to get to work."

"He could have fallen in, given that he couldn't swim," Val said.

"That was the original assumption, but there are too many unanswered questions, like the dead alligator and the missing gun. Oh, and if I haven't said it already, the deceased was wearing a holster for a sidearm. If he fell in, he was probably wearing his gun, not just an empty holster, when he fell. Let's assume that somehow or other, he made it to the island, encountered the alligator, and then–what?–shot it with a gun that was sopping wet from being submerged? And doc said that he would not have been able at that point to shoot the alligator with such pinpoint accuracy. No, if he shot the alligator, he would have had to do it before he fell in the water."

"Maybe the alligator attacked him."

"It was shot in the back of the head."

"Maybe the alligator was backing up toward him."

Sam smiled, "And maybe he was trying to ride it like a cowboy."

"Back to the serious issue, so far we have a deceased male who is a photographer…"

"Very famous wildlife and bird photographer," Sam interrupted. "I have a short bio of him that I'll share with you. It's based on an obit from *The New York Times*."

"An obit in the *Times*? Well, I am impressed. Is he from New York?"

"No, home is in New Jersey."

"I think that's close enough. To continue, a very important wildlife photographer is found deceased on an island in the middle of a pond with no evidence as to how he got there and no indication that he had a way off the island," Val said. "Someone, possibly him, shot an alligator that was found deceased and lying next to him. Why do we think that there was someone else there beside the deceased?"

"Indirect evidence such as the absence of a watercraft suggests that at some time someone else was on the island with him."

"OK, death of deceased probably caused by heart attack provoked by a near drowning. I assume that one earlier theory was that he tried to swim across and climb out, but you're telling me that he couldn't swim, so that's probably not the case."

"Correct. And even if he swam back, it would be difficult to climb up the side to get to safe ground. On another note, from what I've read, he is considered to be an excellent photographer, but a real jerk when it comes to anything personal. Got a phone call yesterday afternoon from a woman who said that a friend of a friend of hers…"

"Friend of a friend?"

"Yes, a friend of a friend of hers was said to have had his career as a photographer almost destroyed by the deceased and had suggested he might not be able to control himself if he ever saw him again. This friend of a friend was in town over the last weekend, meaning both he and the deceased could have crossed paths. This friend of a friend was planning on having breakfast with the local friend on Monday, the day the deceased was found, but cut his trip short and abruptly returned home to Santa Fe, New Mexico."

"I think I followed that. Do we have the name of the friend of a friend?"

"Yes, his name, the friend's name, and the name of the woman who called. The two women live in Egret Bay, but in different houses."

"Any other leads?"

"Not yet, but, based on the secondhand story, the deceased could well have made enough enemies that we should be able to find a few. If we can find out who else knew he was around here on Sunday and Monday, it should limit the number of potential suspects. There can't be that many people in town who have had a run-in with him. We have one potential suspect already, this friend of a friend."

"Well, it might except for one small thing."

"And that is?"

"My dear husband Deke complained all last week that there was to be a meeting of some climate scientists and wildlife artists and writers here in Egret Bay over the weekend. He was upset that participation was by invitation only. He really wanted to attend and talk to some of the participants, a few of whom–please note the correct, I think, use of 'whom'–he knew by name."

Sam groaned. "You got to be kidding me. How many people are we talking about?"

"I don't know. Deke told me it was held in the small conference room of the old Fillmore Hotel, not a huge space, so we're talking modest numbers, but large enough."

"Who organized it?"

"I think the Egret Bay Bird Society arranged the meeting. They have a grant of some sort to develop what Deke called a "citizen scientist" project utilizing school children on both sides of the border to document the effect of climate change on bird and insect migration."

"And you think that we may have suspects among those attending this meeting?" Sam asked.

"It seems like an odd coincidence when a bunch of nature-involved people arrive in town over the same weekend that the deceased visited. And not only that, but I think the Bird Society owns, or at least manages, that rookery, and they are also the ones who arranged the meeting. I think we need to start somewhere and that's a logical place. Of course, the deceased could have brought his problems and his companions with him, but until we know his history, we have no idea where to look."

"If we have no idea, where do we start," Sam asked.

"I'm not sure," Val said. "I assume there have been trips out to the island, investigation team, photos, that kind of thing. Didn't the sheriff's office do that?"

"Yes, there have been three trips to the scene."

"Three?"

"Yes, one to verify that the deceased was deceased. No one got off the boat on that one. Then one to take the M.E. to certify the death, along with a couple of crime scene deputies, and one to take the body off. Oh, and a fourth to remove the alligator."

"And what about access to the island? Can anyone go there?"

"Not really. From what I understand, it's not that difficult to get into the general observation areas around the pond, but there are some impediments to getting to the island itself. I've never been around there. I found a map online and it helped a little." Sam brought an image up on his screen and Val moved her chair over to take a look.

"See, here's the island in the middle of the pond," Sam said, pointing to the map and tracing it as he talked. "The area is surrounded by trees, mostly oaks I assume since it's called Oak Grove on the map. You can see where you come in over here," as he indicated a gate off of a two-way street. "Then you drive up this narrow road to the parking lot and get access to the rookery by going by the ticket booth, here, up a set of stairs, here, to a path that goes all the way around the pond."

"That's just a path?"

"Looks that way."

"There must be a way to drive close to the pond," Val said. She stared at the map. "There is a place back here," pointing to the back of the pond, "where it looks like there is a gate."

Sam looked where she was pointing. "Looks that way."

"Why a gate? I don't see any road attached to it."

"No idea."

"And doesn't that label say, 'boat house' up here," pointing at map, "next to the gate? How would someone get a boat back there?" Val said.

"By helicopter?" Sam asked with a grin.

"So we need to get that information and then, what, visit on our own?" Val said. "And what about suspects? Do we have any suspects with the possible exception of the friend of a friend that you got the phone call about?"

"No, but given the circumstances, as I said earlier, it would be logical to think that if anyone was out there with Burton, it was someone from his world, someone into birds or photography or nature. I can't imagine this as a crime of opportunity. Who else would be out there who would just happen upon him in the middle of nowhere?"

"Alligator poachers?" Val asked.

"Hadn't thought of that," Sam said. "Don't know if that's a problem."

"Maybe we can start at the Bird Society and get some background before we start off," Val said. "I'm not sure where else to begin. Then we need to talk to those who took a boat out to the island. And we need to know how someone gets to that back gate."

"OK, I'll call the Bird Society and see if they are open," Sam said.

"Yes, let's try and do that this morning. Give me time to come up to speed, and then we can drive over."

The Egret Bay Bird Society's office took up almost half of a small shopping plaza that was also occupied by a dentist, two attorneys, and an accounting firm. The Society's office was located on the corner, and its large exterior windows overlooked a parking lot on both sides. The only birds that Val could see were grackles, but whoever designed the plaza had the good sense to plant a couple of crape myrtles to break up the monotony of the parking lot. Val and Sam's arrival into a small reception area was announced by a door chime that sounded like a chirping bird.

"That's cute, and appropriate," Val said to the young woman behind the reception desk.

"I love it," she replied. "Perks me up every time I hear it. Are you the detectives that called a short time ago to see Mr. Wallace?"

"We are. I'm Detective Val Forster and this is Detective Sam Pierson." She looked at the name plate on the desk, "And you are Adeline Alvarez?"

"Yes ma'am," the young woman said, as she stood up and walked toward a door at the rear of the room. She opened it, stuck her head in and said, "Vince, the detectives are here to see you."

A man appeared almost immediately, "Vince Wallace," he said as he walked over, sticking his hand out in greeting first to Sam and then Val. "Come on back. I'm really curious to find out how I can help you. I'm assuming this is about Lester Burton. I can't imagine anything else that has happened recently that would bring a couple of detectives to see us."

"Do you own or manage the rookery?" Val asked as she and Sam followed Wallace through the door and into a rather large conference room.

"The Bird Society owns the land where the rookery is located and is responsible for its maintenance. The pond there was originally a dredge pond that supplied dirt for a railroad project. Years ago, the pond began to fill with enough water that it became a water source for nearby industries. When those industries closed, it was abandoned and slowly the island in the middle became a popular roosting place for waterbirds. We approached the railroad people, who still owned it, and they donated the pond and the wooded acreage around it to us, with the provision that we maintain it. We named it the Bridges' Rookery after Thomas Bridges, the president of the railroad at that time, but most people just refer to it as 'the rookery' now. It's taken some time and a lot of grants and goodwill, but it's our pride and joy. We were all very upset to hear that someone had died there, and even more upset when we learned who it was."

The three sat at one end of a conference table filled with stacks of paper, brochures, flyers, and books. An open legal pad next to a pen suggested that Wallace had been working there when they arrived. "There's a lot of follow-up from the meeting," Wallace said, waving his hand at a pile of paper and tablets near the legal pad. "I'm trying to get everything organized so we can send out a summary of proceedings to the participants."

"To get started," Val said, "was Burton one of the attendees at your meeting?"

"No, he wasn't. He joined a group of us, four or five, at Fillmore Hotel bar after the afternoon session on Friday. We were rather surprised to see him."

"Did he say why he was here?"

"Just said that he was passing through and thought he might see some old friends because of the meeting and wanted to say hello."

"And were there old friends?"

Wallace hesitated and then said, "Old acquaintances. But I don't think anyone who was there in the bar at that time was what one might call a 'friend.'"

"After all the time he was involved in wildlife photography," Sam said, as though he were unaware of the controversy about Burton's behavior, "why wouldn't he have some friends in the birding community?"

"Burton didn't make friends easily and those that he made, he soon lost. I'm sure others will tell you the same thing, except no one wants to speak ill of the dead. The truth of the matter is that he was a wonderful photographer, but a royal pain in the ass if you had to spend any time with him. Sorry if that sounds harsh."

"We have heard some rumors along that line," Sam continued, "but no one went into detail as to what was so dislikeable about him."

"Well, he was not a good conversationalist unless the conversation was about him. That wouldn't be so bad if he talked about his adventures and his photography, but he mostly avoided anything of substance, saving those tidbits for his speaking engagements. Reminds me of an old joke about the man who talked on and on about himself, and then said, 'But enough about me. What about you? What do you think of me?'"

That made both Val and Sam smile. "But surely," Val said, "that's not enough to warrant such dislike. There are a lot of boring and egotistical people out there, but while they may be avoided, they are not called, to quote you, 'a royal pain in the ass.'"

"That's true. But it wasn't just his ego that turned people off. It was mostly his behavior in the field that led to such dislike."

"In the field?" Sam asked.

"Stop me if you know all this, but there are certain rules and behaviors that are supposed to be observed when a group of people are birding, whether with binoculars or a camera. You respect the birds. You don't stress them or disturb their habitat. You respect the people you are birding with. You share observations. You take turns if the birding situation is in a confined space. That kind of thing. Burton ignored those rules. He was, without a doubt, the most unethical birder I've ever met. Even when he was on a trek in some foreign country, stories followed him back here. He would belittle the native residents who accompanied him, accuse them of theft if he couldn't find a piece of equipment, shortchange them in payment. My guess is that he seldom returned to many of the exotic locations because he couldn't find anyone to assist him the second time around. He carried a lot of equipment and going it alone was not his style."

"Someone mentioned a fellow named MacPherson," Sam said. "Said that Burton really screwed him royally."

"Oh, yes. MacPherson was here for the meeting. Let me interject here that he is a friend of mine. He's the one who talked me into submitting an application to the feds in response to a RFP–request for proposal–for a climate change project involving young people. That's what this meeting last week was about. We propose to use junior high and high school kids to monitor the arrival or disappearance of specified birds, plants, and insects along the border, both in the U.S. and Mexico. The meeting was our initial planning session–who to involve up front, how to work with the Mexican educators, that kind of thing. But that's not why you're here. Sorry. Back to Anders–that's MacPherson's first name–and Burton. It's a well-known story among nature photographers."

"We're just trying to get a take on Burton right now," Val said. "These stories help. They might be important. Could you give us a little detail."

"Well, to start, Anders is a very good nature photographer. His images are sensitive and educational, leaning more towards the informative than the spectacular. Burton's work is more towards the spectacular. Back in the early 2000s, Anders was just beginning to get attention; Burton was already the best-known nature photographer in the U.S., mostly because he was an early genius in self-promotion. His photos were in Audubon and Sierra Club publications, in *National Geo-*

graphic, on calendars, and even Christmas cards. He was also a genius as a photographer. There are, for example, a few wonderful photos of egrets and herons by bird photographers showing birds that have scooped up a snake for dinner and the snake has wrapped itself around the bird's bill, making swallowing the meal a little difficult. But Burton got the photo, perfectly in focus and with the absolutely correct composition and depth of field, of the snake rearing back and staring eye-to-eye at the bird while the bird is staring at the snake. Sizing each other up. Wonderful."

"And MacPherson?" Sam said, impatient for the Burton-McPherson story to continue.

"Yes, MacPherson," Wallace said. "Anders took a photograph to die for. There is a family of birds known as Nightjar. Stop me if you know all about Nightjars and I'll skip the introduction." He looked at the two detectives, and getting no response, he continued. "They can be found all over the world. We call them Nighthawks here. They eat in flight, scooping up insects with a wide gaping mouth. They are difficult to photograph because, well, it's night and they're flying, and they are very quick. But there are some nice photos out there. Anders, however, got one of a Chuck-will's-widow..."

"A what?" Sam said.

"Chuck-will's-widow, a Nighthawk species, named after its cry, you know, 'chuck-will-widow, chuck-will-willow.'" He mimicked the call in a slightly higher voice. "That's common, to name a bird after its call. Like Bobwhite or Whippoorwill. Anyway, he got this photo of a Chuck-will's-widow, flying toward him, mouth agape, and zeroing in on a luna moth. It is an unbelievable photo. I have a copy around here, but just try and picture it. A black background, a mottled brown-and-black bird, a pink gaping mouth, and a large lime-green moth. A shot of a lifetime, well-composed, technically excellent. Took best bird photo in national and international competition, made Anders' reputation, and put him, regretfully, in competition with Burton."

"I take it Burton didn't like that from what you've said so far," Sam said.

"No, didn't like it at all. He admitted it was a fine photo, said he wished he had taken it, but then started questioning it, but with subtlety. 'The green of the moth looks a little off, I've never seen a Nighthawk mouth that pink, the depth-of-field seems uneven,' comments that made people look twice at Anders' work. They didn't really agree with Burton, but there was now a doubt. After all, MacPherson was an unfamiliar name, and all the prominent wildlife photographers knew of Burton's work. Was the Nighthawk photo too perfect? How about MacPherson's other work, was it too perfect too? Or was this photo an anomaly? Anders survived Burton's campaign against him, but the doubt, the question, was always there. Did this guy cheat on his best-known photograph? Anders went into a deep funk. It took him a year or two to come back and start photographing again, but he believes his post-Burton-incident work is inferior to his early work. I don't agree. I think he is not only as good, but even better, but how do you convince someone when they are beyond convincing?"

"That's a sad story," Val said. "I can see why there is no love lost on MacPherson's side. Do you know whether the two of them saw each other last week when they were here?"

"I don't know, but I think Anders would have avoided Burton if he knew he was around."

"MacPherson wasn't in the bar with you on Friday evening?"

"No, he wasn't."

"Are there other stories like this? Any of them associated with any of the other people at the meeting?"

"Not that I know of, but that doesn't mean they haven't been exposed to his behavior. Just that the encounters were not as publicly devastating as Anders' was."

"Do you know if Mr. MacPherson is still in town?"

"He left Sunday night–or was it Monday morning? Anyway, he lives in Sante Fe, New Mexico. I can give you his contact information. He won't be happy having his past troubles stirred all up again, but I realize you have to look into such things. Nice man. Takes care to avoid disturbing nature when he's out and about. Walks around things, not through them."

"We need a list of all the participants."

"Yes, I have a spreadsheet. I'll ask Adeline to print one out for you."

"How many are we talking about?"

"We invited fourteen people to attend and four couldn't make it, so ten plus Adeline and me. So that's twelve."

"And where are they from. Are they all local?"

Wallace looked at a list on a sheet of paper on his desk. "Four plus Adeline and me from Egret Bay, four from the greater Houston area, and two, including Anders, from elsewhere. Anders, as I said, now lives in New Mexico, but he spent many years in the Corpus Christie area. The other out-of-towner, Ralph Cook, is an excellent birder who specializes in Southwestern birds. He lives in Rockport."

"Did the participants stay here overnight?"

"We made room reservations for four, two of them from Houston, two for those living out of the area. The others didn't ask for lodging reimbursement so they either live here, stayed with friends or family, or commuted."

"Who were the people who live in Egret Bay and were present at the meeting?"

"The four local attendees include two environmental scientists, Eric and Phil Wright, and the Aiellos—Mike's an author of kids' nature books and his wife, Marie, is an artist that illustrates most of his books."

"And as far as you know, they were here for the entire meeting?"

"The Aiellos were. The Wrights flew out Sunday right after we finished. They were going to Washington state and planned to stay there for a week or so."

"The Wrights—father and son? Brothers?" Sam asked.

"Neither of those," Wallace said with a smile. "They are a married couple."

"Give us a little background on the other attendees, would you? You say that the Wrights are environmental scientists and the Aiellos write children's books. MacPherson is a photographer. Cook is a birder. What about the others?"

"Well, Kamal Kapoor is a freelance videographer from Houston. He specializes in videos of conference proceedings. Kamal stayed here during the meeting. Mildred Dvorkin is, for want of a better title, a historian who specialized in nature-related policy and law. She has been writing articles on South Texas and northern Mexico bird life for years and has a book out that is a collection of her essays from the past thirty years. She is also a fine photographer and uses her own photos as illustrations of her essays. She uses a wheelchair and travels with her husband. They stayed here during the meeting. Pete–Peter–Turner is a botanist, more precisely an agronomist, from Houston. He used to teach at Texas A&M but now has his own consulting company. Aaron Hoffman is a professor at the University of Houston, an entomologist who specializes in pollinating insects. Aaron and Anders are close friends. They worked together recently on a pamphlet on beetles of the Rio Grande Valley."

"And what about the people who work here?" Sam asked. "I mean besides you and Ms. Alvarez. And your board members, since I assume the Society is a non-profit. Are any of them acquainted with or have known problems with Burton?"

"There are just six of us employed fulltime. Me, Adeline, Lainey Gomez–she's someone you have to talk to since she manages the rookery for us–a public relations and marketing coordinator who also works as a grant writer, a volunteer coordinator and event manager, and a bookkeeper who also works with Adeline as general staff. As you can see, most of us wear more than one hat. We hire people for specific skills and then broaden their expertise and convert them into naturalists," Wallace said with a smile. "Lainey, for example, started as a volunteer and then worked her way up to being a damn good rookery manager. Adeline started as a receptionist and is now listed as project coordinator on the grant. We contract for maintenance services with the company that owns this complex, and we have a volunteer who administers our website. It's a rather loose organization, with most employees assuming responsibilities outside of their formal job specifications. And then we have about two dozen deeply committed volunteers from among our membership who assure that everything we try to do gets done."

"Would you add the names of your staff and their contact information to the list? Phone numbers will be fine."

"Sure, no problem."

"Were any of your volunteers associated with the meeting in any way?"

"A few of them helped with putting together the grant application, but they weren't present at the meeting. We did invite them to join us at the social gatherings and a few took advantage of that."

"For such an involved organization," Sam said, "I'm surprise that you have such a small staff."

"As I said, we rely heavily on dedicated volunteers, but you're right in that we are sometimes overwhelmed. This grant we received is now taking a lot of time on top of our normal tasks. Once we get the planning completed, we have the funds to hire three additional positions. They're temporary, tied to the grant for three years, but with luck and a little additional funding we may be able to hire them permanently if they work out. The rookery, for instance, needs another full-time person. We are working Lainey in excess of her forty hours a week during the peak migratory and roosting months. And Adelaide is taking on additional work with the grant over and above working as my assistant."

"That's helpful, thanks," Val said. "We have a couple of other questions to ask you about the rookery itself. We looked at the map online and it shows a gate and a boat house at the back of the pond, but how can someone get there if the only access to the back is by a foot path?"

"There is a street at the rear of our land that isn't shown on the map. It leads to the county maintenance yard. We built a gravel road that leads off that street and connects with the foot path around the pond at the gate shown on the map. There is a small parking area there for anyone who needs to get to the back of the pond. That road isn't included in the online map because we don't want people to use that as an alternative way to get to the rookery."

"And how many people know about that road?" Sam asked.

"Outside of our staff, just the volunteers and people we hire to help maintain the rookery area."

"And that would be how many people, as a guess."

"We have about a dozen active volunteers at the rookery, another four or five that fill in now and then, and maybe, at most, in a good year, a half-dozen workers from businesses that we contract with to provide technical expertise and skills related to maintenance."

"What's a good year?" Val asked.

"One without a hurricane or tropical storm," Wallace answered with a grin.

"And, just for the record, where were you Monday morning from, say 5:00 to 9:00?"

"In bed until a little before 6:00. Adeline and I and Kamal met at 7:30 for breakfast to double- check our list of follow-up items."

"And both Adeline and Kapoor were on time at the breakfast?"

"Actually, they were both there when I arrived. I was a few minutes late."

The detectives thanked Wallace for his information and told him that they would be in contact if they had furthers questions. They said goodbye to Adeline and walked out into the muggy heat of a June day along the Gulf Coast.

Val looked at her watch as they left. "We have time for lunch if you're hungry. Something relatively healthy. I've been eating Deke's barbecue for most of the last few days."

"Poor you," Sam said. "We're only a couple of blocks from the Oy Vey Deli. Haven't been there for a while. I'm sure you can find a healthy sandwich or salad. I'm thinking of a Reuben."

They spent their lunch talking about what was becoming known as "the Burton Case."

There was a phone message from the police department's administrative office waiting for Val when they returned. A local attorney had called the chief about a case Val had handled some months back. "I'm being told to call the attorney as soon as possible and answer his questions as long as my answers can be confirmed by the record." She sighed. "I need to refresh myself on what the record says. I'll be in archives if you need me."

Sam decided to use the time while Val was gone to look into some of the information that Wallace had given them. He first searched for the photo by MacPherson. What was that bird's name? He looked at his notes. Nightjar? It was something like that, but that should do. He started with "MacPherson" and "photograph," and "nightjar." And there it was. Talk about weird. That was one strange critter. Looked like a cross between a bird and a frog. But he had to admit that the photograph was certainly eye-catching. That wide pink mouth and the bright green of the moth. The interesting thing was that he was not sure that the moth would be caught. He didn't know enough about how fast the bird was going or how evasive the moth could be. That tension made the photo for him. He was used to seeing images of hunters and the hunted on TV, the lion bringing down a zebra, or the snake ready to strike at the mouse, but he knew little about birds. Outside of the more common sights around town–the pelican with his beak full of fish, the seagulls eating French fries–he realized he didn't notice much or think much about birds. Except when that white blob splattered on his windshield.

He continued his search on MacPherson. Lives in Santa Fe, New Mexico. They already knew that. He's 62 years old, had been a professional photographer for almost forty years. Started with wildlife, then mostly birds, and for the past ten years he had specialized in macro photography, whatever that is. Sam looked it up. Ah, close-up photography, often of small subjects. His website listed quite a few workshops MacPherson had attended along with workshops that he had taught. The most recent workshop was titled "Bugs Close Up." Five days. Price:

$3,000. Wow, Sam thought. He had never considered that one could make a living photographing insects.

Just as he got up to get something to drink, the phone rang. It was the M.E.'s office. All three bullets were from the same gun. That answered one question. He wished they could all be this easy to answer. He opened his notes and began typing them up, trying to find some order in them.

Val returned from her visit to the archives a bit before 3:00. She tossed her notebook on her desk and plopped into her chair with a sigh.

"Find what you were looking for?" Sam asked.

"Yes. And I called the attorney from the archives, just to make sure I had the wording correct. He's trying to get yet another postponement. If this keeps up, the young woman we believe to be the only surviving witness in this case will have retired and be living on Social Security."

Sam just looked at her. He knew her well enough at this point to be aware that the best thing to do was keep quiet.

She swung her chair around to face the desk, moved the notebook to the side, and pulled out her notepad. "Find anything of interest while I was gone?"

"Yup, just got a call that confirmed all three bullets were from the same gun."

"So it's possible that someone else was there besides Burton and that person shot the alligator and Burton," Val said.

"But we're working so far on the assumption that the firearm used belonged to Burton. And if Burton was shot after he got out of the water, then when was the alligator shot? Since it was shot in the back of the head, I've been assuming that it was on the island when it was killed, not bobbing in the water."

"We will have to come back to that," Val said. "Continue."

"I've gone over the notes we received from the sheriff's department. Doug Fraser, one of the deputies that responded to the initial call at the rookery, is actually attached to CSI, but he was on the road, along with Deputy Jefferson, and they were the closest deputies to the scene

Monday morning, so the dispatch sent them. He's sent over photos that Deputy Jefferson–also attached to CSI–took on the first excursion to the island, the one where they confirmed that both Burton and the alligator were deceased."

He rolled his chair over to Val's desk and laid the photos out in front of her. They showed the island from two different locations. All of them looked like they had been taken from a boat. In one, it was difficult to see Burton and the alligator because of shrubbery. The other was a much clearer image of the two bodies on a shrub-free area at the edge of the pond. Burton's feet and the end of the alligator's tail were in the water. It was difficult to confirm if the two were alive or dead from the distance of the first two shots, but the third, a close-up of the heads of Burton and the alligator, allowed little doubt that both were deceased.

"To summarize to date, the sheriff's office was leaning towards this being an accidental death and were ready to file it as such as soon as the M.E. gave them the OK," Sam said. "They notified us, just in case, but they didn't expect we would have to be involved. As I told you, I called Evelyn Bowers, who I remembered from the art gallery case last year, when I saw she had been among the first to see the body, but it was just pro forma. I had previously bought the idea that it was probably an accidental death, someone falling into the water and drowning. However, that changed when the full M.E. report came through.

"Also, the written report from the sheriff's office said they had no luck finding a next of kin. Burton's been divorced three times and no known kids. They did talk to the manager of Burton's photography and travel business, a guy by the name of...," he looked at his notes, "Terrance Easley. Easley said he'd inform Burton's work associates. No mention of whether he did so." He put a check mark on his notepad. "We need to follow up there," he said.

"They found a keycard in Burton's wallet," Sam continued, "so it was easy to find out where he was staying in town–the Mariner Inn–and access the room. There were keys to a rental car on the dresser and the car was still in the hotel lot. They had it towed and looked through it.

Again, nothing unusual in what they found. They took fingerprints on both driver and passenger sides of car, back side doors, and trunk, but really don't expect much to come of that except to confirm that it was Burton's rental and that he had driven it. Nothing of note in it except a six-pack container of water on the back seat with two bottles missing."

"Burton obviously didn't drive to the rookery himself," Val said. "At least not if that was the only car that he had access to. We need to check with the desk to see if someone came by for him at any time."

Sam made a note of that. "Nothing else of immediate interest in the room," he continued, looking at the sheriff's notes. "Some photography equipment–lenses, I think they said–but no camera. They assumed that he took the camera with him, but it's been verified that no camera was found at the scene. Clothing, personal items. There was a pair of good shoes, a dress shirt and slacks, jacket. Burton was wearing outdoor clothing when discovered. Khaki shirt and pants, hiking boots that probably didn't help him any once he was in the water. They boxed up some odds and ends that might be informative: local bird guides, a bird identification book, and maps of birding locations."

"So, no camera, no gun, and–did they find a cellphone?"

"No."

"...and no cellphone. Do they think the missing stuff is all in the pond?"

"That is a possibility. I have no idea how deep the water is. There may be valuable evidence in the camera or cellphone."

"Any other keys?" Val asked.

Sam checked over the notes. "Yes, there was a larger set of keys in the hotel room, probably belonging to home and business. It looks like he was planning on returning to the hotel rather than heading home immediately after his excursion to the pond. He left his hotel room, taking his keycard and his camera, but left the key to the rental car and some personal items in the room. He had the room reserved until Wednesday."

"I wonder what he was planning to do on Tuesday, after the excursion to the rookery and before taking off on Wednesday," Val said.

"At this point, no idea. On another note," Sam continued, "I spent some time looking into MacPherson. That photo Wallace told us about is really quite striking. Lots of color. Pretty sure the moth didn't get away, but not positive. Not much more about him on his business site. Haven't checked out more personal sites yet."

"And he lives in New Mexico?"

"Yes, his home and his business are both located in Santa Fe."

"Where do you think we should go from here?" Val asked.

"I've only just started looking at the list of the people who were here for the meeting and their contact information. I think we need to find out if any of the rest of them had a major grudge against Burton. Need to talk to MacPherson for sure. I've made a copy of the list for you. I thought maybe we could divvy it up and see if we can find anything else of a suspicious nature."

They separated the names of the ten attendees and information on each under three major categories: locals living in Egret Bay, those living in the greater Houston area, and those living in the rest of Texas or out of state. As Wallace had told them, four of the ten were locals, plus the two employees from the Bird Society. Another four were from the greater Houston area, including the videographer, Kapoor, who had breakfast with Wallace and Adeline on Monday morning. The other two, including MacPherson, were in the third category. At this point there was no reason why they should exclude women. Two of the attendees were women, but a note for one of them said she used a wheelchair. Val remembered Wallace saying that one of the participants used a wheelchair. Given the scenario so far, they might have to consider the possibility of an accomplice for her. To make all this easier, Sam developed a chart while Val, impatient to proceed, began looking up information on the individuals listed on the sheet they had gotten from the Bird Society.

"Birders, that's a new term for me," Sam said. "I always called them birdwatchers, but apparently there is a difference from what I've gathered online."

"Yes, people who travel to China or elsewhere in order to see a bird on their checklist are definitely more than birdwatchers. Not sure where the differentiation begins, however," Val said as she looked at the table Sam had prepared.

Attendee	Location Monday Morning
LOCAL (4)	
Eric Wright, environ. scientist	Flew out Sunday night
Phil Wright, environ. scientist	Flew out Sunday night
Sam Aiello, author children's books	
Marie Aiello, illustrator children's books	
HOUSTON AREA (4)	
Kamal Kapoor, videographer	Breakfast 7:30 am
Mildred Dvorkin, historian & photographer	Note: uses wheelchair
Aaron Hoffman, professor, entomologist	
Peter Turner, agronomist, consultant	
OUT OF AREA (2)	
Anders MacPherson, photographer, NM	Flew home Monday a.m.

Ralph Cook, birder, Rockport, TX	
STAFF (2)	
Vince Wallace, exec. dir., Bird Society	Breakfast 7:30 am
Adeline Alvarez, admin. asst. Bird Society	Breakfast 7:30 am

"I am really impressed," Val said as she looked at the chart. "What about the other people who work for the Bird Society? They weren't involved in the meeting, but that doesn't mean that they weren't involved with Burton. I agree, however, that we should target the most obvious first, anyone who has a history with Burton for sure. I still think we should start with MacPherson, even though Wallace said he flew out early Monday morning. He may be able to give us some insights into why Burton was here."

Given an assumed time of death between 5:00 and 7:00 AM, they decided to postpone questioning Wallace, Adeline, and Kapoor. It might be difficult to make a 7:30 breakfast meeting. It was currently dark at 5:00 and for some time afterwards. Sam offered to check sunrise stats to see how early Burton could have been able to see well enough to get around the rookery. They had doubts he would have traveled to the island on a boat in the dark.

As for the rest of the attendees, they decided to start with MacPherson and the Houston attendees, minus Kapoor since they knew where he was Monday morning. It's possible that some of them might have alibis for Monday morning and could be crossed off the list–at least for now.

"OK, let's start with MacPherson, Turner, Hoffman, and Dvorkin. Then we can go from there. I think we definitely need to ask CSI and

Forensics to begin searching the pond for Burton's camera and other missing items. We also need to get over there and take a look at the site and it would be helpful if we can do that while they're doing their search."

"I'll put in the request now," Sam said as he stretched. "We probably won't have an answer to that today. We can give them a follow-up call when we get in tomorrow morning."

"OK, tomorrow, first thing."

CHAPTER 4

Thursday Morning

Val arrived at the office a little before 8:00, followed shortly after by Sam. Checking her phone messages, she found that a call to the sheriff's office would not be necessary. Someone at the county office had been working late and a message had come in just after midnight. It was brief, saying only that in compliance with a request from Homicide Division, Egret Bay Police Department, a diver would be at the rookery at 9:30 AM and if Homicide wanted to come watch the fun, they were welcome to do so.

"Do you know how to get there?" Val asked.

"There's GPS."

"The last time I used that it took me to a dead-end road."

"There's an area road map on the same website that has the layout of the rookery for people who don't trust technology," Sam said.

She pulled up the page and checked on the map, then jotted down the address. "It shouldn't be difficult to get there," she said. "It's only about a twenty-minute drive to the turnoff. If we leave a little before 9:00, we should have no trouble arriving by the time they get started. When we're finished there, we can explore the road leading to the rear of the pond."

"Not sure I'd want to go diving in that water," Sam said. "You saw the photos the sheriff's office sent over. That gator was pretty big."

"Think of all the cowboy boots that could be made with that hide. Such a waste of good boot material," Val said.

"Or alligator gumbo."

"Is there such a thing?"

"I'm sure there must be. I understand that it's very nutritious, so why not?"

"And don't tell me it tastes like chicken," Val said.

"I don't know. Never eaten it. But if tuna can be called 'the chicken of the sea,' I don't know why alligator can't be called the chicken of the bayou, or–better yet–chicken of the swamp."

They reached the parking lot at the rookery with ten minutes to spare.

"Something stinks," Sam said as he got out of the car.

"Not used to ammonia?" Val asked. "I imagine that's the bird droppings. Reminds me of poultry farms."

"Don't want to think about that. I prefer my chicken smelling like it's been deep-fried."

Val pulled out a can of bug spray and doused her exposed skin. She tossed it to Sam, who was already warding off mosquitoes. "Glad I had this in the car," she said. "We're going to need it. Open the back door and grab a couple of bottles of water to take with us."

They stopped by the ticket booth and picked up a printed copy of the rookery map they had seen on the web. Val asked the woman there if she was the one who had been on duty Monday morning.

"No, that was Doris. She works every Monday, Wednesday, and Friday morning."

They walked through the woods and up the stairs, stopping when they reached the top. Looking through the brush between the path and the edge of the pond, they could see the birds on the island were obviously disturbed, making strange noises, flying around, and jumping in and out of the nests in the trees and on what looked to be man-made platforms. The detectives walked to a nearby viewing platform just as a metal boat with a small outboard motor appeared, heading toward a clearing on the island across from where they were standing. There were three passengers. From the photos they had seen earlier, Val identified the clearing, the only place across from them that was devoid of brush and other greenery, as the crime scene–if there was a crime. She tried to visualize it as she had seen it in the photos, with Burton's body and the alligator lying there. There were enough small shrubs around the clearing that the bodies would have been partially hidden from some vantage points. She wondered if Evelyn and Trudi had been the only early morning visitors who had stopped to look at the island carefully. She and Sam watched as the boat slowed and then edged up to the clearing. The man in the front of the boat jumped out and tied the boat to one of the small bushes. The other two then joined him and pulled the boat a few feet onto the island.

"My Lord," Sam said, as birds continued squawking and flying around in alarm. "I have never seen so many birds all at once except those black ones in the Walmart parking lot."

"Certainly not so many large birds," Val said. "Look at that," pointing to a bird flying by not far from them, "How pink it is! I've seen spoonbills before, but never this close. And all those beautiful white birds!"

Sam walked down the path paralleling the pond until he came to a larger viewing platform. "Come here, Val," he called. "We can get a good view of the search from here." He waved at the three men on the island. One of them was donning a wetsuit.

"The water sure looks muddy," he said as Val joined him. "I wonder if they can see anything in that muck."

"I don't recognize that guy getting into the wetsuit. Do you?" Val asked. "Wish I had brought binoculars. Wasn't thinking."

"No, I don't remember him. One of the others is Doug Fraser, the deputy that was here for the discovery. I think the other guy works in Forensics, but not positive."

"Maybe the fellow in the wetsuit is from Houston," Val said. "They've helped us out with underwater recovery in the past. If I'm right, he may be the diver who helped us last year with recovering the body of that elderly man who drove his golf cart into the deep end of the municipal swimming pool."

"How deep do you think the water is here?" Sam asked.

"Don't know, but I'm assuming it's deep enough that Burton couldn't stand up in it and walk to shore if he fell in."

"He may not have been able to walk out if he had a heart attack."

"But the M.E. says that probably happened after he got out of the water. We know he got out somehow. The question is, how did he get in?"

"Ah, they brought equipment," Sam said as they watched the man in the wetsuit pull on his facemask as he walked across the sand. He was carrying a bright yellow wand. He stepped into the water and immediately disappeared before rising to the surface.

"Yup," Sam said. "The water there is too deep to walk in."

The man in the water began taking short dives using his wand to search the pond's bottom. He then made a deeper dive and rose to the surface holding a handgun. One of the men on shore carefully stepped toward the water, grasped the gun with a gloved hand, and immediately enclosed it inside a plastic bag. The diver then started searching again, but without much luck, until he made another quick dive. This time he came up holding a camera with what looked like a short lens attached. It too was placed in a plastic bag. The diver said something to one of the men onshore, who gingerly moved over towards the boat. He pulled out what looked like a kid's beach toy, an orange box made of narrow slats on the bottom and side and open at the top. He handed it to the diver. The diver left the wand on the beach and dove down again with the box.

"I wonder if he's going to try scooping the bottom," Sam said.

"So far, we have a handgun and a camera–hopefully *the* gun and *the* camera–so the only thing we know is missing and may be down there is the phone."

"Which may not be lying flat and therefore can't be picked up by the underwater metal detector," a woman said from behind them. They turned to look at her.

"I'm Doris Gibson," the woman said. "I'm the one that was here on Monday with the two ladies that discovered the body. I just dropped by the ticket booth to pick up sunglasses that I left there and was told you were here and had inquired after me."

"And you're familiar with underwater metal detectors?" Val asked.

"Yes, my father and my husband are both ardent detectorists. You know, those people who wander around looking for stuff that other people dropped. When my two men get together, that's all they talk about. From their conversation, I understand the phones tend to drop with the heaviest end, where the camera is, pointing down. In soft sand and mud, they stand upright, rather than lie flat. Their signal may be too weak to detect with the wand. If they think there is a good chance there is a phone down there somewhere, they bring out the scoop."

"Well, we're glad you came up here. We wanted to talk to you anyway, and we really appreciate your insights into what's going on over there on the island."

A shout from Sam immediately drew their attention. "He's got it!" They could see the diver handing the basket to one of the men onshore while the other held out his arm for the diver to grab onto as he pulled himself onto the clearing. The man with the basket reached in with his gloved hand and pulled out a cellphone, dripping muddy water as he held it up before bagging it.

The diver stripped out of his wetsuit as Fraser and the other deputy placed all three bagged items in a larger zip bag and labeled it. They then all carefully climbed back into the boat. Val noticed that the boat looked rather unstable and rocked back and forth as each man stepped in, carefully balancing himself before sitting down on one of the boat's benches. If Burton went to the island in that boat or one like it, he must have been uncomfortable with such instability, Val thought. Maybe they were all wrong in their assumptions. Perhaps Burton had fallen out of the boat either coming or going. But if he fell out on his way over to the island, his gun might have been too wet to have been used to kill the alligator. If he fell out when they were leaving, he could not have shot himself after he somehow climbed back on the island. Didn't make sense. Scratch that theory.

"I assume Burton was wearing a life jacket when he was in the boat coming over," she said, more or less to herself. "If so, I wonder why he took it off. And where it is." Sam heard her comment and replied that the other person could have taken the life jacket when he left.

"Or 'she,'" Val corrected him. "We aren't yet sure that the missing person is a male or even if there was more than one. If they used that boat, we now know that there could not have been more than four people involved since that's about all the benches in that boat will hold."

"*If* they used that boat," Sam said.

"Yes, there's that," Val said with a sigh.

The man who had been the diver turned on the motor and the retrieval party slowly made their way around the edge of the island and then out of view, with the birds continuing to squawk and fly about.

"Where are they going?" Val asked Doris.

"To the other side of the pond. They keep the jon boat there."

"Jon boat?"

"That flat-bottomed boat you just saw."

"And you can get over to the boat by taking the back road on the county property?"

"Yes, but it's gated and locked, so access is limited."

"And the boat is stored in the boat house?"

"Not usually, only in bad weather. There are quite a few other things stored in the boat house, mostly maintenance and safety items. The boat is covered and left out so it's ready to use. No need to be super-concerned as long as the gate is kept locked."

"You've been over there?"

"Yes, both my husband and I assisted with clean-up after that storm last year."

"How would someone get access to the jon boat if they couldn't unlock the gate?"

"Well, anyone could if they were agile enough to climb over the gate. It's a traditional swing gate. The bottom bar is set a little higher off the ground than usual so the gate doesn't impede wildlife, so I guess if someone was skinny enough, they could wiggle underneath if they wanted to. There's a channel at one side that is dug deep so big alligators can travel around the side of the gate, but I'm not sure I would use that to get to the other side."

"Could a person bring their own boat and somehow get it over–or under–the gate?" Val asked.

"Under, I don't think so. I guess if it's really small, like a kayak, you could get it under. The bottom bar is only a little over a foot off the ground. That's why wiggling under is only an option for someone skinny. I certainly wouldn't want to try. Probably get stuck half-way. As for going over, it would depend on the weight of the boat. A lightweight boat, inflatable or fiberglass, is not really suggested where there are alligators and possibly tree debris in the water. You might use a smaller jon boat. But I think it would take at least two people, one to lift and one to help it over."

"You seem to know a lot about boats as well as metal detectors," Val said.

"I was raised in a family of fishermen–and women. We moved around a lot but always settled next to the Gulf or a bayou. It's in my blood, I guess."

"Do you have a few minutes for us to ask you some more questions? It will save you having to drop by the station."

"Sure. We can sit here if you want. There's not enough room for all of us in the ticket booth."

"First of all," Val said, "please tell us, in as much detail as you can, what you saw and did on Monday after you were informed there might be a dead body on the island."

"Well, it started when one of the visitors, Evelyn, showed up at the ticket booth. She told me that there was possibly an injured or dead person lying on the island next to an alligator. We hear all sorts of stories about turtles being mistaken for half-eaten people floating in the water and such, so I am not usually concerned about such reports. But Evelyn was very calm and specific, not at all hysterical, about what she had seen. She told me she had looked closer using her binoculars, and that another woman had verified her concern, so I gave her more credence than most. I put up the sign on the booth that instructs visitors to continue on in and pay upon exiting, locked up, and followed Evelyn back to where another woman, Trudi, was waiting."

"Were there other visitors around there at that time as well as Evelyn and Trudi?" Val asked.

"Only five or six, and they didn't stay long. One of them got a text message that there had been some interesting birds over in the oaks down by the highway, so most of them hightailed it out of the rookery. It was very early for just casual visitors."

"Sorry to interrupt," Val said. "Go ahead."

"Well, my first look at the island was partially obscured by some small bushes. So we moved down the path to a new viewing platform. We had a much better view from there. I could see that there was a human body lying on the sand, feet submerged in the water. It was a man and he looked dead or possibly unconscious. An alligator was lying next to him, about three or four feet away. Its tail was partially in the water. It wasn't moving, but they are very still, you know, when they are basking.

"I didn't want to upset the two women, especially the older one because she looked so anxious, so I handed my binoculars–which are stronger than the ones the ladies were using–to the younger one, Evelyn, just to confirm what I saw. She took a deep breath and handed the binoculars back to me, which I took as an agreement that she also saw that there was someone either dead or in distress on the island. I immediately called the rookery's manager, Lainey, who said she would call 911 for an ambulance and then call the sheriff's office and ask them to send someone since the rookery is in the county, which is the sheriff's responsibility. Lainey said she'd leave immediately–she lives nearby–and drive over to the back gate to wait for whoever was on the way."

"But when the deputies came, they didn't go immediately to the back gate, did they?" Val asked. "They joined you at the viewing platform and saw what you saw from the platform before they went over to the island."

"Yes, they didn't know about the road to the back of the pond, so I told them how to walk around the pond to get to the other side to meet Lainey. The ambulance arrived at the back gate shortly after that and the four of them–Lainey, the two deputies, and an EMT–got in the jon boat and came around to the front of the island. They then confirmed that there was one dead male and one dead alligator without getting out of the boat. Lainey told me that the EMT then called the examiner's office so someone could come over for an official certification of death."

"And what did you do then?"

"I went back to the ticket booth. I had been gone for almost an hour at this point and was concerned about visitors piling up waiting to pay for admission. Of course, I was pretty sure that most people would read the sign and just go on ahead up the path and stop and pay on the way back, but you never know."

"And do you think many people arrived while you were gone?"

"It was getting pretty hot. The rookery is still full of nests, but the peak migration season is mostly over. I talked to one party of four who left not long after I returned to the booth. They wanted to know what all the excitement was over on the island. Apparently, they could see the alligator and the boat from where they were standing, but not the body. I told them that we needed to move the alligator because it was dead. They left a twenty-dollar bill to pay for their visit even though I waved them on through. I was pretty upset by the time I had a chance to sit and think about what happened."

"You volunteer here, or are you an employee?" Val asked.

"I'm a volunteer, three mornings a week."

"And when do you open up?"

"I get here at 7:00 and open the gate so I can get in and then I leave it open. Sometimes there is a car or two waiting, but most of the time people don't show up until around 7:30 or even later."

"Was there anyone waiting on Monday morning?"

"No, the first visitors didn't arrive until after 7:30. The two ladies were among the first. They got here about 8:00."

"And you then go to the ticket booth?"

"First, I unlock the restrooms, check to make sure there aren't any snakes or other critters that managed to get in there overnight. Then I unlock the ticket booth and set up for the day."

"And none of the early visitors came back and said anything about what was going on, or about the bodies?" Sam asked.

"No, they were probably looking at the birds flying about. The birds seemed disturbed and uneasy so I thought maybe there was a coyote or other predator on the island. And the visitors may have gone to a different viewing platform, one of those reached by going in the other direction from where the ladies had been, in which case they would not have seen that area with the bodies. I understand from Evelyn–the younger of the two ladies–that she was intentionally looking for alligators along the island's shore because her friend Trudi seemed so excited about possibly seeing one."

"We'll contact the sheriff's office to get an update on their search today," Val said. "And we need to talk to Ms. Gomez."

"Lainey left Tuesday for a wedding in Louisiana. She was going to cancel the trip because of the death, but Vince, the director of the Bird Society, told her to go ahead. He wasn't sure there were many question that he or someone else couldn't answer, and we could always call her if we needed to. She won't be back until tomorrow."

"We have her phone number on a list Mr. Wallace gave us. We will call her if something urgent comes up. Otherwise we can talk to her tomorrow." Val handed Doris a copy of her business card. "If you talk to her before she returns, please emphasize that we need to talk to her as soon as possible, while events are still fresh in her mind."

As they walked back to their car, Sam asked "Did you notice that the diver needed help to get out of the pond? We also need to consider that Burton may have fallen out of the boat. I noticed that it's very unstable, especially for those getting in."

"I thought about that, but it doesn't fit in with the scenario we have so far, especially if he was wearing a life jacket. And then there is the problem of the gun." She explained her earlier thoughts concerning a wet firearm.

"Maybe it wasn't his gun, but someone else's."

"Yes, possibly, but since he had a holster, we're almost sure he had a gun at some point. And the M.E. is convinced that Burton's bullet wound occurred *after* he got out of the water. It just doesn't follow any logical chain of events."

"Yeah, you're right. But we shouldn't rule it out. The scenario might change."

"I agree," Val said. "Now let's take a look at the other entrance. We're going right by the CSI labs on our way back. They'll have some paperwork and other things to do after their visit this morning, so it may be too early to talk to them now."

"OK," Sam said. "That will work. And we can get some lunch to give the sheriff's crew a little more time. I saw a little Mexican café on our way over here. On our right going back, about half mile from here," Sam said.

"Nice to know your food radar even works outside Egret Bay city limits. Sounds good. First stop, back gate. Second stop, café."

After returning to the parking lot, they drove out to the paved road, and then back to the highway. Instead of turning towards Egret Cove, however, they headed in the other direction until they saw a sign, "County Maintenance," that pointed to the right. They followed the road until they could see the maintenance yard buildings ahead of them and a well-maintained gravel road swinging off to their right towards an oak grove. The gravel road ended at a small paved parking area large enough for two or three vehicles. The gate, located just beyond the parking area, reminded her of the one her grandfather had used on his ranch, about five feet high with metal tubes running from end to end. The tubes were strengthened by a rigid set of flat crossbars that spanned from the upper end of one side to the lower end of the other. While climbing over would be relatively easy, as Doris Gibson had told them, and going under possible but limited by the person's size, going around would be a different issue. One end of the gate sat next to a rock outcropping and the other end stopped at the edge of a gully with a couple of feet of water in it. She assumed that was the channel Doris told them about that allowed alligators to get around the gate if they were too big to travel under the bottom tube. The rest of the tubes were about eight inches apart, with a larger tube spanning the top. There was a latch with a keyed lock on the side abutting the rock. Good planning, she thought. Wouldn't want to have to unlock the gate on the other side if there was an alligator making its way around.

"Well, shall we?" she said to Sam as she put a foot on the bottom tube and began climbing over. He followed her, keeping to the side near the rock. He had obviously had the same idea about the possible alligator passage. On the other side of the gate, the road narrowed, but the ruts deepened.

"Lots of heavy traffic here," Sam said.

"Probably from maintenance crews," Val said. "I imagine there is quite a lot of upkeep necessary to keep the island free of debris, what with the storms and all."

There was a large windowless resin shed sitting on a concrete slab not far from the gate. The two sides of the shed door joined in the middle and were secured by a keyed lock. A boat encased in a tight-fitting gray cover sat across from the shed, tethered to a metal post by a hefty rope. Next to the boat was a storage chest anchored to another metal post by a similar rope. Sam took photos of the shed and the boat with his cellphone.

"And what's the chest for," Sam asked as he walked over to it.

"I imagine it's used to put things in, like maybe the cover when the boat is taken out."

Sam lifted the lid of the chest and stood for a moment staring into it.

"Well, here's something interesting," he said. Val walked over next to him and looked in. "Life vests," Sam said. He reached in and moved the top vest to the side. "There are only three here," he said.

"And we think the boat seats four. You'd think there would be enough life vests for four people," Val said. "We are also almost positive that Burton wore a life vest. Unless he brought his own, four minus three means that the vest he used may be missing. We need to find out how many vests are usually kept here."

Sam went back to the boat and bent over one end of it to raise it. It came up easier than he expected and threw him a little off balance. "Not very heavy," he said, "but I wouldn't want to have to lift something like this over the gate. It may be fairly light weight, but it's pretty big. You'd need at least two people on each side to get it over safely."

Sam wandered back in the direction of the gate, turning onto a narrow path that angled off just before the gate and led toward the pond. Sam followed it a little ways, stopping to take a couple of pictures. "This must be the footpath that goes around the pond to and from the viewing area, the one that the deputies followed on Monday," he called back to Val. He walked on a short ways and then came back to where she was standing. "If you follow that path, you can see some of the viewing platforms."

"How easy is that path to travel on?" Val asked.

"It's quite overgrown from what I could see from the short ways I walked, but it's pretty easy to follow."

"Snakes," Val said.

"What do you mean, 'snakes'?" Sam asked.

"A narrow, overgrown path through the woods next to a pond. Sounds like it might not be the safest way to get to the platforms, although the deputies didn't seem to have any problem. I wouldn't want to walk it. I'm sure there must be water moccasins around here."

"You mean cottonmouths?"

"Are they the same thing? I always thought they were two different things."

"One and the same," Sam said. "And I don't think they lurk in the grass waiting for something edible to come along. It's more likely that they would be found on logs or rocks soaking up the sun when they weren't actively hunting."

"It's the actively hunting part that bothers me," Val said.

"Tell you what. You take the car back to the main parking lot and wait for me. I will follow the path around and take some photos as I go. We can compare them with the ones Deputy Jefferson took and the ones the sheriff's CSI agent took. Don't know what good that will do, but it's worth a try. If I'm not at the lot in a half hour, call the ER and have them set up some antivenom for me."

Val returned his grin. "OK. But take a stick with you to beat the bushes if you hear something wiggling around up ahead of you."

Sam looked around and finally found a straight stick on the ground. "See you on the other side," he said as he walked off toward the path, swinging the stick as he went.

Val returned to the car and drove back to the main parking lot. She noticed that there were only three cars parked there, all three of them relatively new SUVs with Texas license plates. She got out and walked over to the ticket booth. The woman she had spoken to earlier was gone, and a man was there that she had not seen before. "Good afternoon," he said. "Welcome."

"Thanks," Val said. She showed him her badge. "I'm just waiting here for my partner. I thought Doris might be here," she said, knowing that Doris didn't work on Thursdays. It was a good way to start a conversation, however.

"No, Doris only works Monday, Wednesday, and Friday," the man said. "I'm Warren. I work starting at noon on Tuesday and Thursday. Are you here about the guy that was killed over on the island?"

"Yes, but we're not sure he was killed. We're still investigating what happened."

"Really shook Doris up. That's all she could talk about for a couple of days."

Val nodded. She remembered that Doris had said she was upset when Monday's events were behind her.

"Not very busy today," she said.

"No. We've had a few lookers come around earlier, wanted to see where the dead fellow was found. They didn't stay long. They didn't seem to know anything about the gator. That big guy that was found with the dead photographer was almost always basking on that little clearing during sunny days, but of course he's not around anymore."

His comment reminded Val that the news reports she had read still didn't mention the alligator. "You mean he went to the same area every day to bask?"

"Every sunny day. Sometimes you could even find him there on rainy days. But not if it was cold. Don't know where he went when it was cold."

"Were people aware of the chance that he might be there? Did he have a fan club or such?"

"The regulars knew to look for him, but most people who come here don't come again, or don't come frequently. And some don't like the alligators, although most are fascinated with them. I miss him. I used to be able to tell people who wanted to see a gator where they could find one and they were often excited, especially if they came from the north where there aren't any such creatures."

"Do you think that alligator would be upset if there was a boat tied up next to his favorite basking spot or that people were wandering around him?"

"Could be, but somehow, I doubt it. He was a pretty big guy, and he was used to people showing up now and then and didn't seem to mind them. They eat at night mostly, you know. They aren't looking for food during the day. He just wanted to catch a few rays and warm up some after a night of hunting."

"Did he have a name?"

"Not officially. Most just called him 'the big guy.' I called him 'The Hulk,' after the green comic book character. Well, actually, my grandson called him that first and it just sort of stuck."

Just then she heard someone coming down the steps by the booth.

"You made it safely," she said as Sam walked over toward her. "See anything interesting?" She turned to Warren and explained that they had been over on the other side of the rookery where the boat was located, and her partner had taken the path back to see if he could find anything of interest to their investigation."

"See any snakes?" Warren asked.

"No," Sam said. "But my partner here was concerned about cottonmouths."

"Oh, you mean moccasins," Warren said. "They're not very aggressive, unless you step on them. They don't like that."

"Do you have many cases of snakebites?"

"No, haven't had one in months, maybe years. Fire ants, that's what gets people. Also those garden spiders, the big ones with yellow stripes. They like to spin webs over the trails and people sometimes walk right into a web. One guy threatened to sue us for having a spider get in his wife's hair, sending her into hysterics."

"And any problem with alligators?"

"Had one bite a poacher a few years back. Guy was lucky. Gator let go almost at once and swam off. Let him off with one hell of a bruise and about twenty stitches, though."

"You have poachers?"

"I think that's why we put the gate up at the back, to keep poachers from driving in at night and trying to catch a gator. Haven't had that kind of trouble for quite some while, however."

Val thanked Warren for his insights and then the two detectives returned to the car.

"Poachers, I've made a few jokes about them, but hadn't thought about them seriously," Val said. "Do you think Burton might have hired a poacher to take him to the island?"

"Where would he find one?" Sam said. "I doubt they advertise."

"Hey, who knows? Probably have a business site online," Val said. "It's almost 1:00. Lunch. And then back to the wilds of civilization."

CHAPTER 5

Thursday Afternoon

The sheriff's department had been housed for years at the old and rather ornate Fillmore County Courthouse in downtown Egret Bay. Now his whole department was located in an annex to the new Justice Building situated on the major highway leading in and out of the town. "Justice," as it was called by most people who worked or had business there, had been built to expand the county jail, the number and size of courtrooms, the sheriff's headquarters, the M.E. facilities and morgue, and the Crime Scene Investigation unit, including Forensics.

Val and Sam flashed their badges for the deputy sheriff stationed at the electronic gates just beyond the entrance. They were then buzzed through to the foyer. "Not many people around," Val said as she pushed the up button at the elevator bank. "Must not be any major trials going on."

They got off on the third floor. Double glass doors marked Crime Scene Investigation Department were located just opposite the elevators. One of the women at the front desk looked up at the two as they entered. "How can we help you?" she asked.

"Is the crew that was out this morning investigating the death at the rookery back yet?" Val asked, showing her badge.

"Deputy Fraser is back. He came in almost an hour ago, just before I left for lunch. I think he's still in the lab. Not sure about anyone else since I just got back."

"We'd like to talk to him," Val said to the woman at the front desk.

"Down the hall and the CSI offices are on your right. I'll let him know you're here," the woman said as she buzzed them in through another glass door leading into a long wide hallway.

"Fancy, fancy," Sam whispered as they headed toward the CSI offices. "One would think this was Fort Knox."

"You're just jealous that we don't have someone sitting at a desk to buzz us in at the office."

"Twice," Sam said. "Once at the front door and then again up here."

Val opened the door marked Crime Scene & Forensics Unit and they stepped into another reception area and asked for Deputy Fraser. The man at the desk pushed an intercom button at his desk. "Detectives from Egret Bay homicide to see you," he said. "Great, send them through," came a quick reply.

"How did you know who we were?" Sam asked him.

"They called back from the front desk," he replied. He pointed to another hallway behind him. "Conference room third door down."

Sam leaned toward Val as they walked down the hall and whispered, "So why do they have such ritzy surroundings and we have trouble getting new chairs for our waiting room?"

"That's because the sheriff is elected and the police chief is appointed," she whispered back.

"What's that got to do with it?"

"Think about it," she said as she opened the door to the conference room. Deputy Fraser was sitting at a large table surrounded by cushioned chairs with armrests. He waved at Sam and then stood up, leaning across the table to shake hands and introduce himself to Val. He motioned for the two to take seats on either side of him. "This damn table is so large that it's hard to hold a conversation if we sit opposite each other," he said.

"Yeah, I hate that," Sam said as Val looked at him and frowned. Fraser was either unaware of the sarcasm or chose to ignore it.

"If I understand it correctly," Val said to Fraser, "you were one of the deputies that responded to the call from the rookery's manager, Ms. Gomez, reporting the presence of a body on the island beach."

"Yes, that's correct."

"And you also were part of the first crew that traveled to the island and then again when the crime scene unit searched the pond for the gun and other items."

"Yes, that's correct, first responders to the scene. Deputy Jefferson and I were on our way back from a meeting in Houston and we were only about a mile from the turnoff to the rookery when the call came through, so the dispatcher sent us there. We weren't that concerned, figuring that some debris had washed up on the island or such. That's happened a couple of times before. Once it was a dead coyote that had been partially consumed by an alligator and someone thought it was a dog and wanted its remains removed for burial."

"But when you got there...?"

"It was obvious when we looked with binoculars that the body on the island was human. From the platform, it looked intact, so we immediately thought that it was some guy who leaned over the viewing platform's railing and toppled into the water. It was the alligator next to it that left us confused. That was unusual, to say the least."

"You two then took the path around the pond to meet Ms. Gomez. We understand she used a boat kept on the other side of the island to take you two and an EMT to the scene where the deceased and the alligator were located. Is that correct?"

"Yes. Ms. Gomez used the motor to get around to the front of the island and then slowed down when the bodies could be seen clearly. We were hesitant to get too close, both because of the alligator—we certainly didn't want to startle it—and fear of muddying the scene in the off chance it was a criminal investigation."

"And that's when you discovered that both the person and the alligator were dead."

"Yes. Weird. Very weird," Fraser said.

"Did any of you get out of the boat?"

"No, we called the medical examiner's office to let him know what we had found. He said he would leave immediately and bring a CSI deputy with a camera to document the scene. I was going to tell him that my primary assignment was with CSI and that Deputy Jefferson had a camera and she was already taking pictures, but he hung up before I could tell him. I knew by then that we weren't going to leave the boat to document the scene, so it's probably good that someone else was coming to do that. I wasn't feeling well and was a little dizzy, so I was just as happy that we weren't getting out."

"And then you all returned to where the boat had been originally located?"

"Yes."

"And then what did you do?"

"I got out," Fraser said, "but Ms. Gomez and Deputy Jefferson stayed with the boat to wait for the M.E. The EMT returned to the ambulance and then came back and said the ambulance would stay put unless they got a call."

"So you didn't go on the boat with the M.E. back to the site where the deceased was located?"

"No, as I said, I was feeling dizzy with the heat. The EMT said he thought I was dehydrating, so I drank some water and stayed on shore. Dana–Deputy Jefferson–said that rather than taking the path back, I should wait until the M.E. was finished and we could get a ride back to the parking lot with the M.E. or with Ms. Gomez. I went down the path a short ways to where there was a place I could sit down and watched them from there. Once they reached the area, the M.E. and the CSI cameraman got off the boat. Deputy Jefferson and Ms. Gomez stayed on the boat."

"How long did you watch them?"

"Not long. Ten, fifteen minutes maybe. They weren't there very long."

"And did you see the M.E. examine the deceased?"

"Not clearly. There were too many bushes in the way. I understand from Deputy Jefferson that the M.E. had a little difficult getting off the boat and onto the beach. I didn't see that, however. She said that Ms. Gomez had taken the boat right up to the landing, but there was nothing for the doc to hold onto when he stepped off. He staggered a step and that made him trip over the alligator, and he fell down between the alligator and the deceased. Geez, she told me, I should have heard him swear," he said with a grin. "The cameraman was up on the beachy area doing his work, photographing the deceased, the alligator, and the environment. Dana–Deputy Jefferson–said that the doc first took a quick look at the alligator to confirm it was dead and, according to Deputy Jefferson, that's when he saw that it had been shot twice, once through the eye and once through the back of the neck.

"As I said, I couldn't see exactly what was going on because of the shrubbery, but I did see all three standing there, looking around, probably to see if there was anything there that they should photograph and bag. I moved down the path a little further and could see much better. I saw the doc bending over the deceased, possibly looking through his pockets. He then turned the deceased over, face up. I couldn't see all the details from where I was, but when the doc was taking me back to our car in the parking lot, he said that when he turned the deceased over, he realized that he had been shot in the thigh. He also saw that the deceased was wearing a sidearm holster, but it was empty. He said that he found a camera lens cap in the deceased's front pocket and decided to expand the search area to look for a camera as well as a handgun, with no luck. They also looked for and did not find a cellphone. The M.E. said that he had certified the death, initially marking it as due to unknown causes. We had all been pretty sure it was an accidental drowning up to that point, but the absence of the gun, camera, and phone made us uncertain.

"The doc had pulled a wallet out of the deceased's back pocket, but he didn't examine it. Just bagged it. When I looked at it after we got back to the lab, I had trouble separating the items in it because they were wet and stuck together. His driver's license was behind a protective sleeve, so we had an I.D. The name didn't mean anything to me. I understand he was pretty well-known, however."

"Well-known to a select group of people apparently," Val said. "When was the body removed?"

"I understand Ms. Gomez made another trip to take two EMTs over after the M.E. left. I heard that they had a difficult time getting the body bag into the boat and came close to capsizing it. There wasn't room for all of them so one of the EMTs stayed on the island until Ms. Gomez returned to take him back. Then they had to figure out how to remove the alligator. They ended up contacting animal control and a couple of those guys had to go out there by themselves. All they brought back to Forensics was the head. One of the animal control vets then extracted the bullets and sent them to us. He said that whoever shot the gator knew exactly how to do it and was taking a major chance if all he had was a handgun. No idea what they did with the rest of the alligator. I'm glad they took photos when the M.E. was over there. The three following trips–to obtain the deceased and then the alligator and then this morning to search the pond–certainly muddied the crime scene, if it was a crime."

"You think not?" Val asked.

"As I said, I didn't think so at the time, but the more we looked at it, the more I began to think it might be. Obviously, they wouldn't have asked for you two to help if others in our office weren't also concerned about it."

"And you returned this morning during the search of the pond, right?"

"Yes, with two bottles of water and two bottles of a sports drink. I don't think I've ever experienced dehydration before and didn't want to risk it again."

"Who was the guy in the wetsuit?" Sam asked.

"He's a diver from Houston. He's helped us out before. They have all the latest devices for underwater searches, like that really cool metal detector that he used to find the gun and the camera at the bottom of the pond."

"And who else was with you?" Val asked.

"Another deputy from CSI. He went to take another look around and assist in recovery in case anything was found in the pond."

"And since Ms. Gomez is out of town, who was that who took you over there?"

"The diver. He knew how to handle the boat and had permission from the organization that owns the land."

"And since you've had a quick look at the items recovered this morning, is there anything you can report about those items?" Val asked.

"Forensics is looking at them right now. The only thing I know is that there are four rounds missing in the handgun and three accounted for: two in the alligator's head and one in the deceased's leg. A handgun is not a firearm that I associate with killing alligators, but there were no other injuries found on the alligator."

"Four rounds missing?"

"Yes, but of course we don't know that that the chambers were all filled to begin with."

"Any evidence that the deceased fired the gun?"

"Lab's working on that but doc doubts there will be any residue left on the deceased's hand–if he fired the gun–because of his dip in the water. However, an empty holster suggests that he had a gun on the island at some time, so we're assuming it's his."

"And the camera?" Val asked.

"Somewhat of a surprise. You'd expect a professional photographer to use one of those top-of-the-line camera costing thousands with one of those super scopes sticking out in front of it, but the lab guy working on the deceased's camera–assuming the camera we found was his–said that although it was a quality camera, it had a 50-millimeter prime lens–that is, a fixed lens. No zoom like you often see wildlife photographers use. Of course, he may have been traveling light. I imagine a professional would choose to use a tripod with one of those big lenses. Taking a tripod was probably out of the question. Too much baggage."

"Any images survive the water bath?" Sam asked.

"Working on it."

"And the phone?"

"Working on it. Forensics says that they think its password-protected, so that presents another hurdle."

"What about fingerprints or other clues–fabric threads, etc.–on the boat?"

"We didn't even try. By the time we got there, any evidence would have been compromised by the people who used the boat on Monday. We did check for residuals–threads, discernable shoe prints, and such–but no luck."

"How do you think he got to the island?" Sam asked.

"I can see only one explanation outside of the possibility that he just fell in the water from one of the viewing platforms: the deceased and at least one other person drove out to the back gate and came in that way. The front gate was locked if the M.E.'s time of death is correct. If they had come in through the front gate, they would have had to park outside, climb the gate, walk through the parking lot to the stairs, up the stairs to the path, and then around the pond to the back. And then do the same coming back. No, they came in the back way. I'd bet on it."

"And do you think that Burton and whoever was with him used the rookery's jon boat to get over to the island?" Val asked.

"Makes sense. It's possible that one of them knew the code for the lock on the gate and brought in their own boat, but why? If they knew the code, they certainly knew the jon boat would be available for them to use."

"When you got to the back of the pond the first time over, was the boat covered?"

"No, I don't think so. It was just sitting there ready to go. However, Ms. Gomez was already there and she could have uncovered it."

"Did you notice if it had water in it or was otherwise wet from a recent trip?" Sam asked.

"No. I wish we had looked more carefully when we arrived there. We were in such a hurry to get out to the island that I don't think any of us stopped to look at the condition of the boat. We just got in it and took off."

"So you think at least one person involved in the incident had inside knowledge of the boat being available and accessible."

"Yes, that's my theory."

"That might limit possibilities," Sam said.

"Do you personally think someone planned this in advance?" Val asked Fraser.

"Off hand, I would say yes, but the question is what is meant by 'this.' Burton's death? The excursion to the island? We have no idea why they were out there. The doc has said since he finished the autopsy that he believes the death occurred under suspicious circumstances. Maybe the images in the camera will give us a clue if we can retrieve them. Ditto for the phone. We'll just have to wait and see."

"The M.E. has been hesitant about revealing the presence of an alligator. Can we mention the alligator now, as far as the sheriff's office is concerned?" Val asked.

"That's entirely up to you," Fraser said.

"Is Deputy Jefferson around?" Sam asked.

"She's been assigned fulltime to the drug task force and hasn't been around much. You can leave her a message," Fraser said, writing her number on his card and handing it to Val.

The detectives decided to stop by the Mariner Inn on the way back to their office to see if they could turn up any evidence that someone picked Burton up late Sunday night or early Monday morning. The manager pulled up the front desk video covering midnight to noon on Monday, but the only visitors were people checking in. There were no phone calls to Burton's room. The last entry on his bill was a room-service scotch and soda at 12:20 AM. He didn't stop by the desk when he left, whenever that was, so he may have used the side door to the parking lot going out. The items that had been left in his room indicated that he planned to return.

"OK, what's next?" Val asked Sam after they had returned to their office.

He checked his notes. "Well, we have Ms. Baldwin's account of what she and Ms. Olson saw when they discovered the body, and we have Doris Gibson's account of the same. We'll probably have to wait until tomorrow to talk to Ms. Gomez about her trips out to the island. Deputy Fraser has given us his account of his two trips, and now we have his update on CSI and forensics activities. Next on the list is contacting MacPherson. Deputy Jefferson, the EMT on scene, and the Houstonians."

Val checked her watch. "It's almost 4:00, a little late to get started here. But it's only 3:00 in Santa Fe. We can probably get a call in to MacPherson."

Sam looked at the list of meeting participants. "There are three phone numbers for MacPherson. One at home, one business, and one cell," Sam said.

"It's a Thursday afternoon. Let's try the business first."

There was an answer on the third ring. "MacPherson Photography, Mac speaking."

"Mr. MacPherson," Val said, "this is Detective Val Forster, with the Homicide Division of the Egret Bay Police Department."

"I was wondering how long it would be before you contacted me, Detective. There seems to be some rumors floating around someone had done him in, but it wasn't me. What else would you like to know?"

"Just a couple of other questions if you have a few minutes."

"Go ahead. I knew this was coming and I'd like to get it over with," MacPherson said.

"When you just said that Burton 'had been done in,' what do you mean by that?"

"Well, I heard he had been killed. Shot."

"You heard he had been shot?"

"Yes, that's what a couple of people told me, that he was shot."

"That rumor is incorrect."

"Then how did he die?"

"He died as a result of complications of almost drowning," Val said.

There was a pause before MacPherson spoke again. "I don't know what to say to that. I can't imagine that Burton's ghost is satisfied with such a pedestrian demise. Eaten by piranhas, yes; gored by a rabid rhino, yes. But drowning? Not in line with his character."

"And what is his character?"

"As an example, I happened to be in Tanzania at Lake Manyara about ten years ago to photograph the magnificent gathering of flamingos at the lake. My guide was a young man, English but raised in Tanzania. He told me that he had acted as a guide for Burton the previous year and would never work for him again. When I asked why, he told me that after Burton had taken multiple photos of the flamingos feeding, he wanted to take one of them flying. The guide told him that they would not fly off in the midst of feeding unless there was cause, like a predator. At that point, Burton pulled out a pistol from his holster and fired a shot into the air that startled the birds and then another a little lower when they lifted from the water. That second shot wounded a bird that was just taking off and it fell back in the water, thrashing around in pain. Burton ignored it, lifted his camera and got the flight shots he wanted. Once the birds had resettled, Burton turned and walked away, leaving the wounded bird for someone else to put out of its misery." He paused again. "Given that memory, maybe Burton dying from almost drowning is karma."

"Why didn't stories like that ruin his reputation?" Sam asked.

"Who would believe me if I said anything ugly about Burton? Everyone has probably heard about our history. I would just look like someone with an ax to grind. He never acted like that around people who didn't pose a threat, those he didn't consider his competition. Other photographers who relied on his largesse didn't speak out, nor did birders who were afraid to get blackballed for criticizing a well-known personality. But word gets around anyway."

"Did you see Burton while you were in Egret Bay?"

"Did I see him? Yes, I saw him in a local restaurant. I left and ate elsewhere."

"So you knew he was there?"

"I didn't know before I saw him. He was not on the program schedule. I don't think I would have participated if he had been."

"Was there any interaction between the two of you?"

"No. I don't think he saw me at the restaurant, and I was just as happy that way."

"But weren't some of those at the meeting aware of the history of the two of you and knew that you were both in town?" Val asked. "Didn't someone say something?"

"A couple of friends warned me that he was there, but Vince assured me that it was not because he had been invited to the meeting."

"And do you know if he tried to join anyway?"

"No, although I understand he showed up at the bar on Friday evening. I wasn't there."

"When did you leave Egret Bay?" Val asked.

"On Monday morning. I had a flight around 10:30 a.m. out of Intercontinental."

"I understand you had a breakfast meeting scheduled for Monday morning that you cancelled."

"Boy, word gets around, doesn't it? Yes, I was supposed to have breakfast with a friend that lives in Egret Bay, but I was uncomfortable about Burton being in town and wanted to get out of there as soon as I could."

"Did you drive to the airport?"

"No, I used a limo to get from airport to Egret Bay, used taxis around town, and the limo service again to get to the airport on Monday morning."

"What time did the limo pick you up?"

"About 6:30. There were three other stops along the way, and we got to the airport about 9:15 or so."

"And where did you stay while you were in town?"

"At a B&B, Pelican Inn, on–appropriately–Pelican Street."

"Not the Fillmore where the meeting was held?"

"No. I'm working on a magazine article and wanted some peace and quiet."

"You arrived on what day?" Sam asked.

"I came late Thursday evening. Couldn't get a decent flight schedule on Friday morning."

"And you saw Burton on what day?"

MacPherson paused and then said, "That must have been Saturday lunch. At that downtown coffee shop, the Foghorn or some such name."

"One other thing," Val said. "In the flamingo story, you said that Burton drew a pistol from his holster. Do you know if he usually traveled armed?"

"I am pretty sure he was usually armed when he was in foreign countries, especially if the area he was traveling in was known for having dangerous animals...or people. I'll give this much to him: he had nerves of steel. He went places, did things, took risks that I would never consider. He would do anything, almost anything, to get a good photograph."

"Do you know if he was a good marksman?"

"No, I don't know, but I would assume that he was, just because he did most physical things well. He was, for example, an excellent rock climber."

"Were you aware that he didn't know how to swim?"

"Good gosh, no! Can't believe that. I guess that helps explain his demise. But it's hard to believe that he lacked such a basic skill."

"One last question," Sam said. "Was there anyone else at the meeting that you know of who had a similar antipathy towards Burton?"

"No. I doubt he had friends there, but I don't know of anyone else with a personal grudge." He paused. "I take that back. Mildred, that is,

Mildred Dvorkin, disliked him for personal reasons. I don't know why. When I asked her once, that's what she said, that there were personal reasons."

Sam quickly looked over his list. "She's listed as a wildlife historian from Houston. Isn't she the one using a wheelchair?"

"Yes, she has some limitations to getting around, but she knows about every law, regulation, excursion, and natural disaster that's affected wildlife along the southern border. She's also a capable birder, a good photographer, and a community activist for improved outdoor amenities for those with disabilities. Quite the lady. Her husband's a pretty good birder too."

"I would assume that access is an important consideration when you are discussing birding-related activities," Val said.

"Yes, indeed. We haven't paid much attention to that. Which is strange and rather shortsighted, given that so many birders are retired individuals, not all of them in the best of physical health."

"Thank you for your time," Val said. "We appreciate your insights. We will contact you if we have more questions. Also, please feel free to call us if you think of anything else that may help us. I have your email and I'll send you our contact information. We're asking everyone to write down what they did and where they were while in Egret Bay and send that to me."

"I'll do that and get it to you by tomorrow at the latest," MacPherson said. "Happy to help."

Val and Sam looked at each other after hanging up. "He says he didn't rent a car. Let's say that he did or that he found some other form of transportation. Do you think that time schedule, if it checks out, would allow him to get to the rookery, go back to lodging, clean up if necessary, and still catch a 6:30 a.m. limo?" Val asked.

"Can't see how," Sam said. "Can't ignore his animosity towards Burton, but...."

"Yeah. I agree. So let's check his timeline for Monday morning just to make sure. Gulf Limo is the only company that serves the various lodgings in town and both Houston airports. Also I think Mildred Dvorkin should be next on our list to call."

"Well, a woman in a wheelchair is not likely to have traveled out to the island in a small metal boat."

"No, but someone else could do so on her behalf. It depends on what the personal issue is that she declined to explain to MacPherson. It could be a minor thing that just hit her all wrong, or it could have been something as devious as the treatment he gave MacPherson," Val said. "One thing is certainly coming to the fore: Burton was not a very nice man. I remember something my grandmother said when I saw a cat walking down the alley in back of our house with a baby cottontail rabbit in its mouth. I was so upset, and she said something like 'nature red in tooth and claw.' It stuck with me, as young as I was, but I really didn't understand the implications until some years later when it was in a poem we studied in an English lit class. We like to think of nature as the great Mother, nurturing and all that, but it's dog eat dog out there sometimes. We certainly see that in our line of work."

"Good Lord, but you are philosophical today, Detective Forster."

"It was the poor flamingo that Burton shot. I've always been upset hearing sad stories involving animals. Next up, Ms. Dvorkin."

The call was answered on the third ring. "Dvorkins," a female voice said.

Val put the phone on speaker and introduced herself and Sam. "We're calling the participants of the birding meeting last weekend regarding the death of Lester Burton. Do you have a few minutes to talk to us?"

"Yes, I can do that. I was wondering if someone would call. I don't have to be anywhere this afternoon."

"Thank you. Were you in Egret Bay for the entire meeting?"

"Yes, well almost. I travel with my husband, and we couldn't leave until he got home from work shortly before 4:00. What with the traffic and all, we didn't get to the meeting until just before dinner on Friday, missing the afternoon discussion. But we were there for the rest of the meeting."

"I understand that you aren't one of Mr. Burton's fans," Val said.

"You understand correctly. He didn't have a lot of fans, so I am not alone. But I made no bones about my dislike of him."

"Did you know that Mr. Burton stopped by to say hello to the group at the bar after the afternoon discussion?"

"I heard that later. It's the only time I've been thankful about Houston traffic slowing us down."

"And where did you stay?"

"At the Fillmore. They have a wonderful accessibility suite."

"And you left when?"

"I was really tired at the end of the day Sunday, so we stayed over and drove home the next morning after breakfast."

"Which would have been about…?"

"We left around 9:30 or 10:00. We were home before noon."

"Did you eat breakfast in the hotel restaurant?"

"No, we went to that little restaurant on the road out of town. What was the name of that place? Just a second…" They could hear her call to her husband, but her voice was muffled. She came back on, "The Egg House. How could I forget that?"

"Can I ask why you disliked Mr. Burton?"

"It's rather personal."

"We won't share anything you tell us unless it's pertinent to the case. But this is, you understand, potentially a homicide inquiry, and we have to ask such questions."

"I understand. I really don't want this to get out among my birder friends. Do you know that I use a wheelchair?"

"Yes, we do. But that's all we know of you except that you've been called an excellent photographer as well as a historian of bird-related activities along the border."

"Well, that's nice. I just don't want people focusing on my attempts to photograph birds from a wheelchair instead of focusing on me as a bird photographer, if that makes any sense."

"All the sense in the world."

"Some years ago I was at a birding conference in the Rio Grande Valley. I was very excited because they have some wonderful birds that are seen along the border, Green Jays and Chachalacas and other exotic species. I had only been using a wheelchair for a year or so at that time, ever since I broke my back in an auto accident. I was pretty sensitive about being a burden to other birders, so when I signed up for a field trip to a well-known drip, I...."

"I'm sorry to interrupt," Sam said. "Did you say drip?"

"Yes, sorry. Birds are attracted to the sound of water. This particular drip was a natural pond that had been altered so that the water flowing into the pond ran over some rocks and then ended in a steady drip into the water below. That noise attracts birds. The pond is shallow so that birds can bathe and drink in it."

"Thanks," Sam said, "so continue. You signed up for a field trip...."

"Yes, and I got there early and with my husband's help, I found a spot in the corner of the viewing area where I could see what was going on and not obstruct the view of other people who would have to work around me. Although I had been writing about wildlife along the border for years, I was relatively new to photography. I had taken it up after my accident. I can't easily maneuver around other people, so getting a spot upfront is important. Also, while I can't take a picture if anyone is in front of me, people behind me can shoot over me so I'm not in their way. As others began to gather, Burton arrived. He was late for some reason and perturbed to find other people there. So he pushed his way through, reached down and undid the brakes on my chair. Then he pulled my chair back into the crowd, stopped it, reset the brakes, and stepped in front of me, standing where I had been sitting in the front row. It happened so fast–I was so confused about what was going on–that I didn't say anything until he turned to leave after taking only a couple of shoots. I whispered, because I didn't want to disturb the birds.

"Why did you do that?" I asked him. He ignored me, if he even heard. The other birders seemed to think that he and I knew each other, which we didn't, and they were enthralled by the birds that were visiting the drip, many of them species that some had never seen before. They moved forward, filling the space that I, and then Burton, had occupied, blocking my view. It took a couple of minutes for them to realize what had happened. One of them turned around and started to push me back where I had been, but by then I was so upset that I started to cry and told him to leave me alone. I rolled back to the path and waited for my husband, who was on another field trip, to come and get me. I was mortified, hurt, angry, and never, in my whole life, felt more used and useless."

"That falls in line with other things we're hearing about him," Val said. "I'm finding it difficult to understand how a man can do such disgraceful things and get away with it."

"His editors loved him," Dvorkin said. "His readers admired him, other photographers depended on his good graces with major publishers, and he was a very good photographer, among the best. Who was going to put up a stink? And how would it spread? Rumors and tales make their rounds, but few birders travel to meetings far from their home–it can be quite expensive–so my guess is that most birders do the majority of their birding close to home and therefore outside the gossip chains."

"And your husband was with you most of the time you were in Egret Bay?"

"Yes, we did everything together. Ever since that episode with Burton, he goes with me on field trips."

"Have they ever met, your husband and Burton?"

"No, thank heavens."

"I'll give you my email address," Val said. "Would you write down where you and your husband were and what you did between the time you arrived and 10:00 AM on Monday and send it to us. We need to know where you stayed, where you ate, when you were in meetings, that kind of thing. We're asking all participants to do that. You're not being singled out."

"I understand. One question. You said, 'this is potentially a homicide inquiry.' Do you think someone murdered Burton?"

"We're uncertain," Val said. "That's why this is an investigation. There are a lot of unanswered questions about his death." She gave Ms. Dvorkin her email address and phone numbers where she and Sam could be reached, and they ended the call.

"OK," Val said. "Let's write this up and then I think we should call it a day. Any questions?"

"Yes," he said looking at his notes. "What's a Chachalaca?"

CHAPTER 6

Friday

Sam was already in the office when Val arrived. He had just gotten off the phone with Gulf Limo. "Looks like MacPherson is in the clear, at least for now," he said. "Talked to the dispatcher and she put me through to the driver who picked MacPherson up. The driver said he got there a few minutes early and MacPherson was outside on the curb waiting for him. That would have been a little before 6:30."

"It would be difficult," Val said, "to do whatever was done on the island and get back here ready to go by 6:30 when the limo picked him up."

"OK, that strengthens MacPherson's alibi for now."

"And talking about timing," Sam said, "following up on our questions yesterday morning, sunrise Monday was at 6:30. But there's this thing called civil twilight where it is light enough to be out and about without need for artificial light. That period lasts for thirty to forty minutes before the sun actually rises, which takes us back to 5:50. Anything earlier than that would probably call for some type of light such as a lantern or flashlight."

"If that's the case," Val said, "whoever was there would only have, what, a little over an hour once they got there to open or climb the gate, launch the boat, travel to the front of the island, do whatever needed to be done on the island, and then travel out of sight of the viewing platforms before 7:00. They could then finish their trip, tying up the boat, getting back to the car, and driving away, all out of sight of anyone on the viewing platforms."

"They could use artificial light to climb the gate and launch the boat," Sam said.

"Yes, that would give them a little more time at the front end. But it might draw attention from any employee using the county road. And could Burton take photos before sunrise? If not, that means that he wouldn't want to be there on the island before 6:00-6:30. I have no idea how much light he would need."

"But 7:00 is not really an accurate end time for their expedition," Sam said. "Ms. Gibson opens the front gate at 7:00. Let's say someone was waiting for her and they follow her in. Both cars have to park, then the visitors have to wait while she checks the restroom and opens the ticket booth, then the visitors have to climb up to the path. So we're at 7:15 or 7:20 at the earliest."

"She said no one was waiting for her to open the gate on Monday and it was around a half hour before someone came."

"So the first visitor to the viewing platforms would have been around 7:45."

"But could Burton and/or others be sure of that when they were setting the timeline?" Val asked.

"Probably not. But even if a visitor got up on the path by the viewing platforms at, say, 7:15, the timetable we've come up with for Burton–at boat by 6:00, on island by 6:10 to 6:20, off island by 6:45 to 7:00–works just fine. However, that timeline does not include Burton's time in the water."

"But even if he was in the water for five to ten minutes, heading to the back of the island could have started as late at 7:10, even if the first visitor came in with Ms. Gibson," Val said.

"Boy, that's cutting it close," Sam said.

"I think I agree with you," Val said. "Whatever their timeline, it must have been interrupted by Burton's time in the water. That makes me even more convinced that his near drowning was just happenstance, something they did not foresee. I would imagine that would take a few minutes and then a few more minutes to get out of the pond...."

"...and get shot," Sam added.

"Yes, and then get shot. If we're on the right track, the drowning was not part of the plan."

"Which reminds me of another thing," Sam said, paging through his notes. "I called the B&B where MacPherson was staying first thing this morning. They confirmed that he didn't have a car and that he used taxis to get around when he was here. I called the taxi company and they said they had no record of any trip from anywhere to the rookery between midnight and 8:00 AM on Monday."

"Good thinking. However, everything we learn puts our best suspect further out of reach. Might as well put MacPherson at the bottom of the list."

"OK, next? Call the plant guy and the bug guy?" Sam asked.

"Plant guy and bug guy, geez. I looked them up. They're both PhDs in their field and need to be treated with a little respect."

"OK, Dr. Plant Guy and Dr. Bug Guy. Regardless of how they are addressed, they both live close enough that they could have driven home on Sunday if the meeting ended at a decent hour. Wonder what time it got over on Sunday," Sam said.

"We didn't ask that, did we? MacPherson waited until Monday morning to fly out, so I guess I just assumed the meeting lasted all day Sunday. We need to get the meeting agenda."

"I'll give the bird people a call and have them send one over," Sam said as he checked through his notes for their phone number. The call didn't last long. "Not open yet," he said. "Coming in at nine."

Val checked her watch. "That's not long from now. Let's get a copy of the agenda and then we can call...," she looks at the table Sam had developed, "Dr. Turner and Dr. Hoffman." She called the Egret Bay Bird Society a few minutes after 9:00 and Adeline promptly answered the phone. The meeting agenda was in Val's inbox a few minutes later.

"That's nice," Val said. "I wish everyone was so rapid in their assistance." She looked over the agenda. "Ah," she said, "informal lunch on Friday at 1:00 followed by a meeting scheduled for three hours that started at 2:00 with a break halfway through. Topic was discussion of the meeting's purpose and goals. There was an informal dinner afterwards. The meeting with Burton in the bar must have taken place between the time the meeting got over and the time they went to dinner. Then they met Saturday morning at 10:00, followed by an open lunch hour, and then another three-hour get-together on Saturday afternoon, 1:30 to 4:30, followed by refreshments at 5:00 and dinner at 6:00. Sunday morning free, lunch at noon, then wrap-up session 1:30 to 4:30. That's a little late to get to a Houston airport, especially if you're flying out of Intercontinental. Even if you skipped the dinner, you couldn't stay through the full wrap-up and catch a flight that went out before, say, 8:00 that evening."

"But not too late to leave if you live in the Houston area and can drive home," Sam said.

"Let's call Dr. Turner, the botanist, first and then Dr. Hoffman, the entomologist. If we can't reach them, we can leave a message and have them call us. If we don't hear from them before we leave this evening, we can call them tonight at home. We need to know when they headed home."

"And, as I've mentioned, they could have gone home Sunday evening and then come back early Monday morning," Sam said. "Unlike MacPherson, they live close enough to make that possible."

"Yes, there is that," Val said with a sigh. "We need to get their Monday morning activities as well, all the way up to noon."

The calls to the two Houstonians resulted in having to leave messages, but both called back within the hour. Val wasn't surprised at the rapid response. She imagined that they were both eager to get information about the state of the investigation. Dr. Turner told them that he was an admirer of Burton because of the photographer's habit of including botanical images in his wildlife photos. "Just like Audubon did," he said. He had commuted each day to the meeting, staying for dinner on Sunday and then driving home. After he got home, he went out with his girlfriend for a drink and then she had come back to his place to spend the night with him. He shared her name and phone number so Val could confirm he had been in Houston Sunday night through Monday morning.

Dr. Hoffman, the entomologist, had decided the trip twice a day through Houston traffic was a little too much, so he had stayed with his brother in Egret Bay. He left right after the wrap-up meeting on Sunday in order to get home in time to have dinner with his wife. He had no appointments scheduled for Monday morning, so he had slept in until after 8:00 and then he and his wife had run errands and gone grocery shopping before he left for a faculty meeting. He had seen some of Burton's photos in wildlife magazines and thought his photos of arthropods leaned toward the sensational rather than towards scientific accuracy. He knew about the past history between Burton and MacPherson, who was a friend of his. "It's difficult to have much respect for Burton," he said, "once you've heard the Chuck-will's-widow story. Still, I can't help but be sorry that Burton had met such an anticlimactic end."

"You must know by now that he was found next to an alligator on an island rookery," Sam said. "It's in all recent newspapers. That doesn't sound very anticlimactic to me."

"Yes, the alligator certainly lends something to the story. I'm surprised they didn't mention that at the beginning. But, even with the alligator, it may have been anticlimactic for Burton. I called Anders after I first heard about Burton's death and then again after I heard about the alligator. He said that it would have been more appropriate if Burton had wrestled the alligator to death and then died, victorious, from the exertion."

Hanging up from the call, Val opened her notebook and made a few entries. "It's still morning," she said. "What can we do to make the most of the rest of the day? Who should we interview next? Ms. Gomez is coming back today, and I want to compare her story of the initial trip to the island with what we got from Deputy Fraser as well as her account of the rest of the trips. I'd also really like to know if Forensics has found anything of interest in Burton's phone or camera. I wonder...," but she cut off as the phone rang. "Maybe this is them." She picked up the receiver and gave Sam a thumbs-up as she put the phone on speaker.

"There's good news and bad news," they heard Deputy Fraser say.

"Let's start with the good," Val said.

"Our forensics people think that the cellphone still contains usable data in spite of its bath in muddy water."

"And the bad news," Sam said, "is that it's password protected, and we can't access it."

"Well, yes and no," the deputy said. "Getting a search warrant is probably possible since this is now an active homicide inquiry. But we know Apple won't be much help with the password. However, the Texas Rangers have access to the equipment that's necessary to try and extract whatever is in there if we can get a warrant. But they are backlogged, as usual, and there is low priority for this case because there is no indication that the public at large is in danger. On top of that, there is the cost. Recovery can be expensive and even if we had the funds, we might not get the information for weeks or even months. Even high-priority cases are lagging in recovery time."

"So, in other words," Val said, "we might as well have left it in the water."

"Not entirely. Forensics wants to go ahead and get a warrant. They are willing to tinker with it to see if they can extract any information. Without the advanced equipment, the chances are low, but they are willing to give it a try. You know Forensics. They hate to give up on something."

"And the camera?"

"Apparently the real culprit for the camera is not the water bath, but the sand. They tell me that we're fortunate that the pond isn't salt water. The camera body itself is damaged, both inside and out. The mainboard–that's what Forensics calls it–is toast. However, the contact strips on the memory card are gold-plated, which is good."

"And what does all this mean?" Sam asked.

"It means that if you're patient and speak nicely to everyone in CSI and Forensics, we might be able to save at least some of the photos. Not as valuable as phone records in tracking conversations, travel, and other things, but there may be something of interest."

"Like a photo of whoever else was on the island?" Val said.

"That only happens in your dreams," the deputy replied. "But who knows?"

Val took the phone off speaker and hung up. "The Shadow knows," she said.

"Where did that come from?" Sam asked.

"I think it's from an old radio program. My grandmother used to say that whenever we said, 'Who knows?' She would look at us and in a very deep and solemn voice she would say, 'The Shadow knows.' I hadn't really thought of that for ages. I must be regressing."

"It's a little early for lunch," Sam said. "But what say we catch something, call it brunch, and come back just in case Ms. Gomez gives us a call."

"Good idea. I'm hungry," Val said. "Had a small healthy breakfast and it didn't fill me up sufficiently."

Sam picked up his notebook and phone. "Healthy breakfasts are a bad way to start the day," he said.

They had not been back but a few minutes when Lainey Gomez called. "I just got home," she said, "but Doris said that it was important that I call you as soon as I got here. Will this take long? I haven't had lunch yet."

"No, I don't think it will take long," Val said, putting the phone on speaker. "If it takes longer than I anticipate, we will make an appointment for later today or tomorrow. I just want to go over what you saw on the trip over to the rookery with the deputy sheriffs and an EMT."

"Have you talked to them?"

"We've talked to one of the deputies and will be talking to the other deputy and the EMT as soon as we can reach them. Everyone sees some things differently. We want as complete a picture as possible. For instance, when you got to the jon boat on the first visit to the island, was it wet or were there signs that it had been used recently?"

"Yes, there were small puddles inside. Whoever last used it didn't put the cover back over it, but that was no surprise. Some users are too lazy. A few just turn the boat over so it won't fill with rainwater, but then the person who next uses it has to check for snakes under it before turning it upright. I couldn't remember if it had rained since I had last been there, but there were other things to think about."

"And when was the last time you were over there?"

"About a week earlier, just to check things out."

"Was the cover on the boat during that visit?"

"Yes, it was. If it hadn't been, I would have covered it."

"Do you know who was over there in the interim?"

"No, I don't."

"Do you keep a sign-in sheet?"

"Anyone going back there is supposed to notify me. They don't always do that, but we try to enforce it. You might check with the Bird Society office to see if anyone called there."

"Tell us what happened the first time you traveled over to the island on Monday."

"If it had just been me, I would have tried to row over, but with all of us on board that was out of the question. I had to use the motor, which really upset the birds. They were already skittish, probably from the events earlier that morning. As we came around to the front of the island, we could see the man and the alligator, and I slowed down as much as I could. Didn't want to upset the alligator by coming in too quickly."

"If I understand correctly, you didn't go all the way to where the bodies were."

"No, we stopped short and used our binoculars to see if there was any chance the man was still alive."

"And you could tell he wasn't?"

"Yes, his eyes were open and staring and there were flies crawling over his face. His clothes were all wet and muddy."

"And the alligator?" Sam asked.

"The eye on the side we were looking at was bloody and the flies were all over him too."

"Someone from the boat called Ms. Gibson over at the viewing platform," Val said.

"That was the young male deputy."

"And could you see the two older women who were with Ms. Gibson?"

"Yes, there were three women watching us from the viewing platform. Doris and two women I didn't know."

"And we understand you stayed and took the medical examiner and a couple of others out for a second visit."

"Yes, I took the medical examiner and the female deputy who had been on the first trip and one other person, who was an investigator of some sort. He had a camera and was taking pictures."

"All this happened over what period of time?" Val asked.

"I was notified of the bodies about 8:30-8:45 and didn't get home until past noon."

"Just for the record, what were you doing when you received the initial call from Ms. Gibson?"

"I was taking care of the chickens."

"Chickens?" Sam asked.

"Yes, we have a half-dozen laying hens and I was cleaning out their coop. I think a snake or some other predator tried to get in sometime during the night and upset the ladies. There was bedding and feathers all over the place."

"But the hens are OK?" Val asked.

"Yes, thank heavens."

"Who takes care of them when you're gone?"

"My son. He lives in Egret Bay. The hens were my husband's hobby, and I inherited them after he died. When the ones I have now die, I'm getting out of the chicken business."

"You don't plan on eating them?"

"They are more pets and egg layers than dinner."

"Getting back to Monday," Sam said, clearing his throat to get their attention, "did you get out of the boat on the visit with the medical examiner?"

"No, I stayed with the boat every time I was there. There was a fuss when the examiner fell–I think he tripped over the alligator–and I was glad he wasn't hurt because that would have meant yet more trips."

"Were you with the team that brought Mr. Burton's body in?" Val asked.

"Yes, I took two EMTs out to transport the body back to the ambulance. They were able to get the body bag in the boat, but there was not enough room for both EMTs, the body, and me. I took one EMT and the body back and then made another trip to pick up the remaining EMT."

"That just left the alligator."

"I know the animal control people who went on that trip. One is a volunteer at the rookery and I trust him with the jon boat. I went home and left him in charge. There was another fellow–big, young, hefty–with him. Besides, there wouldn't have been room for me."

"There was room in that boat for the alligator?"

"I think they ended up towing him back and then drove their truck in to load him. I understand that he was big enough that they had trouble putting him in the back of his truck but eventually managed to haul him in."

"Were you there when they arrived?"

"Yes, but I left when they got there. I was exhausted."

"One other thing," Sam said. "Shots were fired that morning. They must have made a lot of noise in that relatively quiet environment. Did anyone report them?"

"The people who live around there are used to periodically hearing gunshots. They go in their back yards and practice shooting at tin cans and bottles. They hunt around here in season. This is the country. Gunshots are not necessarily the exception."

"This has been very helpful, Ms. Gomez. We will probably want to talk to you a little more, but we can make an appointment for that and let you go for now."

"That's fine. I'd like to get this cleared up and behind us."

"First time I've heard someone use chickens as an alibi," Sam said after Val hung up.

Sam and Val had been talking for a few minutes about the conversation with Gomez when Val's phone rang.

"Detective Forster, this is Officer Perez in Intake. I have a rather upset woman on the line who wants to talk to someone in Homicide."

"Rosie, what are you doing in Intake?"

"Broke my foot."

"Antsy to get back in your squad car?"

"Yes, ma'am. Sure am."

"Well good luck and take care. Go ahead and put the call through."

"Homicide, Detective Forster," she said.

"For God's sake, will you try and help me and not transfer me somewhere else. I've been transferred too many times already."

"Well, I can try and help," Val said. "What are you calling about?"

"I'm calling about Les. Lester Burton."

"Mr. Burton, yes." Val reached over and put her phone on speaker. Sam looked over as soon as he heard the name Burton. "This may be the right place. What about Mr. Burton?"

"I'm his partner–was his partner–actually his fiancée–but I don't like that term because it sounds so stuffy. I'm trying to find out what happened to him, and I keep getting the run around. I keep hearing 'He had a heart attack, he almost drowned, he was on an island.' All I know is that he is dead, and I don't know where he is and what I should do." She sounded on the verge of breaking out in tears.

"Where are you calling from, Ms...?"

"Adkins. Sonya Adkins. I'm at Les's home in Medford, New Jersey, but I'm flying to Houston tomorrow morning. No one called me. I only found out about Les when a friend called me on Wednesday to offer condolences and I asked her what for. Talk about a shock! I've been beside myself ever since. Can you please tell me what happened to him?"

"I'm sorry no one contacted you, Ms. Adkins," Val said. "We've been trying to find his family and acquaintances, and the only persons the sheriff's office talked to is his business manager."

"Terry? Oh, he wouldn't mention me. He thinks I'm a gold digger or something."

"But you say you are Mr. Burton's fiancée?" Val asked.

There was a pause, and then the caller continued. "Yes, I see–I think–what you're suggesting. I'm just someone who calls up out of the blue and tells you I was engaged to be married to someone who's in the news. I don't know how to prove our relationship, especially over the telephone. I can bring photographs and correspondence from him. He sends...sent...me postcards from the places he visited. I got one from Houston that arrived just yesterday."

"I'm glad you understand our caution. We would like to talk to you when you get here. Bring whatever you have that speaks to your relationship. Any legal documents are best, but everything helps. All we can tell you at this point is what is classified as public information, but I'd be glad to answer any questions you have within that constraint. You say you got a postcard from Houston. Did he stay over in Houston before he traveled down here last week?"

"Yes, he flew out there last Wednesday. The last I heard from him was that Sunday evening."

Val went over the known facts of Burton's death and the circumstances of his death that had already been cleared for the press.

"But you don't know who else was on the island with him?" Sonya said.

"No. We don't even know why he was there. I'm sorry for your loss and realize how hard this must be for you. Can I ask you a few questions that might help?"

"Yes, of course. Whatever I can do."

"Are there any other next of kin that we need to notify?"

"He has one nephew and three nieces. The rest of his family–his parents and his brother, the father of the nephew and nieces–have all passed away. I have their contact information."

"We will need that, thank you. Do you know why he was in Houston?"

"It was a business meeting. Les is," she paused, "was trying to raise money for a project he's been working on in Ecuador. He wants to purchase a birding business of some sort and turn it into an ecotourism center. It's a lot of money, more than he has, so he's partnered with a few others who are willing to invest in it. One of the investors is creating problems, and Les wanted to talk to another investor who lives in Houston and is a friend of his to see if they could find a solution."

"What do you know of this project?" Val asked.

"Not much. I know he was very excited about it. He reduced his photography business and turned his attention to what he calls–called–'the Ecuadorian project.' He asked me if I would be interested in moving to Ecuador. I told him that if he was moving to Ecuador, I'd move with him. He said that it was only a possibility, not a probability, but that he wanted to make sure I was supportive."

"This investor of his might have some idea as to why he was on that island. Perhaps we could talk to him," Val said.

"I think I have a contact number. I'll check and make sure I bring that with me. His name is Salvadore–but Les calls him Sally–Rios."

Val sat up straight in her chair and stared at Sam, who responded with a perplexed look.

"That might be of some help, Ms. Adkins. You say you will be flying in tomorrow?"

"Yes, I'm coming in late morning to Houston Hobby Airport. I thought I'd rent a car and drive down to Egret Bay."

"That would work out fine. Why don't you get settled down here and then come to the police station and ask for Detective Val Forster or Sam Pierson in Homicide Division and we can continue this conversation."

"I'll do that. Thank you so much. It will be so good to get some answers."

The conversation ended and Val let out a deep breath.

"What's up?" Sam said.

"Sally Rios."

"Who's Sally Rios?"

"That's right, that was before you came here. Sally Rios has been connected with the drug trade throughout southeast Texas. He is one of the people that the feds have been trying to put behind bars for years."

"But what would he have to do with a bird photographer? Or as an investor with an ecotourism site? And, even more important right now, do you think he's part of the case the sheriff's office is helping to put together?"

"Don't know. No idea. Nada. I do know we have to get an answer about how we should handle this information before Ms. Adkins gets here tomorrow. Let's see if we can get ahold of the deputies over at the sheriff's office. If they think it's important, they can walk it up the line there and we can run it by the chief here. This may be nothing, but somehow, I doubt it."

To Val's surprise, her call to Doug Fraser was answered almost immediately. "Fraser" was all he said as he answered.

"Val Forster over at Homicide. Any chance the two of us can meet with you and Deputy Jefferson this morning?"

"I can talk now. Don't know about her."

"We would really like to do this in person if you don't mind, and we'd like to have Deputy Jefferson there if possible."

"Sounds serious."

"May be or maybe not. Just got a piece of news we'd like to bounce off you."

"Let me call Dana. I'll get back with you shortly."

He called back only five minutes later. "We can do it right now if you can get over here. Dana's been on call today, so her schedule is uncertain."

"Fifteen minutes," Val said. "Same meeting room as last time?"

"Yes, fine. They will kick us out if they want the space."

When the detectives entered the conference room, both deputies were present with their coffee cups in front of them. Two additional cups of coffee were sitting in front of a couple of empty chairs with packets of cream and sugar beside them. "If you want sweetener, you're out of luck," Fraser said. "It's sugar or nothing."

"This will do just fine, thank you," Val said.

After introducing Sam and herself to Deputy Jefferson, Val took a sip of coffee and then immediately started into the reason for the meeting.

"Does Salvadore Rios, aka 'Sally,' ring a bell with either of you?"

"Where did that come up?" Jefferson asked, frowning.

"His name surfaced in our rookery death investigation. He had business dealings with the deceased."

"The photographer?"

"Yes," Val said. "Given your current investigation, I wanted to see if there was any problem with our following up on this lead."

"Tell me more," Jefferson said.

"Not a lot to tell," Val said. "As soon as his name came up, I dropped any line of further inquiry until we could talk to you. Burton, the photographer, was–according to his fiancée–an acquaintance of Rios', who was–again, according to her–an investor in an ecotourism project that Burton was putting together in Ecuador."

"Come again?" Fraser said.

"Yes, I know it sounds weird," Val said, "but that's the story so far. Burton was supposedly in Houston last week meeting with Rios about some type of conflict with one of the other investors, and then he came down here to Egret Bay when that meeting was over. We have no specific idea at this point as to why he came down here. I mean, was the rookery the primary reason he came down or did he go to the rookery because of something else he found out when he was here? The fiancée is coming into Houston tomorrow. We expect her late morning to early afternoon. My question is, do we say, 'It's too bad about Mr. Burton's project, and we hope that it is far enough along that it can be finished,' and move on to other topics, or do we try and get more information on Burton's relationship with Rios and the nature of the project? Do we need to look into it a little deeper, over and above the investigation into Burton's death?"

Fraser turned toward Jefferson and asked her if she knew if Rios was tied to anything in Ecuador.

"I really don't know. That's a question for the higher-ups. We're just ancillary crew down here. The question is, why would Rios be friends with a bird photographer? Seems like a strange combination. This could be a wild goose chase–no pun intended–that detracts from the investigations already underway."

"Yes, it could be. Or not," Val said. "Burton travels all over the world with, as I understand it, lots of local contacts."

"And," Sam added, "while he's not well-liked by many, he is probably a person of some importance in second- and third-world countries that are trying to boost tourism. And many of those countries are also part of the growing drug cartel problem."

"Not well-liked?" Jefferson asked.

"He's not easy to get along with, pushes his way around, ignores birding ethics, that kind of thing," Sam said, realizing that he had never before referred to "birding ethics."

"Rios has a legitimate–or what passes as legitimate–business as a building contractor," Jefferson said. "But I've never heard anyone say anything about his dabbling in tourism. If you can stay around here for a while, I'll try and get an answer to your question about your conversation with his fiancée as quickly as possible. I'd like to get that answer while you're here. Once I'm called, you won't be able to get ahold of me, perhaps for a few days."

Val looked at Sam and they both shrugged. "We'll wait," Val said. "I don't want to go into the meeting with Adkins without knowing what direction to take with her. We also have a few questions about your rookery visits, so perhaps we can ask those when you return, if you're still free."

"If the rest of you have a plan for moving forward, am I done here?" Fraser asked. "If yes, I'll take off." Seeing the two detectives nod in the affirmative, he rose and left the room.

"I'm going to also excuse myself then," Jefferson said. "I'll let you know if I'm called or if there will be any delay in getting back to you."

"Thanks," Val said. "We can wait for a while. There are some things we need to talk about with each other. We'll be fine."

After Jefferson left, the two detectives sat facing each other without saying anything for a minute. Then Val broke the silence. "What does Rios gain by an acquaintance with Burton?"

"Photographs for his home?" Sam said. "Seriously, nowhere in my research on Burton have I come across even a murmur of his being affiliated with anything shady. If he was, you'd think that would come out somewhere, especially given the number of people who dislike him."

"He probably goes to a lot of countries that are part of the worldwide drug industry. Wouldn't surprise me to find out he'd been to Columbia, Mexico, Bolivia, Nigeria maybe," Val said.

"Yes, but he'd have to travel commercially, and that can potentially be high risk for him if he's doing anything shady," Sam said." "That may not be a problem once he leaves the big cities, however. He probably goes to remote locations and may travel by boat or train, where security would be less rigorous."

"It's a stretch.... I guess all of this is a stretch right now. I wonder if he still uses film or if he shoots all digital."

"What difference would that make?" Sam asked.

"Well, let's say that Burton is working with Rios in the drug trade or some other illegal activity as a sideline in his capacity as a photographer. If he's shooting digitally, he can electronically send whatever photos he's taking anywhere in the world. He wouldn't have to carry film, negatives, or photos through security or customs. If he's shooting film, he can carry the images back as undeveloped film, something that customs may pass right through since I don't think that film can go through X-rays. If I remember, it needs a hand check. He may be well enough known at airports to get special treatment and not be questioned."

"Ah, I see. He doesn't have to be carrying drugs," Sam said. "How about diamonds, for instance? Or gold?"

"Wow," Val exclaimed. "They leave us alone for a few minutes and we've solved the case." At that they both raised their coffee cups and toasted each other. "Here's to Homicide," Val declared. She sighed. "This is taking us off the track we were on. It makes so much more sense that whoever else was on the island was not some hit man—or woman—but someone who had a particular grudge against Burton and took advantage of the opportunity to settle accounts."

"Yes, I simply don't believe that it was just a coincidence that Burton was in town the same weekend as the meeting," Sam said. "And I also don't think the Bird Society meeting itself was why he was here. Why would someone planning a project in Ecuador want to show up and hope to be invited to participate in a meeting that's planning to teach kids about birds and bugs?"

"You think he came here to meet someone who was participating in the meeting?"

"Well, that makes some sense," Sam said. "It gives him a motive for coming down here."

"And along that same line," Val said, "where are we on establishing which meeting participants were still in town on Monday morning?"

Sam took out his notebook and turned to his last entry. (1) "Wallace, Alvarez, and Kapoor–the videographer–were at breakfast at 7:30. Wallace says he was a little late. Not sure what 'little' means. We now think that it could be possible for someone to be at the rookery and still make it back by 7:30, but only if there were no delays, like Burton's falling in the pond or having to stop and change clothes because they've gotten wet and muddy. For all we know, Burton may not have been the only person who fell in the pond. If someone tried to rescue him, they'd probably be as dirty as he was when we found him. The timing would be close though. (2) The Wright couple, Mr. and Mr., flew out Sunday night and aren't back yet. (3) Anders MacPherson was still in town but was standing on the curb in Egret Bay at 6:30. (4) Dvorkin and her husband were here and went home to Houston after breakfast on Monday. Possibility, but only for him, not for her because of wheelchair. (5) Of the two Houston professors, one went home Sunday night–need to check his alibi with his girlfriend–and the other says he also left Sunday night and 'slept in on Monday' before running errands with his wife. (6) That leaves the Aiello couple, who live here, and the wildlife artist Ralph Cook from Rockport. Haven't talked to them and need to check alibis for a few of the rest."

"Let's check alibis first to see if we can indeed scratch off those who say they weren't here on Monday morning. Then we can talk to the three remaining and do any cleanup work on the others as necessary," Val said.

The door to the room opened and Deputy Jefferson came in and sat down next to them. "There seems to be some agreement between my boss and your boss that you should limit any discussion of Rios with Burton's fiancée to Rios' role in the birding project. They will talk to the feds to confirm that and let you know if there are any changes in the plan. If the feds agree, then sometime after she leaves, you should call Rios, again limit the talk to the Ecuadorian project. He may well be aware that Burton's fiancée is in the area, and that she's planning on coming down here and talking to you. If so, he may think it's strange if you don't call him. If she has the number for a personal phone, not business, try and get it from her. We only have numbers that we've identified as used for business. I'm to stress to you that Rios is not one of the people we are targeting, but he is friends with others in the drug trade and could therefore be dragged into the investigation, so you have to limit your conversation to Burton and if he knows why Burton was coming down here, and that's it. Nothing more unless he volunteers information."

"And when do you expect that this conversation will take place?" Sam asked.

"As soon as we get clearance from the feds. I imagine you're in a bit of a hurry to do this, but it shouldn't be done until after you've talked to the fiancée and gotten as much of the background as you can. So maybe Sunday. They may want to have someone from our office there with you when you call because of the connection between the two cases. And maybe someone from the DEA as well."

"OK, we'll look at Sunday," Val said. "As long as you are still here, do you have a few minutes so we can ask about your activities at the rookery last Monday?"

The deputy looked at her watch and nodded. "Unless they call me, I have time."

"We'll make this as short as possible. If we have follow-up questions, we'll talk more later. To start with, we understand that you and Deputy Fraser were asked to respond to a call the sheriff's office got from Lainey Gomez, the manager at the rookery, about what looked like a body on the island at the pond."

"Yes, we were sent out there with the expectation that it was a false alarm. We've heard stories about things like that a few times in the past, usually because of a basking alligator."

"But it wasn't a false alarm."

"No, it was definitely a man, but we had no idea as to whether he was dead or just injured. So we took the path around the lake to meet Ms. Gomez, who had access to a boat. She had already called 911 before coming over to the rookery, and we waited for a couple of minutes until an ambulance arrived and one of the EMTs joined us. The four of us—me, Deputy Fraser, the EMT, and Ms. Gomez—went around the island to where the body was located. It was quite obvious when we got there that both the man and the alligator were deceased."

"When you were there, did you see anyone on any of the observation platforms across from the island?"

"Just the three women that we spoke to when we arrived."

"And when you determined that both the man and the alligator were dead, was that when you called the M.E.?"

"Actually, Deputy Fraser called him and gave him a heads-up when we were hiking around the lake to get to the boat. We were already concerned from our view on the platform that the man there was deceased. And then I called the M.E. again and said we were sure the man was dead and that we needed him to certify that because of the strange circumstances."

"And when you got back from your first trip to confirm that the man was deceased, did the EMT leave while you stayed around until the M.E. got there?"

"The EMT went back to the ambulance in case they got another call. If they weren't needed elsewhere, he said they would stay to transport the deceased back to town. Deputy Fraser was not feeling well, and both the EMT and me were concerned about him being dehydrated or suffering from heat-stroke, so he stayed behind when the M.E. got there and the four of us—this time, Ms. Gomez, the M.E., a CSI deputy who came with the M.E., and me—went out there."

"You all got out of the boat when you reached the scene?"

"No, Ms. Gomez and I stayed in the boat, but the other two got out. They didn't seem to need me and I would have been in the way. There wasn't a lot of room on that little beachy area for three people to maneuver."

"And I understand the M.E. tripped on the alligator."

Jefferson smiled at that. "Swore like a trooper. I think the cameraman got a few good shots of that."

"And how long were you there?"

"I'm not sure. I took a few pictures, the M.E. did his thing, and the cameraman did his. At this point, we all still believed it was probably an accidental death. We thought that the man had fallen into the pond and tried to swim over to the island—I don't think he could have climbed back up that steep bank to one of the observation platforms—and had a heart attack or stroke or something. Maybe from fright when the alligator joined him. We didn't know at that time that the alligator and the deceased were both shot, only that they were dead. When the M.E. turned the deceased over, he said that he could see that he had been shot in the thigh but had no obvious serious—that is, potentially fatal—injuries. The deceased was wearing a holster, but there was no firearm in the vicinity. If the deceased had shot the alligator when it came ashore and before he died, I would think that the firearm would still be around there somewhere, but they couldn't find it. That was when the M.E. said that he was beginning to think that this was not an accidental death, that the deceased had not simply fallen or jumped into the water from one of the observation platforms."

"Would you jump into a pond that was full of alligators?" Sam asked.

"Sober, no, but under the influence or sufficiently depressed...people sometimes, as you know, do strange things." She paused. "The M.E. asked Ms. Gomez how deep the water was at the edge of the island, and she said that it was pretty deep. The spring rains had brought the water level up. She wasn't sure how deep the water was over at the bluff where the platforms were, but, as I said, the bluff is quite steep and high, so it would be very difficult to climb out of the water on that side, even if the water was fairly shallow."

She looked at phone as it began to vibrate. "I have to go."

"Boy, this is getting crazier and crazier," Val said after the deputy had left the room. "Let's go back to the office and write all this up while it's fresh in our minds. And then we can go home."

"I'm scheduled to have the day off tomorrow," Sam said.

"Ms. Adkins won't be in until noon at earliest. Why don't you take the morning off and I'll call you when I hear from her or if the chief wants you in."

"That'll work. Thanks."

CHAPTER 7

Saturday

Val came in a little early to see if there was a message or text from the chief confirming what she had heard from Deputy Jefferson. There wasn't. She would continue to assume that the phone call to Rios would take place the next day, probably in the morning.

Although Val tried to avoid sharing details from her work with her husband, this case was different. She had decided the previous evening to bring him up to date. Deke was an enthusiastic birder, even though he admitted to being slow in identifying certain species. He kept a life list of birds he had seen, with a little star next to those that he had identified in their yard. That, to her, meant he was a birder, not a birdwatcher–terms she knew and had used, although interchangeably–but now had distinction. He loved to talk about his experiences "in the field," as he put it. And he had been a big help by letting them know about the meeting in Egret Bay at the same time that Burton was in town. She was still convinced that somehow the two were related, but she was no closer to finding out how than she was when the case opened.

Val thought about her conversation with Deke on Saturday morning as she looked at her notes, trying to decide what to do next. As they sat at the table after dinner, Val had pushed the list of the people who had attended the meeting towards him. "Do you know any of these people?" she asked. She hoped he would say 'no' so that nobody could accuse her of conflict of interest if one of his friends turned out to be the person who left Burton on the island. On the other hand, she hoped he'd say 'yes' because that might bring new insight into the case from a person that she knew she could trust.

He looked it over carefully. "Yes," he responded, "I know a few. Vince Wallace, of course, because I've been to some of the Bird Society meetings and events. The Aiellos, although I know him better than her. He's a curmudgeony sort of guy, but he writes great books on birds and wildlife for children. His wife illustrates them. She's a very good artist. Her work reminds me of the watercolor paintings in the old Peter Rabbit books." He continued down the list. "I've met Eric Wright. I didn't know he had gotten married. He was with another guy, possibly this Phil, his husband, at the birding festival last year. I took a class in gull identification from Eric. It was interesting but didn't do me much good. Too much to learn and I guess I wasn't dedicated enough." He pushed the list back to Val. "That's about it. Why? Are they on your list of suspects?"

"No, most everyone at the meeting is in the clear for now. I haven't personally met any of them except the Bird Society people. Everything has been by phone. I still have to contact the Aiellos and a few other people. The Wrights won't be back until sometime next week. They're birding in Washington state. We've confirmed they flew there Sunday, so they are currently in the clear. I'm just trying to get a handle on the birding community, whether they would band together to protect a favored brother–or sister–that they think may have been responsible for Burton's death."

"From what I've seen," Deke had said, "it's a close fellowship where people never run out of things to talk about related to birds and nature. There can be a spirit of competition, but usually in goodwill, at least among those who treat it as a hobby or avocation. I can't really speak about what it's like at the top. The people I know always have a bird or a birding site or a piece of birding behavior to discuss or to crow about, pun intended. I can't imagine any of them keeping quiet about something suspicious to protect someone else in the birding community. It's not like cops," he said with a grin, not being able to resist needling Val, knowing how much the "blue wall of silence" bothered her.

"Yeah, thanks," she said. "Appreciate that reminder."

Later that evening, she was going through the day's mail when Deke called her over to a window looking out on the backyard. "Look, Val. We have a visitor at the birdbath!" She could see a very large brownish bird perched on the side of the bath, periodically dipping its beak into the water.

"What is that?" she asked.

"A red-shouldered hawk, I think," Deke answered. "Isn't it beautiful?"

"Doesn't it eat other birds?"

"Yes, of course. It's a raptor. It also eats mice and rats and snakes."

"Well, if it eats rats, I'm president of its fan club," she said.

"I don't think it wantonly kills," Deke said. "Mostly to eat and protect itself and its young."

"People kill for the same reason," Val said with a sigh, "but it's the 'wantonly' that keeps me employed."

Val's contemplations were interrupted by her office phone ringing. She hoped that someone was returning one of her calls.

"Detective Valerie Forster, Homicide Division, Egret Bay Police Department."

"This is Terrance Easley, Les Burton's business manager. You've been trying to reach me."

"Yes, indeed. Thank you for returning my call. I believe that you were the first person that the Fillmore County Sheriff's office contacted after Mr. Burton's death."

"I think so. They were asking all sorts of questions that indicated that they really didn't know much about him. Was he married? Where was he employed? That kind of thing. Have you found out what happened to him? There's very little information in the newspapers, but the rumor mill is chugging out theories."

"All we know is that he fell into a deep pond and came close to dying but managed to get out. At some point shortly after he got out of the water, he had a heart attack that killed him."

"Ah, geez. Les was scared to death of water. What on earth was he doing that he fell into a pond? Why wasn't he wearing a life preserver? He never went out on the water without one, except maybe if he was on a yacht or a liner, something big, and even then, I bet he had one in his cabin."

"That's what want to find out. We're trying to put together a scenario of what Mr. Burton was doing in the week or so before he died. We know he went to Houston to meet with a friend who was also an investor in a project Mr. Burton was involved in. Do you know anything about that meeting?"

"That was with that Rios guy. I told Les to stay away from him, that I didn't trust him. I never trust a fellow who has lots of money and is unwilling to say where it comes from. But Les really seemed to like the guy. If he didn't like him and trust him, he wouldn't have gone into business with him."

"What kind of business?"

"Something about developing a birding preserve or tourism spot in Ecuador."

"And you weren't involved with that?"

"No, I mostly handled all of Les's travels, his book deals, online workshops, that kind of thing. I never got involved with his personal business side."

"Did you talk to him at all during his recent trip?"

"Yes, he called from Houston the day before he went down to your town, said he had to take some photos of something or other and that he'd be back early the next week. We're working on a new book and he's been falling behind on it because of this Ecuador thing. He didn't seem very happy about the assignment in your town. Said he thought the photo excursion was totally unnecessary."

"Pictures of something or other? Did he say what?"

"No, and I didn't ask. He seemed to resent it when I asked too many questions about his personal life or business not related to Burton Photography."

"I've talked to Ms. Adkins and she doesn't seem to be able to tell us much about his business deals either. Did Mr. Burton usually keep things so close that he didn't share them with others."

"Well, he may have shared them with his attorney, Audrey Brennan, but I'm just as happy that he didn't share them with Sonya. Don't trust that woman. That doesn't mean I think she might be involved in Les's death, but I'm willing to bet that she will benefit by it."

"Did Mr. Burton have a sizeable estate as far as you know?"

"He had a sizable amount of property and of course the entire gallery of his work. I think he still had copyrights to all of it. You have to talk to his attorney about that. Out of my job description. Right now I'm trying to figure out where I stand in all this. Guess I better start looking for another job. It's a shame. I really liked working with Les."

"You got along with him? I understand he was difficult at times."

"Yeah, sure. He was pretty much a perfectionist. I just stayed out of his way as much as I could when he was in one of his moods, but I liked the kind of job I had, scheduling things, travel arrangements, that kind of thing."

She thanked him for calling, said she would contact him again if she had other questions and went back to planning her day. Who else did they need to contact? The Aiellos, husband and wife, and Ralph Cook, the artist from Rockport. And then there was the EMT who had been on the initial trip to the island. And they really should talk to Kapoor—how had they somehow skipped over him? Probably by seeing him as part of the staff. However, if anyone knew what went on at the meeting, he did since he had recorded all the sessions. And they could ask him how late Vince was to breakfast on Monday morning. And who decided to meet at 7:30 instead of 8:00 or 8:30. If Vince had been the person at the rookery with Burton, one would think he would suggest breakfast later in the morning in order to avoid being so squeezed for time—if their assumptions about the schedule that morning were correct.

The Wrights' presence on the Sunday flight had been confirmed. No way they could have gotten back by Monday morning. Mildred Dvorkin could be counted out, but her husband could have gone to the rookery. Doesn't seem likely, however. And it would be difficult to prove without further evidence since they are each other's alibi. She had learned over time that no one's alibi could be crossed off permanently until a case was closed. She had made mistakes in the past by doing so and then having to backtrack.

Anders MacPherson, like the Bird Society people, had a confirmable timeline. He had to be available at 6:30 for the limo to Hobby Airport. And he was.

And now there is this monkey wrench of Salvador Rios. She thought it was pretty farfetched to believe that he or someone in his employ would arrange to pick up Burton, take him to a secluded birding spot, take him out to the island, attempt to drown him, possibly shoot an alligator—still didn't know for sure who shot it—and get away safely. Still, the connection of Rios and Burton being acquainted was intriguing.

The staff and volunteers at the rookery certainly had access to the sanctuary and its resources, including the jon boat. But motive? None of the individuals associated with the Bird Society had been at the meeting except Wallace and Alverez, not even Gomez or their event manager.

She wished that they had started working on this case earlier. However, no one had seen the potential link between Burton and the meeting's participants until Wednesday afternoon, two days after Burton's body had been discovered. It was pure luck that she knew about the Bird Society meeting. But if the case had been assigned to them on Tuesday and she had been called back to work, they still might not know any more than they did now, even if they had knowledge of the meeting. They could have started talking to the attendees a day earlier, but she wasn't sure that would have changed anything. Nevertheless, the two-day delay meant that the other person—or people—involved in what happened on Monday morning had plenty of time to cover their tracks before Homicide seriously started working on it. She had suspicions that the crime investigation team had not put their best efforts into their initial examination of the scene on Monday, believing it was an accidental death. And having the M.E. trip over the alligator and muddle the scene didn't help. If there were any footprints near Burton's body, they were gone after that. A dead man, a dead alligator. It was pretty weird, something to talk about. Thankfully, Forensics seemed to be taking it seriously now. She hoped they'd get something from the camera—or from the phone—that would help them understand what Burton was doing out there to begin with.

She decided that she would start the morning phone calls with the EMT who had been at the scene. Maybe he had seen something the others missed. She called the non-emergency services number at the county health district and asked to speak to someone who could tell her the name of the EMT who answered a call outside the city limits at approximately 8:00 AM on Monday. The person who answered said that information was in the main office, which was closed. However, he would ask those currently on call if any of them had been on a run Monday morning.

"Tell them it concerns a deceased man and an alligator," Val said.

There was a pause at the other end. "An alligator? I know who answered a call that included an alligator. We all do. Gave us something to talk about all day. His name is Freddy Richard." She pronounced his last name *Ree-shard*. "That's spelled R-i-c-h-a-r-d. He's Cajun. He's on a non-emergency transport right now, but I'll have him call you when he returns." So Val was stuck waiting for a call from the chief and from the EMT.

Val was beginning to look at her notes in preparation for calling the Aiellos when the chief's call came through. He told her that in his discussions with the sheriff's office and the DEA, they had agreed that Val should call Rios from her office phone after talking to the woman who was the source of information regarding the connection between the two men. "It's possible," he said, "that his fiancée may have mentioned contacting Homicide, so any call Rios gets in connection with Burton's death will have to be from your phone number and extension. Any other number might be suspect. See if you can get a private number for him. He may suspect something if we call him on his business line. If you do manage to get that number, we'll arrange for someone from the sheriff's office and probably a federal agent to be at the station tomorrow morning about 10:00 to listen in on the call just to make sure it doesn't infringe on their investigation." He paused and then continued, "Your job will be to try and find out what the relationship is between Rios and the deceased that might have a bearing on his death. What exactly is this project that the deceased was working on and why is everybody skirting around that? As long as the discussion focused on trying to find out why the deceased was in Egret Bay over the weekend, there should be minimal distrust on Rios' end about the call."

"Tomorrow is Sunday morning. What if Rios is not in when I call?" Val had asked.

"If you call him on his personal phone, not a business line, you can leave a message. Tell him what it's about. Ask him to call you and–if you don't answer, which you won't if you see his number pop up–tell him to leave you a message about what's a good time for you to call him back. That will allow you to regroup and call him at that time. I think he'll follow through on this if Burton was really a personal friend."

As soon as she hung up, she called Sam to bring him up to date.

"Do you get the idea that Rios is a target in their investigation?" he asked.

"Hard to tell, but there seems to be no doubt he is at least on the periphery. I certainly don't want to be the person who screws up that investigation."

"Should be interesting," Sam said.

OK, next on the list, the Aiellos. Marie Aiello answered the phone on the second ring. "Hello," she said with some trepidation, probably seeing the police department listed as the caller. Val quickly told her that she was calling all of the birding meeting attendees as follow-up to the investigation into the death of Lester Burton.

"I have a couple of questions I'd like to ask you and your husband. Is this a good time?"

"Our kids are coming over in a few minutes and we're taking them out to brunch," Marie said. Val could hear someone in the background saying something indistinct.

"It's the police calling about Lester Burton," Marie said, her voice muffled, probably covering the phone. The voice in the background continued.

"My husband, Mike, wants to know if we can talk to you later today. The kids are just pulling into the driveway."

"Yes, of course," Val said. "What time?"

"We'll be around all afternoon. Any time after 2:00 would be fine."

"That would work," Val said, thinking that she could wait and call after Ms. Adkins' visit. "We have a meeting early this afternoon. I'll call you when it's over."

So, next stop, Ralph Cook. No one answered after six or seven rings. She was waiting for the voicemail to kick in when someone said a slightly-out-of-breath "Hello."

"Ralph Cook?" Val asked.

"Yes, that's me."

Val again quickly explained her reason for calling and asked if this was a good time to answer a few questions about Lester Burton.

"Yes, fine. I'm just getting myself a cup of coffee. Give me a second to get the creamer and I'll be right with you."

He quickly returned to the phone. She could hear his spoon clinking against the cup as he stirred in the creamer.

"Vince Wallace told me to expect a call. I guess this means that you haven't figured out yet who was involved in Burton's death."

"No, we're still in the middle of the investigation. Right now I'm trying to establish where all the meeting attendees were last Monday morning and if any of them saw or talked to Burton while he was in town."

"Well, I was on my way home by about 8:00-8:30. Had breakfast in Egret Cove and then packed up and left."

"What time was breakfast and where?"

"I picked up a McDonald's breakfast about 7:00, 7:15ish, took it back to my room to watch the news."

"You were by yourself?"

"Yes. My wife couldn't come."

"Just to cover all bases, do you have a receipt from McDonald's?"

"Not the sales receipt, but I paid with my debit card, so it'll be on there."

"And where did you stay?"

"At the Best Western. I do have my receipt from there if you need it."

"Not at the Freemont with the others?"

"No, I wanted some privacy after being with those people all day. The Bird Society picked up my hotel bill anyway."

"Thanks. We'd like a copy of your debit card payment to McDonald's and proof of your check-out time from the hotel. We're asking everyone to account for their movements while in town."

"No problem. I can understand why you're asking these questions. I assume because of the questions that there has been no arrest made yet in Les's death?"

"No, not yet. Did you know him well?" Val asked.

"No, not really. I've talked to him a few times. Had a beer with him on Saturday night at that little bar next to the hotel. He was sitting by himself, so I went over and joined him. We just talked about bird things."

"I don't have any reason to believe otherwise, but was he sober?"

"Yes, very. I think he only had one beer and then said he had to call it a night. Look, I know what people say about him. A lot of people didn't seem to like him. With a few, I even had the impression that his death was met with a shrug. Too bad. That was all. But he seemed like an OK guy to me. Very serious and intense, but all in all, I think he was just a very competitive person who probably rubbed some people wrong."

"Did he say why he was in town?"

"Something about trying to get some photos to close a contract he was working on."

"Did he say what kind of contract?"

"No, I didn't ask and he didn't offer." He paused. "It's really a shame, what happened to him. I have one of his photos of a Green Jay up on my wall. Not an original; it's a poster. I thought he had taken the photo down my way, along the Rio Grande. I mentioned it to him, and he said that he had taken the photo in Ecuador. I'm sort of jealous. I've never been to Ecuador, but it's on my list. Really, really want to visit the Galapagos."

"Well, that makes two of us. Thanks for your information and insights." She gave him her contact information and said she'd call him back if for some reason she had questions, thanked him, and told him to have a nice day. Then she hung up and sat there, thinking about what he had said. Here was another person that seemed to get along with Burton just fine. And then there are all those other stories about Burton and none of them good. Of course, if anyone had left him stranded on the island, they might say that they liked or admired him to deflect suspicion. But Cook had sounded sincere about his feelings. And there was another mention of Ecuador.

It was really quiet around the station. Val had paperwork to do and the morning was moving on. She decided to spend her time working on her report, bringing the Burton case up to date. The Aiellos were the last of the bird meeting attendees that needed to be contacted regarding their whereabouts between 6:00 and 8:00 on Monday morning. So far, they had crossed off MacPherson, Vince Wallace, Adeline Alvarez, and Kamal Kapoor–although there was still a question about Wallace arriving late–the Wrights, Mildred Dvorkin–they could probably cross her husband off as well–Pete Turner and Aaron Hoffman–if their alibis held up–and probably Ralph Cook. If the Aiellos were also cleared, she and Sam would have to rethink their theory about a connection between the attendees at the meeting and Burton. Or they would have to rethink their timeline surrounding his death.

That didn't mean they didn't have any more interviews. Kapoor and the Wrights might give some new insights. Had any of them ever talked to Burton and, if so, what about? What other rumors were circulating out there? Was there anyone else visiting in town that weekend that could have known Burton but was not part of the Bird Society meeting?

Her phone rang. It was only 10:00, a little too early for Ms. Adkins.

"This is Freddy Richard," the caller said. "You left a message to call you."

"Yes, indeed. I understand that you were the EMT with the ambulance that responded to the call from the bird rookery on Monday."

"Yes, there were three of us, but Muriel and Xavier, my partners on that run, stayed with the ambulance in case we had a call. There wasn't room for them on the boat anyway."

"And you went in the boat with two sheriff's deputies and a woman from the rookery over to the island where the deceased was located."

"Yes, the deceased and the alligator. That was one of the strangest runs I've been on, and I've been doing this for six years now."

"But you didn't get out of the boat."

"No, didn't have to. It was obvious that the man was dead. We thought the alligator was too, but our attention was mostly on the man."

"What did you do then?"

"Well, I called the M.E. office from the boat and said we needed a certification of death. We thought it was an accident, some guy falling into the water, but we knew that the M.E. would have to come take a look, especially because of the alligator right beside him. We couldn't figure out what it was doing there. The deceased would have to be transported back to town, of course, so when we got back on land, I went to the ambulance to see if there was any reason we couldn't wait. We decided to wait as long as there wasn't another call. We called dispatch and got clearance on that, so we sat and waited.

"The M.E. arrived about a half-hour later, maybe a little less, went out to the rookery with two CSI deputies, one of them a female deputy who had gone out with us on the initial trip. The M.E. called me and said that it was going to be difficult getting the deceased off the island and to the ambulance. He wanted to know if we could stay around a little longer and if I and one of my partners, could handle that. I told him we had already discussed this with dispatch and that we'd hang around as long as we could. We got a call a few minutes later and thought we would have to leave, but the call was cancelled. So Xavier and me and the rookery manager–Lainey, I think her name is–went back over after the M.E. returned. Xavier and me were able to get the body in a body bag and get it on the boat–it was a little tricky–but Xavier had to stay there because there wasn't room for him. Lainey and Muriel helped me get the body bag in the ambulance and then Lainey went back for Xavier. All in all, it was almost two hours from the time we arrived until we were ready to bring the deceased back to town."

"Did you see anyone else there at the rookery over where the viewing platforms are located when you were going over in the boat?"

"There were some women with binoculars watching us from one of the platforms. Oh, and a guy further down near the other end of the pond."

"What guy?" Val asked.

"He might have been another deputy. He was dressed in what looked like khaki and he was watching us through binoculars."

"And where did you say he was?"

"He was farther down from where the women were standing."

"What else can you tell us about him?"

"Not much. My attention was focused on the body on the island."

"Thank you," Val said. "No one has mentioned seeing anyone observing what was going on that day. We will most definitely check."

Maybe we have an eyewitness, Val thought as she finished the call. Wouldn't that be nice? She was almost positive that there were only two deputies that responded to the first call. Certainly they would have mentioned if there was someone else with them. But if it wasn't a deputy, who was it and how long had he been standing there? She made one more phone call, this one to Evelyn Baldwin.

Evelyn answered the call almost immediately. Val made sure this was a good time to talk and was assured that it was. No cake baking or kids coming over. Val didn't want to ask questions if Evelyn was distracted.

"I'm just calling to once more ask if you remember anyone else wandering around at the rookery while you were there."

"I did see a few when we first arrived, but that was all."

"Did you see any individuals, that is, someone all by themselves?"

"I don't remember seeing anyone but that small group."

"If someone came after you arrived, would they have to walk by where you were standing?"

"Where we were at the start, yes. But not necessarily after we moved down to the other platform. When we arrived, we were viewing the island from a platform right next to the stairs coming up. But then we moved toward the far end of the island, leaving the stairs behind us. Anyone could have come up and gone in the other direction and we would not have seen them. And because people tend to talk in what I call a 'library voice' when they are at the rookery, we may not have heard them either."

"But if they turned and went the other direction, the direction you took?"

"We were pretty preoccupied. Nevertheless, I would think someone coming by, even if we didn't notice them, would wonder what we were doing, what we were looking at. They would probably think that we were looking at something exciting over at the rookery that they wanted to look at too."

"I don't want to bother Ms. Olsen," Val said. "But would you double-check with her about other people that might have been there when you were? I think she would be much less anxious talking to you."

"I'd be happy to. I'll call you if she saw anything I haven't already told you about."

"Thank you so much," Val said. She hung up, made a note: One, talk to Kapoor; two, who was the guy watching the activity on the island?

It was close to noon when Val's phone rang again. She hoped it was Adkins.

"Egret Bay Police, Homicide Division, Detective Forster speaking."

"This is Sonya Adkins."

"Yes, we were waiting for your call. Are you still in Houston?"

"No, I rented a car and I've just checked in to the Mariner Inn. I think that's where Les stayed when he was here."

"Yes, that's right. I'm sorry, this must be very hard on you. We would, however, like to talk to you as soon as possible."

"I need to get something to eat. I missed breakfast. Tell me where to meet you and how to get there and I can be there in a half-hour, forty-five minutes. I really want to talk to you too."

Val gave her the directions to the police station and told her that they would let the front desk know to expect her and that either she or Detective Pierson would come out and meet her.

She called Sam to let him know she had heard from Adkins.

"Do I have time for a quick shower?" he asked.

"You have a half-hour."

"I'm not very dirty. I think I can make it."

Val called the administration office to make sure the conference room was free and reserved it for two hours. Probably didn't need that much time, but one never knows.

Sam came in, his hair still damp from the shower. Ten minutes later, the front desk called to let them know Adkins had arrived.

Val went out to the lobby to meet her and escort her back to the conference room.

"Have you been to Egret Bay before?" Val asked.

"No, I've been to Houston once and I went to Big Bend with Les about a year ago, but that's it as far as Texas is concerned."

Sam was setting three bottled waters on the table as they entered. Val made the introductions and asked for permission to tape the interview.

Adkins hesitated, and then agreed providing she could get a copy, so she didn't have to take notes.

"First of all," Val said, "is our need to confirm your identity. You say that you are–were–engaged to Mr. Burton. The information that we can share is not all privileged, but there are details that we would prefer stay in-house."

"Yes, you mentioned that in our phone conversation yesterday. So I brought some items that might help in this matter." She opened her rather generously sized purse, pulled out her wallet, and put her driver's license on the table. She then pulled out a business-size brown envelope and removed a small stack of items from it, placing them next to the license. "Here are some papers and also photos of Les and me, most of them taken in the last year or so."

"How long have you known him?" Sam asked.

"We met at a birding festival in Florida two years ago, corresponded online for a while, then got together at another festival a little over a year ago. We've been a couple ever since. He proposed to me at Christmas…last Christmas." She paused and then continued. "I went with him on a couple of his photo trips, and he visited me whenever he could–I lived outside Minneapolis–and then I moved in with him in New Jersey in February."

She pulled a few folded pieces of paper from the envelope. "In April, he revised his will to leave his house and all its contents to me, along with any royalties from his books. He also took out a new life insurance policy for $100,000 with me as beneficiary. He had previously left almost everything to Cornell University for an endowment in ornithological studies, along with a bequest to his nieces and his nephew." She opened the papers and pushed them across the table to Val.

"And this is a copy of his new will?" Val asked.

"Yes."

"And how has that changed from his old will?" Val asked.

"He reduced his legacy to Cornell but continued to leave his studio, which is located on the same block as his home, as well as the property it sits on and all the photographs and equipment in the studio to them."

"And his nieces and nephew?" Sam asked.

"The new will left them $10,000 each, which is only a tenth of what the original will stipulated. The remainder of his estate, outside of the things I've mentioned, he left to an ecotourism park in Ecuador. I think the owners of that park are partners in this project that he's been working so hard on. His attorney estimates that the remainder will be about $100,000. Almost all of Les's assets were tied up in his photography business, home, and studio. He paid for most things up front and had very few debts."

"Did the other heirs, the nieces and nephew, know that their share of the estate had been reduced?"

"I don't know. Not unless the attorney or Les told them."

"Do you have the attorney's contact information?"

"I'll give that to you. What I really want to know now is the circumstances of Les' death," Adkins said. "The newspapers said he had a heart attack, but when I first called here someone said it was a drowning. No one wanted to tell me anything that wasn't public knowledge. That, along with the fact that the Homicide Division is involved, makes me think there is more to this than an accident."

"We are, as I think I mentioned before, not sure exactly what happened. We didn't find any watercraft that could have been used to transport him to the island so we're assuming that he didn't go there by himself and that someone used that craft to leave. Alternatively, although it's a stretch, maybe he swam over...."

Adkins interrupted, "He couldn't swim. He had a phobia about water since he was a child. It was, I think, the only thing that scared him."

"Thank you," Val said, pleased that the water phobia had been confirmed. "So we can rule that out, but that makes the absence of a watercraft even more important."

"But I don't understand why he was on the island. He is very hesitant about getting into small boats and insists on wearing a life jacket. Did he have a life jacket on?"

"No," Val said, "but that doesn't mean he didn't have one on when he arrived at the island." She hesitated, then decided to continue. "There is also the fact that he had been shot..."

"Shot!"

"...yes, in the thigh, but the wound was not life-threatening. We don't know if someone else shot him or if he accidentally discharged his handgun when he climbed out of the pond."

"And what's this about the dead alligator? Do you think Les shot that, too?"

"It's possible. All three bullets, the one from his leg and the two from the alligator, are from the same gun. He was wearing a holster, but there was no firearm found around him. We did, however, find a handgun in the pond that would fit the holster. If all the bullets came from the same gun, we will assume that it was the one that was originally in his holster. Did he usually carry?"

"Not at home, but he did usually carry some type of gun when he was on a photography trip to other countries, especially if there might be dangerous animals or hostile people. But not at home."

"Was he a good shot?" Sam asked.

"Yes, excellent. We went to a shooting range once so Les could try a new rifle he had purchased, and he hit the target almost every time. He has two or three handguns, but I've never seen him use one. He kept his firearms in a locked gun safe in his den. I can't believe that he was shot. Shot, drowning, heart attack...oh, poor Les."

"I'm so sorry to have to tell you all of this, and I wish I could bring some type of closure as to what happened, but I can't yet," Val said as she reached into her jacket pocket and pulled out a couple of tissues. "They're mussed but unused," she said with a small smile as she handed them to Adkins.

"On a different topic, why Ecuador?" Sam asked, eager to change the subject.

"That was his favorite place to visit," Adkins said as she wiped her eyes. "He liked the company that ran the ecotourism program. He periodically took tours there as part of the expanded Galapagos trips, and he loved the wide variety of birds–there are over 1,000 species, he told me. He was planning on writing a book on the birds of Ecuador and the Galapagos once he got the project completed."

"Had you ever been down there?"

"No," Adkins said, looking down at the envelope on the table. "We were going to go there in October."

"And was the investor he met with in Houston also interested in ecotourism or Ecuador?"

"Mr. Rios? I'm not sure exactly what their business arrangement was, but Les thought that Mr. Rios was his best investor, someone who shared his dream."

"Have you talked to Mr. Rios since Mr. Burton died?"

"Yes, I called and told him I was flying down to Houston and would be going to Egret Bay. He told me to call him when I was leaving Houston to go back and maybe we could have dinner together."

"We would like to talk to him to get any knowledge as to why Mr. Burton came down here from Houston, if he came down alone, if he was meeting someone, that kind of thing."

"Anything you can find out that would help make sense is fine with me," Adkins said.

"You said you had a phone number for him."

Adkins opened her purse and pulled out a small notepad and opened her phone to contacts. "I've already written down a couple of numbers you may need. His manager Terry Easley–I think you've already talked to him–and Les's attorney, Audrey Brennan, and I'll add Mr. Rios." She copied a number to the notepad, tore off the page and handed it to Val. "I think the number for Mr. Rios is personal, not a business line," she said. "He asked me what I was planning to do to…you know…take care of Les's body. He offered to send someone to help me if I thought it would help. I told him I would let him know, but I'd really rather do this myself."

"I'll talk to the medical examiner, and we may have to talk to legal regarding that issue."

"...Because I'm not an official relative," Adkins said.

"Yes. Do you have any preferences as to what you would do if we released the body to you?" Val asked.

"I don't know. I know he preferred cremation. We talked about that in reference to a friend of his that died a few months ago, but I couldn't get him to put it in any legal form, including his will. He didn't want to discuss the possibility of his dying. But that's as far as I'd gotten."

"How long do you plan on staying here?" Sam asked.

"No longer than necessary. I can arrange to stay for a couple of days in case you need to talk to me again, but I'd like to return to New Jersey early next week."

Val handed her a business card. "You can email me at that address or text me at the phone number next to my name. The other number goes to the front desk. The medical examiner is at the county building." She reached for the business card and pulled it back to write another number on it. "That's the main number for the medical examiner's office," she said as she returned the card. "Feel free to call either one of us if something occurs to you that you think might help us with our efforts. We'll let you know if we find anything at this end."

Sam escorted Adkins out and then returned to join Val at the office.

"Well, that's interesting," he said. "What happens now that we have a personal number for Sally Rios?"

"The powers-that-be agree that the call should come from us. The chief said that we should try and get a non-business phone number for Rios, and we have. They want to send someone from the sheriff's office and a DEA agent to make sure we don't say something and blow the drug investigation."

"And what else is up for today?"

"I'm supposed to call the Aiellos back this afternoon. And now I want to talk to Burton's attorney. She's an hour ahead of us and it's Saturday, but I can give her a try after I talk to the Aiellos. I need to call the chief and let him know I have the phone number. He may still want us to call tomorrow and I would rather do that than wait until Monday. This has dragged on too long already. Why don't you resume your day off and I'll work the phone here. I'll call you if I hear anything from the chief. However, there's a catch. I haven't had lunch. Pop by Whataburger and bring me something back. While you're gone, I'll call the chief and let him know we have Rios' number, and then you're off for the rest of the day."

"It's a deal."

As soon as she finished eating, Val called the chief's office and left a message. Next, the Aiellos. Mike Aiello answered almost immediately. "Is this a good time now?" Val asked.

"Perfect," he said. "Marie is just finishing up in the kitchen and she'll be out in a minute. I'll put this on speaker so we can both hear what you have to say."

"I'm more interested in hearing what the two of you have to say," Val responded. "I have a few basic questions I need to ask you and then I'd like to listen to anything else that may come to mind."

"I'm here now," a female voice said from the background. "Just let me pull a chair up." Val could hear some rustling and then Mike spoke. "We're ready."

"OK," Val said. "Since you live in town, I'm assuming that you went home every night after the meeting. Did you interact with the other meeting attendees in any way?"

"Well, we had dinner both Friday and Saturday night with some of the others that were there," Mike said. "We skipped the informal dinner on Sunday night and ate at home."

"And lunch?"

"We ate at home except on Saturday. We only had a little over an hour for lunch that day, so we ate in town."

"Did either of you know Les Burton, either personally or by sight?"

"Not personally, no," Mike said, "and not sure I would recognize him, but Marie did."

"Yes, I knew what he looked like," Marie said. "I had seen him at a few other birding festivals, but I never spoke with him. I have a better memory for faces than Mike does, so when we saw him at lunch on Saturday, I pointed him out."

"Yeah, that's right," Mike interjected. "I didn't pay much mind, however."

"Well, that's not unusual," Marie said. "Burton's quite famous, you know. I have used some of his photographs to make sure I get my drawings correct. They are often better than the guidebooks."

"And where was this?" Val asked.

"It was at the Foghorn Café, downtown. It's one of our favorite spots. Burton was there with the young cameraman from the meeting."

"Kamal Kapoor?"

"Yes, that's his name. Nice young man."

"Why are you asking?" Mike asked Val. "Is he a suspect?"

"No, I'm just trying to locate the people who talked to Burton to find out as much as I can as to why he was here and who he met with that might be able to answer that question. No one seems to know for sure why Burton was in town, but I haven't talked to Mr. Kapoor yet."

"My guess is that Burton wanted to horn into the meeting," Mike said. "He has a reputation for wanting to be front and center of everything."

"Oh, Mike," his wife said. "That may be just jealousy talking. He's been so successful, and for some people birding can be rather competitive."

"She's right, as usual," Mike said to Val. "But there are other photographers that I think are just as talented, maybe more so, than Burton, and they don't get the attention he does. Anders, for example–Anders MacPherson. And the Wright brothers were at the meeting because of their work on climate change, but they are also both excellent photographers."

"They are not brothers, Mike," Marie said. "They are married. To each other."

Val jumped in, just in case there needed to be a diversion in the conversation. "You say birding can be competitive. But certainly competition is common in almost all professions. Why should birding and other wildlife interests be any different?"

"Oh, I don't think it is, really," Mike said. "If a well-known shoe salesman, for example, were found shot dead and there was no indication of robbery, I imagine you'd be looking at other shoe salesmen who were competing with him for customers. With birding, the professionals occupy a rather small world, but birding itself has an enormous following. Birding and birdwatching are among the major past times of American adults–adults worldwide–and even some kids. In spite of all the equipment and books and binoculars and cameras and khaki outfits people associate with birders, someone can participate in birding at almost no cost whatsoever and that's what most people do. Hang out a bird feeder, that kind of thing. Few people reach the top, but Burton did. All it takes is one person who is near the top and resents his fame."

"So you think that whoever was involved in his death would be someone from that small world of professional birding," Val asked.

"That's my guess," Mike said. "You're the expert here, but that's my guess."

Val thanked them both for their insights and wished them a pleasant evening. Top of her list: they needed to talk to Kapoor. Why did he have lunch with Burton? She placed a call to Burton's attorney, but there was no answer. She left a message and then began to update her notes to add the new conversations. She contemplated Mike Aiello's opinions about competition. Deke had said something about competition among birders but he seemed to think that it was mostly harmless. When Val finished her notes, she was ready to go home. The call to the attorney had not been returned and she had heard nothing more from the chief or the sheriff's office to cancel the call to Rios. They will just have to play it by ear tomorrow.

CHAPTER 8

Sunday

Both Val and Sam arrived a little after 8:00. Val handed Sam the notes she had made the day before and brought him up to date on her phone conversations with Terrance Easley, Ralph Cook, the Aiellos, and the EMT. "I've put Kapoor and this unknown guy the EMT saw towards the top of our list," she said. "We can talk about this more after the phone call to Rios. The other participants should be here about 10:00."

Val was surprised to see Deputy Jefferson arriving to represent the sheriff's department on the call to Rios. She was under the perception that the deputy was a peripheral member of the drug investigation. Jefferson herself had described her position as 'ancillary crew' when they met earlier. Jefferson must have noticed Val's reaction because she smiled and explained that she had been sent because she was the only person in the sheriff's office who had been involved in both the Burton case and the drug investigation.

It was almost 10:15 when the DEA agent arrived. He waved at Jefferson and put out his hand to Sam.

"Agent Harold Simpson. Wreck on the freeway. Sorry I'm late."

"Detective Sam Pierson, and this is my boss, Detective Val Forster," Sam said with a nod to Val.

"As I understand it," the agent said, pivoting to face Val, "you believe that Salvadore Rios is a friend of your homicide victim and may have been among the last to talk to him before his death."

"The last *friend* known to talk to him before his death," Val corrected, putting the emphasis on 'friend.' "He had other conversations, but no one we have talked to has any concrete idea why he was down here or, more importantly, why he was at the rookery where he died."

"And you think that Rios has that information?"

"According to the deceased's partner–that is, his fiancée–Rios was Lester Burton's business partner and a close friend. How close, we don't know."

"Since I think all three of you have been involved with the homicide case, would you give me a little background on the case," the agent asked.

Val proceeded to give a quick sketch of Burton's death, his reputation, his occupation, and his personal life.

"And you're sure it's a homicide?"

"Right now, our best bet is voluntary or involuntary manslaughter. Nothing yet rises to suggest intentional homicide. Someone–so far, we have no indication of more than one person, although it's possible there may have been one or two others–either participated in trying to drown him, did not assist in his attempts to escape drowning, left him without calling for help as he was dying, or left him dead and fled."

"Not murder, first degree?"

"Not as far as we've been able to ascertain."

The agent nodded. "OK, thanks."

Sam pulled over a couple of chairs for Jefferson and the agent and moved his own chair so they were sitting around Val's desk. She opened her notebook to where she had jotted Rios' phone number and placed the call. To her surprise, it was answered almost immediately.

"Sal here. Who's calling?"

"Mr. Rios, this is Detective Valerie Forster from the Egret Bay Police Department. I'm sorry to bother you on a Sunday morning, but I'm calling in reference to the death of Lester Burton. I understand that he was a friend of yours and a business partner."

"Who gave you this number?"

"Mr. Burton's fiancée, Sonya Adkins. She's arrived in town and we've been talking to her about the case."

"And she told you I was a business partner?"

"She said that you were helping him with a project in Ecuador."

"Yeah, I was. I wonder if it's going anywhere now. Have you determined who was responsible for his death? He was a fine guy, sorry to hear that he had died."

"We are still looking into the case. So far, we have no primary suspects. We're trying to track his movements since he arrived in Texas. We understand from Ms. Adkins that he visited you before he came down here."

"We had a meeting the day he arrived. That was–let's see–Thursday, week ago Thursday. We had dinner together."

"Did he mention why he was coming down here?"

"Something about taking some photos for one of his investors."

"Did he tell you what kind of photos the investor had asked for or whether that was the primary reason he was coming down here? There was a meeting of regional wildlife and climate scientists here that weekend. Did he mention that?"

"No, he didn't specify what he was planning on doing down there, just said that it was an unnecessary request by one of his principal investors and he had tried to get out of it but was not successful. I think I know the guy he was talking about. He can be pretty demanding. If he wanted photos, Les would have to take photos or risk losing essential financial support."

"Can you tell me who that person is?"

"I would prefer not. He is what you call a silent partner. I can call and ask him, but my guess is that he will not want to be involved."

The agent wrote something on a slip of paper and passed it over to Val. "How did they meet?" it said.

Val nodded. "So there is no reason that you could think of why the trip down here could be connected with Mr. Burton's death?" she asked.

"No, I can't think of any connection. Les was just trying to accommodate an investor in order to keep a principal supporter in the fold, so to speak. If he had anything else planned, he didn't tell me about it."

"People keep talking about Mr. Burton's interest in Ecuadorean ecotourism. Can you give me more information about the project he was working on?"

"Is that going to help you any in finding out what happened to him?"

"I really don't know. We're just fishing around. No one else we've talked to seems to know him very well—except Ms. Adkins and she doesn't know much about his business life. We know he had rubbed some people the wrong way and a couple of those people were in town, but they have solid alibis. We're just trying to get a snapshot of what he was like, what kind of enemies he could have had."

"Lot of people were jealous of him, but he didn't seem to have any concerns about someone doing him harm. I've known him for over two years. In fact, we met down in Ecuador."

"Why Ecuador? I'm not very knowledgeable about ecotourism or birds, but it seems like there are places closer to home."

"That project's specifics are still under wraps. No one wants to talk about it until we're sure that it's a go. I certainly am not going to talk about it without the support of the other investors. I mean, Les's death may squash the whole thing, but if they want to go ahead, I don't want to say any more right now. I don't see any connection between the project and Les' death. Nobody associated with the project wins anything by his dying. In fact, most of us may be financially damaged by it."

"On a more personal side, Les has been in love with Ecuadorian birds for years. So have I. That's how we met. My mother was born and raised in Machala—that's in the south part of the country, on the coast—and she used to talk about the birds there until I got so curious that I went down to see for myself. I've been down there four or five times since then. I met Les in a bar in Quito when I was getting ready to come back from a visit down there. He had just finished leading a tour of the Galapagos and was bushed. I bought him a drink and we talked birds, and then he told me about this project he had been dreaming about. We've been corresponding ever since, and I became one of his investors about a year ago. People think it's funny, my liking birds so much. I'm a building contractor and birds never come up in conversations with the people I work with. But it's my mother's doing. She was crazy about them."

"I really appreciate your input, Mr. Rios. I will give you my phone number and extension. If you think of anything that might help us, please don't hesitate to give us a call." She gave him the information, thanked him again, and hung up.

"You silver-tongued devil, you," Sam said.

"That was well-done," was all the DEA agent said.

Deputy Jefferson just smiled and nodded.

Val felt very relieved. That was over.

The group left the Homicide office and headed to the small conference room to discuss the conversation in a more comfortable setting.

"Well, that was a little strange," Deputy Jefferson said. "I really anticipated a conversation of 'yes,' 'no,' 'I can't remember,' but instead he opened up with a rather lengthy story about his love of birds and meeting Burton."

"If you can believe anything he said," Agent Simpson added.

"I tend to," Val said. "Burton does not seem like he was a very nice guy, but he somehow manages to find and hold a few friends. You two," waving at the deputy and the agent, "have not had the opportunity to meet Burton's fiancée, but she comes across as genuinely loving the guy, and now Rios talks about him in the same way, 'nice guy,' 'sorry he died,' and all that. We've all seen this before, really bad guys–and gals–who seem to have connected on some level, selectively, with a few people. Rios with his mother and Burton; Burton with his fiancée and Rios. I may just be looking for something positive out of all this, maybe I'm naïve, but Rio's story sounds true."

"Or maybe this love of birds is just a cover for some other of Rios' operations in Ecuador," the agent said.

"I suppose that's possible," Val said. "Is Rios suspected of having contacts in the Ecuadorian drug cartels?"

"Sorry, can't talk about that here."

"Do you want us to keep you informed of our investigation into Burton's death," Sam asked, "or are you satisfied that it probably has nothing to do with your operation?"

"If you hear any more about Burton's travel to Ecuador–or any other countries south of the U.S. border–or connections with other local residents in relationship to this purported project of his, keep us in the loop. You can always contact Deputy Jefferson," pointing at her, "and she can put you in touch with the sheriff and me or someone else from the DEA. If your investigation just has to do with birds and birdwatchers, there's no need to contact us."

After the agent and Deputy Jefferson had left and the detectives had returned to their office, Sam looked at Val and sighed. "Why do I feel so confused about all this. The more I hear, the more confused I get."

"I hear you," Val replied. "I think it's because of the delay before the case came to us, the absence of evidence at the scene, and we seem to do our best work when we can talk over a case at the beginning so we have a plan of action, not just jumping from this bit of information to that bit. My suggestion is that we start all over again, integrating what we know with what we don't know, and then maybe it will make more sense."

"Sounds good to me," Sam said as he rose to close the door to their office to minimize interruptions. Opening a new file on his computer, he sat back and looked at Val, waiting for her to begin.

"You've been closer to all this than I have," she said. "Interrupt whenever you want with additions, subtractions, comments, and questions. What we know is this: One, a well-known nature photographer named Lester Burton was discovered lying face down on an island rookery located in the middle of a pond by two women who were visiting there. The rookery is a major birding site, and although visits to the rookery have been reduced due to heat and other factors, it is still attracting visitors. When he was first seen, he was lying next to an alligator, and it was uncertain whether one or both of them were alive. Upon closer examination by individuals who took a boat out to the site, it was determined they were both deceased.

"Two, the cause of death was determined to be a heart attack that resulted from Burton's near drowning in the pond. We still don't know how he got in the water, whether he jumped–which is unlikely because he can't swim–lost his balance or was pushed. We do know he was in the water long enough to come close to drowning. He survived the near drowning, only to die from what the M.E. called…let's see here…'a storm of cardiac events.' Burton had some substance under his fingernails, and the lab tests on that are not back yet. Other lab tests for drugs and alcohol are still not back either.

"Three, Burton had been shot in the thigh at some point after he got out of the water. He was not holding the gun at the time it discharged. Trajectory all wrong. However, he could have dropped the gun and had it discharge on impact. I've seen this happen before, even when the safety is on and the trigger wasn't touched. The alligator had been shot twice, once through its eye and once through the back of the head. All three bullets were from same gun. But there were four empty chambers in the gun. Burton was wearing a holster, but no gun was immediately found on the scene."

Sam interrupted. "Because all three bullets were from same gun, it seems reasonable to believe that Burton's missing gun was used to kill the alligator, but we still don't know whether he shot it or someone else shot it. If someone else shot it, how did they get Burton's gun? If someone else had his gun, that person could have shot Burton."

"Yes," Val said. "But it's also possible it was an accidental discharge. We can't ignore that."

"We need to revisit that question after we finish the list," Sam said.

"Yes, let's do that. Four, there could have been a second, or possibly third or fourth, person…"

Sam interrupted again. "If they traveled in the rookery's jon boat, which seems increasingly likely, it's pushing it to have five people aboard. And Burton was probably wearing a life jacket, maybe others as well, making it awfully crowded. So I think three people and Burton are as many as that boat could hold. One of those needed to mind the motor and steer the boat, so three other people max."

"Hadn't thought of that. Someone on that boat knew how to handle it. Doesn't necessarily mean they had used that particular boat before, but they had some skills along that line. Following your reasoning, we'll stick with one but no more than three other persons on the island with Burton. We know he had to travel there in some type of watercraft, but no watercraft was found on the island or adrift in the pond, indicating that whoever was with him had used the watercraft to return to wherever it cast off from."

"What other reasons do we have besides the missing watercraft that makes us believe that there was someone else on the island other than Burton?" Sam asked.

"Good question. One indication is that Burton had to get to the rookery by car. They couldn't have driven in and parked in the larger lot by the ticket booth and walked around because they arrived before the rookery opened, so they had to come in the back way. No unclaimed car was left in that vicinity after his death."

"They could have climbed the front gate and come in that way, but then they would have to walk around the pond," Sam said, "adding to their timetable."

"OK, there are two primary indications that at least one person was there besides Burton: the watercraft missing from the island–it would still be somewhere in the pond if he took it out there all by himself–and the fact that he got to the island without using his rental car or some transportation service. A secondary indication is that we're pretty sure they came in the back way and Burton, not living here, may not have known about that entrance unless someone else told him about it or led him there. Where are we in numbering?"

"Five."

"Five, a camera, handgun, and cellphone were retrieved from the pond near where Burton was found and are believed to belong to him. No fingerprints on any because of the length of time they were immersed. At this point, images from the camera and images and other information from the cellphone have not been recovered."

"And we believe those belonged to Burton because...?" Sam said.

"The handgun because of the empty holster. The camera because he was a photographer who had already mentioned that he needed to take some photos and he would probably have, unlike others today, taken them with a camera and not a cellphone. He was, after all, a professional photographer. And he had a lens cap in his pocket. The cell because who goes anywhere today without a cellphone and," she paused, "no one mentioned a watch, did they? So he could have had his cellphone out because he was using it to check the time."

"...and perhaps dropped it when he fell in the water," Sam added. "You're right. Either he or someone else must have been watching the time. Timing must have been important to them. Continue," Sam said.

"Six, upon talking to individuals who knew Burton, we found out that he had a lot of people who disliked him, and many seem to have good cause."

"Although people may have disliked him, wouldn't he know who they were? Would he have gone out to the island with someone who really disliked him?" Sam asked.

"I don't know," Val said. "I've assumed that he was planning on going out to the rookery before he even got to town because Rios mentioned that Burton had told him he was going to be taking photos. There might have been other places he photographed or planned to photograph, but I'm willing to bet that the rookery was already on his list. We know he was going to take some photos of something that had to do with a project in Ecuador that had a birding and/or ecological component. As far as we know, he didn't go anywhere else to take photos, although there are gaps in what we know of his timeline. Let's continue for now to believe he went out there willingly with someone else, which means either a friend or a person he hired."

"It would have to be someone he trusted," Sam said. "He couldn't swim."

"OK, that would narrow the possibilities a little. Someone that he knew and trusted or at least had no reason not to trust. Where are we?"

"Seven."

"We can trace Burton's movements somewhat. Ms. Adkins says he flew out to Houston on Wednesday. He was in Houston Thursday night having dinner with Rios. On Friday, he shows up at the Fillmore bar after their last session of the day. Doesn't stay. On Saturday he's having lunch at the Foghorn with a man who has been identified as Kamal Kapoor, the videographer who filmed–do we still say 'filmed'?–the meeting. Saturday night Burton had a beer with Ralph Cook, the photographer from Rockport. We don't know where he was or what he did on Sunday except for the little bit of info from his hotel charges and that he talked to Ms. Adkins Sunday night, probably from his cellphone because there is no record of that call at the hotel. Sometime after he ordered room service at 12:20 AM Monday morning, he left the hotel, but not in his rented car. As a side, I guess it's possible the other person or persons were there just to provide transportation, first by car and then by boat. Didn't have to have an alternative reason if that was the case. The next time we pick up Burton, he's lying dead on the rookery island."

"And we have a pretty good timetable for that morning," Sam said. "He needed some light to take photos, so he wouldn't have started while it was still dark. I suppose someone with photography savvy could guess when that would be, but for now we are guessing that he wouldn't have enough light for photos until after 6:00 and maybe as late as 6:30. In order to avoid being seen on the island by visitors to the rookery, the watercraft would have to be out of the view of the observation platforms by 7:15 at the latest."

"And if Burton's unplanned time in the water was not part of their timeline, there must have been some panic on the part of whoever else was on the island." She paused. "And then there is another point," Val said.

"OK, I'll add an eight."

"We also have a person dressed in khaki at the rookery that the EMT saw during the M.E. trip. Could have been a visitor, but no one remembers seeing him wander in. Don't know how we can locate this individual but we need to try."

"Not a lot to go on," Sam said.

"No, I agree. What other questions do we have?"

"It might be helpful if we knew more about the Ecuadorian project, but don't know where that information would come from."

"OK," Val said. "Still waiting to hear from Burton's attorney. We might get some info there."

"Where I'm having problems," Sam said, "is with trying to figure out what went on at the island. We know that time is an issue. They have to be out of sight by 7:00, maybe 7:15 if they know how the place functions, when the first visitors might arrive. They have a relatively short window, maybe at most an hour and a half, to take care of whatever they want to do."

"They?"

"Yes, I don't think we can assume that Burton's activities are driving all the action. Since we don't know who the other person is, it's possible that he or she or they might have reasons for being there as well."

"That's an excellent point," Val said. "That person may just be someone providing transport to the island, but it may also be someone who has a reason to be there independent of Burton, one that Burton may or may not have known about."

"And may have taken advantage of the opportunity provided by Burton's going over there," Sam said.

"Let's look at the transportation issue. If they used the jon boat to get to the island, someone had to know it was there and was available," Val said.

"Can we rule out their bringing their own watercraft?" Sam asked.

"It's beginning to look more and more likely that they used the jon boat rather than bringing their own. A lightweight craft that could be lifted over the gate would probably not be used in a pond with alligators. One bite and, whoops. A heavier one would be difficult for just two, or maybe even three, people. And there was water in the jon boat according to Gomez and it hadn't rained."

"Unless they knew the code for the gate," Sam said. "Who knows that code?"

"We need to get the answer to that. For now, let's assume they didn't know the code. Even if we find out that only a few people know the code, that doesn't limit our investigation. If Burton and his companion or companions didn't know the code, they could just climb over, like we did. However, if they didn't know the code, they probably used the jon boat since getting another boat over the gate is looking like a major undertaking. That means that they had to know the jon boat was there."

Val tapped her pen on her desk. "We're forgetting something here. What items did I tell you to make a note of during past conversations?"

Sam paged back in his notes. "OK, here goes: 'Who was khaki-dressed man at rookery?' That's a newer question. 'What was Burton photographing at rookery?' 'Who knows code to gate on back road?' That just came up again. 'What was Burton's relationship with Rios?' 'Could Sonya Adkins be involved?'"

"Yes, Sonya Adkins. She seems genuine, but we only have her word that she was in New Jersey on Monday morning."

"At this point," Val said, "I can see no reason that the person we're looking for can't be a woman."

"And we're still not absolutely sure," Sam said, "that only one boat went to the island."

"No, geez, we're not. Seems unlikely, but possible. Brings up the question of getting the second boat over the gate, however...unless they knew the code for the lock. So we need to keep that in mind."

"What's next?" Sam asked.

"Let's call Ms. Adkins. Let her know we talked to Rios."

There was no answer on Sonya Adkins' phone, and it rolled over to voice mail. Val left a message asking for a callback. "I wonder if she's been able to find out who is responsible for Burton's remains once we're through with them—which I think we are as soon as we get the report from Forensics—and who can claim the items from his room."

"We haven't looked at those," Sam said.

"That's right, we haven't. How on earth did we miss that? I'm not interested in the clothes, but there were maps and pamphlets or books that might be helpful. Call the crime scene unit and see if they will send those items over to us. Let's have lunch and then come back and tackle those noted items," she said."

Sam quickly agreed. "There is a new Honduran place in town," he said. "How's your Spanish? I was there last week. The food was excellent, but my Spanish is rusty, and no one there spoke English."

"*Mi español es lo suficientemente bueno como para poder leer un menú.*"

"Great. I caught the word 'menu,' so I guess that's a yes."

When they got back to the office, there was a phone message from the M.E. The lab reports had come back on Burton. No signs of drug use, alcohol level was almost normal, no other significant findings except that the residue under the nails was found to include skin cells consistent with those of *Alligator mississippiensis*, the American alligator.

"He was scratching the alligator's back?" Sam said.

"Doubt it," Val said with a grin, "but it's quite possible that he may have grabbed onto the alligator's tail to haul himself out of the water. If I remember correctly from the photos from CSI, the tail was partially submerged in the water."

"What's next?"

"Let's start with the access questions," Val said. She put the phone on speaker and called Lainey Gomez to see who had access to the front and back gates and to the ticket booth.

"The ticket booth is kept locked when not in use," Gomez said. "All the volunteers know the code, as do I and Vince and probably Adeline at the Bird Society. Those same people know the code to the front gate. As for the back gate, that's a little more selective. Vince, of course, and me, and the head of our volunteer maintenance crew. But if anyone else needs access, one of us usually goes there to open the gate. I really don't think anyone opened that gate before I got there that day," Gomez said. "The gate drags a bit and leaves a track in the dirt when it's opened. I usually check just to see if someone has entered since my last visit, and I didn't notice a track. Of course, I had other things on my mind, but that's such a habit that I do it without thinking."

"So you think that Burton and whoever was with him used the jon boat to get out to the island?" Val asked.

"It's the most logical thing."

"Maybe they thought the jon boat was secured, so they brought their own," Val said.

"Or didn't know that the jon boat was there," Sam added.

"Yes, that's possible, but everything else, the use of the back road, the timing of the visit, all that suggests to me that someone knew what they were doing and that the jon boat was available to them," Gomez said.

"And how many people would know that?"

"Oh, oodles, I'm afraid. Anyone who has volunteered in the last five years since we put the gate up and started leaving the boat out by the pond, the workers who helped us build the new platforms after the hurricane tore the old ones down, perhaps visitors that we took out there for some reason. The only people who wouldn't know there was a boat available for their use would have never been there before or did not know someone who had been there before."

"And those people might have brought their own boat?"

"Yes, if they knew there was a gate and didn't know there was a boat, secured or not," Gomez said. "But almost everyone who knew there was a gate was capable of knowing there was a boat. Could be wrong, but I really believe it was a well-planned intrusion. Someone knew what they were doing."

"We have a report that someone was watching the activity going on at the rookery, the boat coming and going. So far, we haven't been able to identify that person. He's male, wearing khaki, had binoculars. Was on one of the far platforms, the newer ones."

"Oh, gee, it could have been anyone. I would imagine that there was so much activity on the island that anyone on that path would be tempted to stop and watch." She paused and then continued.

"There is one other alternative, however," Gomez said. "There used to be a guy who hung around the pond. He was a trespasser of sorts, came in through some other way than the usual paths. People who have lived around here before we took over feel free to roam around here, hunt or fish, just like they did when the railroad owned it. This one guy–he said his name was Tom, just Tom, no last name–funny fellow, usually dressed in camouflage rather than khaki, but no reason why he wouldn't wear khaki–carried an old and probably ineffectual set of binoculars. We were worried about him when he first showed up, but he turned out to be a pretty nice guy, friendly, polite, shy, never bothered anyone, helpful if people got lost, so we let him be. He stopped showing up five, six months ago and we figured that he had moved or died or was ill. He must have been in his sixties at least. I suppose it's possible he's back, but no one working here has mentioned that they've seen him lately."

"And you have no idea where he lives or hangs out."

"No, but some of the businesses around here might know. The gas station, the motel, the post office. Not much around, but it might be worth a try."

Val thanked her and hung up. "Just what we need," she said. "Another possible wild goose chase."

"OK," Val said. "Next, Kapoor. His phone number should be on the list of attendees at the meeting."

"We could drive up and visit him," Sam said, looking at the attendee list. "We have an address." He put the address into his search engine. "Ah, that's his work address. It's in the Galleria area. Don't have a home address." He searched for "Kapoor" and "video" and found a website for Kapoor Video Studio. "The wonders of the internet," he said, searching the site. "According to this, Mr. Kapoor 'provides cutting-edge technology services to enhance marketing, enrich conferencing outcomes, and live-stream public and private events.'"

There were two phone numbers on the website, one listed as work and the other as cell. The same two numbers were on the spreadsheet from the Bird Society. She tried the work number first. Voice mail said to leave a message, but she hung up without leaving one and tried the cellphone. Again, voice mail, but this time she left a message to call her on her cell in connection with inquiries into the death of Lester Burton.

"So now we're waiting on callbacks from Burton's attorney, Mr. Kapoor, and Forensics about the camera and cellphone."

"What's next?" Sam asked.

"What's always next?" Val said. "Paperwork."

The box from the sheriff's office marked "Burton, Lester, Mariner Inn" arrived just after 3:00. Sam picked up the box and took it to an empty desk at the back of the room. "It's quite heavy," he said as he tore off the packing tape. A sturdy-looking bag filled over half of the box. Opening it, they could see a series of padded compartments, two of which contained camera lenses, one quite large and the other a little smaller. An empty pocket was rectangular, possibly large enough for a camera body, and there was a smaller pocket, also empty, for some unknown item.

"Boy, that bag looks like it's custom made," Val said, lifting the smaller lens out and looking at it without having any idea what she should be looking for. Sam lifted the larger lens. "Oh, this is pretty heavy," he said. They carefully placed the lenses back in their respective pockets, checked to make sure there was nothing else in the bag and removed the bag from the box and turned to the other items. Outside of checking in pockets or other potential hiding places–something, no doubt, already carefully done by Forensics–Burton's clothes and personal care items were quickly set aside. Two birding books remained, along with a couple of local maps, a set of keys, and a universal charging cord.

"My notes mention there were two sets of keys," Val said. "They must have returned the other set to the car rental agency. These are definitely personal keys to, what?" as she moved them around the keyring. "Home, car, something that is probably a key to a locker or storage area. Not a lot to go on."

She picked up a folded sheet of paper. "Here's a map of the sanctuary where the rookery is located, but it doesn't look like Burton marked it up. It does show both roads, the one to the parking lot and the one around on the back. The other map is just a general road map of the greater Houston area. I didn't even know they still made road maps. You never see them anymore except in old atlases and urban guidebooks. And he brought a couple of books. One is on the birds of Ecuador and it's in Spanish. Wonder if he was bilingual. Ecuador again. Keeps popping up. The other book, a guide to U.S. birds, is very well-used." Val held up a copy of a bird guide, still in its crime scene packaging, the edges of the cover frayed. "We should take the time to go through it carefully, just in case there is something there."

"I wonder if that is his," Sam said, motioning toward the book. "I haven't gotten the idea that he spent a lot of time chasing birds around the U.S. Most of the stuff mentioned online focuses on foreign and exotic birds."

"No idea," Val said. "And then there are the lenses. Burton came down here with two, probably three, since there was one on the camera that he took to the rookery. I would like to know more about how a professional photographer uses lenses. Why didn't he take one of these two with him as well? Or why did he take the one that he did?"

"We can ask someone from CSI to come over and explain that. They must have a camera expert over there if someone's working on trying to bring up the images on the camera that went into the drink."

"Yes, we could, but they're so busy with their current assignment, that I hesitate to do that. They might not show up for a couple of days. I bet there are some capable photographers over at the Art League. One of the photographers there is related in some way to Doris Gibson. A daughter-in-law, if I remember correctly. She already knows a lot about this case and Doris is involved with it, so maybe she would be willing to help us."

"Why does it matter, the lenses, that is?" Sam asked.

"I don't know if it does. Maybe the lens Burton took was the lightest weight or the smallest. The empty pocket in the camera bag is the smallest pocket there. We're assuming he knew he was going to the island and took the one best suited for the excursion. But it seems as if one of the other two might be better, depending on what he was going to photograph. But what else at this point do we have to go on? We still don't know if this was an accident, a willful disregard for human life, or a murder. All we're pretty sure of is that someone took him to the island and left without him. That leaves a lot of room for conjecture."

"And do you have a contact number for this photographer?"

"I'm sure that Ms. Baldwin has her number. She's a member of the Art League, and I do have Ms. Baldwin's number."

Evelyn Baldwin was home and happy to help. She was also curious why the detectives wanted to talk to an Art League photographer, which Val had expected.

"You may already know this," Evelyn said, "but Milly Gonzalez, the woman I think you're calling about, is the sister of Doris Gibson's daughter-in-law, and I've been kept up to date with what's going on through what Doris has relayed through Angela–her daughter-in-law and Milly's sister–and Angela has told Milly, and Milly–knowing I've been involved since the start–has told me. Is there anything new that you can tell me, or is everything still under wraps?"

Val sighed. She would never get used to the long stories and even longer pedigrees of Texans. "I'm afraid almost everything is, as you put it, 'still under wraps.' I can tell you that we want to ask Milly if she will take the time to give us a lesson on camera lenses. We have once again encountered a case that has taken place in a setting where we don't have much technical background, and we thought she might be of help. We do know about the family connections, which is one of the reasons we decided to ask her because we don't need to give her a lot of background or get a new person involved in our inquiries."

"Well, I'm sure she'll be happy to help. Give me a second and I'll get her phone number."

When Val ended the call, she turned to Sam. "Please don't tell me that Milly Gonzalez's cousin just happens to be married to your kindergarten teacher's brother."

"What on earth brought that on?" he asked.

Val just shrugged and called the number Evelyn had given her. No answer. So Val texted her, figuring that Milly might not bother with the telephone anymore. Sure enough, her text asking Milly to call her resulted in her cell ringing a few minutes later.

"Hi, Detective Forster. This is Milly, calling back as requested."

"Thanks, Milly. I have a favor to ask if you have an hour to spare. We have a few photography questions that you may be able to help us with. When Les Burton came here, he brought three lenses with him. We have the other two here in our office. Neither Detective Pierson nor I know much about camera lenses and why he would choose one over the other when he went to the rookery, and we thought maybe you could help us."

"Sure. I'm free until 7:00 if you want to do it today. Otherwise not until late morning tomorrow. But my sister, Angela, is more of a techie than I am. And if we can't answer your questions, we can suggest people who know more about cameras and lenses than Angela and I do."

"But do any of them have background in bird photography, familiarity with the rookery, and a general knowledge of the events that took place at the rookery the day Mr. Burton's body was found?"

There was a slight pause. "No, probably not all three. The first one, yes, you could get people much more skilled than I am, and some of them may be familiar with the rookery, but I don't know anyone who matches all three."

"And that's why we called you," Val said. "If you feel you can't answer our questions, then we'll try someone else, but I'd like to start with you. And Angela is welcome to join you."

"Great. When would you like us to come by?"

"Today would be wonderful." Val looked at her watch. "How about 4:30?"

"I can do that. I'll call Angela and see if she can come with me."

The front desk called at 4:45 to say there were two women there to see her. Val went to the front to escort them back to the homicide office.

"Sorry we're a few minutes late," Milly said, as she introduced her sister to the detectives. "It never fails. Touching the front doorknob makes the phone ring. I was afraid it was someone asking me to come in early for work, but it wasn't."

"Where do you work?" Val asked.

"I'm a front desk clerk at the Fillmore Hotel."

"Really?" Val said. "So you got to meet the people who were here for the bird meeting."

"I knew some of them before–the locals, mostly–but it was good to meet the others. It's too bad that Burton wasn't invited to participate since he was in town and his name on the list would give it some prestige. I would have loved to have met him. He's a great photographer. I have one of his books on wildlife photography and it's really been helpful."

Another positive assessment of Burton, Val thought. So far, however, the negatives were still winning.

"And Angela, do you have time constraints?" Val asked.

"No, I'm a student at the community college. No classes today. I wanted to come with Milly because she is such a fan of Burton's and I'm not, so we balance each other out."

"Not a fan?" Val asked.

"No, I don't care how talented he is, he's not a very nice human being."

Milly looked at her sister and frowned.

"Milly and I have been round and round with this," Angela said. "We agree on 90% of everything, but this is one exception. I think Milly asked me to come because she thought that I might soften up on my assessment, but I don't think it will work."

Milly just shrugged. "She sees right through me, as usual, but it was worth a try."

The sisters gave each other a quick smile and followed Val over to the desk where they had laid out the items from Burton's hotel room. Milly immediately reached for the bird guide and then quickly withdrew her hand.

"It's OK," Val said, "you can touch any of these things. They have all been cleared."

Milly once more reached for the bag with the bird guide and carefully picked it up. "This is a classic," she said. "One of the first *Peterson Field Guide to Birds*. If it's a first edition and if it were in much better shape, it might be worth hundreds of dollars." She asked if she could remove it from the wrapper, and at Val's nod of approval, took it out, carefully opened it up, and turned to the title page. "Not a first edition, but still...." She set it down very gently.

"Hundreds?" Sam asked. "Did you say hundreds?"

"In good shape, well cared for, yes. Signed, most certainly. This one is probably too used to be worth much, but it was meant to be used and it certainly has been," Milly said. "And it belonged to a famous photographer, which I'm sure means something in terms of value. I've seen the undamaged ones sold online for quite a lot of money."

"And he's just carrying it around with him?" Val asked.

"Yes. A lot of the information in here is now outdated. Flight paths and nesting grounds have certainly changed, but it could be a talisman of sorts, you know, carried for good luck. Or maybe he bought it when he was in Houston. Or someone gave it to him. There are a lot of explanations," Milly said. "Whatever."

"Thank you, Milly. We'll make sure we let his next of kin know about the book. We asked you to come here to look at the lenses and we have a rare book expert as well," Val said.

"Not an expert, no, but I did a paper on early bird guides for an ornithology class and this one started the section on American publications. It's that important. Now, how can we help you with the lenses?"

"We think Burton came here with three lenses. One of them, which the crime scene lab described as," she looked at her notes, "a 50-millimeter prime lens, was attached to a camera he took to the rookery with him. That little piece of information has not yet been published, by the way, so please keep it quiet until you see it in the paper. The other two are in front of you. We've been trying to figure out why he went to the island, and we thought that maybe the lens that he chose would help us."

"Gee, a 50-millimeter prime lens is a strange one—at least I think it's a strange one—for someone who photographs birds," Angela said, looking at her sister as though asking permission to join in the conversation. "'Prime' means that it doesn't zoom, you know, make the image closer or farther away. If you have a camera, Detective Forster, it probably has a zoom lens."

"Yes, the ones I've used for work and the one I have at home all have zoom lenses," Val said.

"Prime lenses also tend to capture more light and have sharper images than zoom lenses," Angela continued. "But if you're photographing birds, you need to be able to follow the bird and keep it in focus, so you would probably use a zoom lens."

"You're suggesting that he didn't go to the island to shoot photos of the birds flying around?" Sam asked.

"Yes, that's my guess." Angela said. "Both of the other two lenses are zoom lenses. If he wanted to shoot wildlife of any kind, I would think he would take one of those. They are, however, very heavy in comparison. Did you find a tripod anywhere? You can hand-hold these, but most photographers use a tripod if they can in order to get cleaner shots because the camera is stabilized."

"No, no tripod. Of course, it could have fallen in the pond," Sam said. "You're suggesting that if Burton was traveling light, he might take the lightest lens and avoid taking a tripod?"

"Yes, that would be a consideration," Angela said, "but it seems to me that he'd really be handicapping himself taking a prime lens unless he planned to photograph more stationary objects. But what do I know in comparison to what he knows...knew?"

"OK, let's go with what you've just told us. What kind of photos do you think you would take if you were on that particular spot on that particular island and were using the lens that Burton used?"

"Gee, I don't know," Angela said. "I'm not that familiar with the rookery. Milly, what do you think?"

"Well, there are some more sedentary subjects. You know, turtles, frogs, basking alligators, the nesting platforms, that kind of thing."

"I don't think that's a good lens for the nesting platforms," Angela said. "If I remember the island correctly, there's not a lot of room to maneuver if you're on the island and trying to take photos of the trees and platforms around you. And you couldn't zoom in to focus on something of particular interest. But if he turned around and shot across the pond to the viewing platforms, that particular lens, especially if it was a wide-angle lens, would be perfect."

Sam interrupted. "Why would photographs like that be of any interest?"

"In the hands of a good photographer, that could be a lovely shot," Milly said. "You have the bank across from the island going up from the water to where the platforms are, the architecture of the platforms, maybe a bird flying by, and perhaps some turtles basking on the tree roots at the base of the bank."

"But would someone like Burton be interested in such an image?" Angela asked her sister.

"He might be taking it for some commercial reason," Milly said. "Maybe someone is thinking of developing a rookery or some other birdwatching attraction and is looking for ideas on how other developers have done it. If you wanted to photograph that, you'd have to do it from the island. You couldn't get a really good shot when you're standing on the path with the observation platforms right in front of you, and you can't shoot from the other side because the island is in the way."

"That's an interesting idea. Do people build rookeries?" Val asked, deciding not to mention the Ecuadorian project. "I got the idea that it's sort of up to the birds where they are going to build their nests. I mean, the island was a rookery before the area was opened up for visitors, wasn't it?"

"Yes, it was probably a pleasant surprise for Vince and the others when they discovered all the nests there. I think they were initially interested in preserving the oaks behind the area with the rookery. It attracts hundreds of migratory birds some years, exhausted from their trip across the Gulf."

"Across the Gulf?" Sam asked.

"Yes, from Yucatan peninsula, mostly. Straight across. That's why these trees along the coast are so welcoming to them. They are very tired, hungry, and thirsty."

"So, to get all this straight," Val said, "you think that Burton chose the lens he did because he was not interested in taking photos of birds, but because he was planning to take photos of more stationary subject matter?"

"Well, yes and no," Angela said. "You can take great shots of almost anything with a prime lens, even a bird in flight. It's just a little trickier. But the fact that he took the prime lens instead of one of the larger and heavier zoom lens suggests to me that he was going to take photos of something that would be best photographed with a prime lens, and the only thing I can think of that he could photograph better with that lens than with a zoom lens while he was on the island is the bank across the pond where the viewing platforms are located."

"And the best reason you can think of to take that kind of shot is....?" Val asked.

"For illustration purposes," Milly said. "Maybe to show the height of the banks or how the viewing platforms are designed?"

"Who would want to know that?"

"Well," said Milly, "anyone who was trying to build a rookery from scratch or update a rookery site for visitors."

Val looked at Sam and then back to Milly. "And who would want to do that?"

"Oh, someone developing an ecotourism park for one. There is a lot of money in those if they are well designed. There's one in Costa Rica I'm saving my money to visit next year."

"Where can we find out more about ecotourism parks?" Sam asked.

Angela said. "Perhaps a photography magazine...or maybe a tourism magazine."

"Are there tourism magazines that focus on ecotourism?"

"I don't know," Milly said. "But there must be, if not in print, then maybe online."

Sam went back to his desk and typed "ecotourism AND magazines" into his search engine.

"Oh, good Lord," he said. "Here's a site that lists the 'top ten' ecotourism magazines, suggesting that there are more than ten. There's also a list of best ecotourism places to visit when you're away from home for business. Val, why don't we get opportunities like this? Take advantage of a trip to Beaumont, for example, and then stretch that out for a hop, skip, and jump to spend a couple of days in Cancun?"

Val ignored Sam and, turning to the sisters, told them how much she appreciated their help. "This information has opened some doors and closed others, but at this point any information is helpful."

"Do you think someone killed him?" Milly asked. "Or is that something we shouldn't ask?"

"We still don't know exactly what happened," Val said. "But we know enough to keep looking. That's about all I can tell you because that's just a truthful summary of where we are at the moment. Oh, and I have one more question to ask you. Do either of you know of an older man who hangs around the rookery area, wears khaki or camo, and carries an old pair of binoculars?"

"Are you talking about Tom?" Milly asked.

"Yes, Tom. Do you know him? Does everyone know him?" Val asked.

The sisters laughed. "No, not everybody knows him," Milly said, "but people who spend a lot of time wandering around the rookery in the early morning hours might bump into him. I've never seen him around later in the day. And I don't really *know* him, only enough to say hello, talk about the weather, that kind of thing. He seems like a nice guy. Once he stopped long enough to tell me that there was a fire ant nest by the path in the direction I was going and that I should be careful. Doris, Angela's mom-in-law, says that he's officially a trespasser, but he was around before they created the pond and knows his way around so well that no one has ever thought of trying to keep him out. Keeping him out might be a challenge."

"Do you know if he lives somewhere around there?"

"Doris told me once when I mentioned seeing him that she thinks he drives an old pickup with a camper on the back," Angela said. "So he could be parked almost anywhere if he's living out of the camper. The gas station or grocery store people may know more. I'm sure that he must trade there. They may not tell you much though. The people who live around here tend to let others be. Someone once told me that he used to poach alligators and other wildlife around the pond."

"You don't think he still does that, do you?" Sam asked.

"No, I think that was in the past. There was no grocery store here until after the rookery opened up. Just a gas station. I'm sure that he has to buy groceries and get gas. I've never seen him carry anything around except that old pair of binoculars. They're more like opera glasses than binoculars."

After the sisters left, Val sighed deeply. "We keep learning things and still get nowhere."

"I don't know about that," Sam said. "We are getting some information about the kinds of photos that Burton may have been taking. We know he had a choice of lenses and must have taken the one he did for a specific reason. We now have a working explanation for that. And we know more about Tom."

"And why does all that get us any closer to finding out what happened on the island that morning?"

Sam shrugged. He picked up his cellphone, grabbed his jacket from the back of his chair, pulled his car keys from his desk drawer, and headed for the door, waving good-bye as he left.

"I take that as a 'hell if I know,'" Val said, joining him in the hallway.

CHAPTER 9

The Second Monday

When Sam arrived at the office, there was a message from Sonya Adkins on his phone announcing that she was heading back to New Jersey on Wednesday. She also said that, thanks to Burton's attorney and the suggestion of a small monetary enhancement, she had notarized copies of documents faxed to her by each of Burton's next of kin attesting to the fact–and here she paused and it sounded as though she was reading the next part of her message–"that they would not dispute Sonya Adkins' taking possession of Lester Burton's remains and subsequently arranging for his burial or other legal disposition of said remains." Adkins added that she would be around and about the rest of the day and would call back a little later in the morning. The detectives were free to call her if they had urgent questions or information about the case.

"Ms. Adkins has permission to claim Burton's body and dispose of it," he said to Val as she entered the office. "Do we have other questions for her?"

"We want to make sure she was not in Texas on Monday morning. We still haven't talked to the attorney. I've left three messages so far and no response. Somehow, I get the feeling she is avoiding us. And if Ms. Adkins finds out from her what Burton was trying to photograph the morning he died, she needs to tell us."

"Do we mention anything about Rios when we talk to her?"

"I'd like to follow up there, but we've been told to keep our hands off him for now. The drug people must be pretty serious. How often have you had a DEA agent show up to monitor a telephone call?"

"So you don't think we can call Rios and ask him where he and/or his primary henchmen were on Monday morning?"

The office phone rang, and Val hurried back to her desk to answer it, putting it on speaker. She mouthed "Sonya Adkins" to Sam, who came over to his desk and sat down.

"Thank you for calling, Ms. Adkins. We got your earlier message. I understand that you have been cleared to claim Mr. Burton's remains," Val said.

"Yes, thank heavens. That's one problem solved. I'm thinking seriously about having Les cremated here in Egret Bay and then sending his ashes to the bird place in Ecuador that he left money to in his will. It seems appropriate. I will probably sell his house; it's much too large for one person, and I have no idea where I will end up."

"We have a couple more questions for you before you leave. We are asking all the people who knew Mr. Burton or who encountered him while he was here to send us information about their location and activities from late Sunday night until mid-morning on Monday."

"That's easy. I was in New Jersey on Sunday. In fact, I had a few friends over for dinner on Sunday night to celebrate one of their birthdays. I can send you the names and contact numbers for them if that will help."

"Yes, it certainly will. Thank you. Send them to the email that's on my business card. Do you still have that?"

"Yes, that's how I got this number. What else?"

"We have not been able to talk to Mr. Burton's attorney. We have left multiple messages, but she hasn't responded. We are especially interested in trying to find out anything we can about the project Mr. Burton was working on in Ecuador. It might help if you contacted the attorney and told her that it is very important that we speak to her. We only have a couple of questions. I don't think any of them impede on attorney-client privilege, but they could be important."

"Have you talked to Terry, his business manager?"

"Yes, but he wasn't much help."

"He probably knows that I plan on firing him when I get back. He doesn't like me—I think it's more truthful to say that he resents me because he thinks I've come between Les and him—but I don't trust him. I can hold off on the firing if you want to talk to him first."

"That might be a good idea. Thank you," Val said.

"I'm sure that there is a lot of mail piling at our home," Adkins said. "There may be some information there. I will go through it carefully and call you if I find anything that may be of interest. I wish I knew Les's password for his email and telephone, but it just never seemed important since he primarily used them only for business and fan mail."

"And no social media?"

"Oh, heavens, no! Les abhorred social media. 'Goblin zone,' he called it."

"Goblin zone?" Val said. "That's a new one to me. I'll have to remember that."

"He had a lovely sense of humor," Sonya said. "He used to come up with all sorts of funny things."

Val and Sam looked at each other and Sam shrugged.

"We will let you know if we find anything of interest at this end."

"Thanks. I really appreciate all your help."

After Val hung up, she looked at Sam. "Has anyone else mentioned his sense of humor?"

"No, I never got the idea that he was frivolous about anything. But I must admit I like goblin zone."

"We can verify her presence in New Jersey when she sends us the names. It would be almost impossible for Ms. Adkins to fly from there to Houston on Sunday night and get to the rookery by 6:00 AM."

"Well, she could have had an accomplice."

Val sighed.

"So what's next?" Sam asks.

"We initially had no theories as to what happened to Burton, and now we can chose among two or three. We know that Burton either fell or was pushed into the water. We can pretty well rule out that he jumped in on his own. So scratch that for now. If someone planned on killing him and knew he couldn't swim, they might have pushed him in to drown. But why didn't they stick around and make sure he didn't get out? They couldn't rely on the cardiac event that killed him. So scratch that for now. On the other hand, if he fell in, why didn't someone help him out? And if they tried to help him out and failed, why didn't they call for help? And if he died in front of them, why didn't they report it? Those questions still need answers. Make a note: We need to ask the M.E. about the time span between getting out of the pond and the beginning of the heart attack."

Sam reached for the phone and dialed the M.E.'s office. One of the assistants answered and Sam left a message to have the M.E. call back with information about the timing of the heart attack after Burton got out of the pond.

"My guess is that they didn't come forward if the drowning was unintentional because they didn't want anyone to know they had been there," he said.

"That works better for me," Val said. "Because if he drowned, everyone would assume he fell in the water while on the island and they would be in the clear. Whoever else was there may not have known that he couldn't swim. That makes the most sense by far, but only if that's all there was to it. We have to throw in a dead alligator and a bullet in Burton's leg."

"OK, let's try the old trilogy. Means, motive, and opportunity. Means and opportunity are pretty set. Regardless of how it happened, the pond was the means and Burton's inability to swim was the opportunity. Whether he fell or was shoved, he died because he almost drowned and that precipitated a heart attack," Sam said.

"Motive?" Val said.

"Well, we know lots of people really disliked him."

"But enough to kill him?"

"It's possible, but not probable. We've cleared just about everyone that was visiting in town that weekend, both those that liked him and those who disliked him, during the time span the M.E. specified."

"If Rios is active in one of the drug cartels, I doubt he would have any qualms about murder if he believed Burton had somehow crossed him," Val said. "He might know that Burton was coming down here to photograph something–against his will, so we've been told–and he might also have known that meant going to the island. But how would he know about the gate, for instance? Or that the jon boat would be there? And why go to the trouble of having someone take him to the island and murder him there when he could simply have him–I don't know–run over crossing a street?"

"What about Sonya Adkins? Do you think Rios and her might be a pair and together planned Burton's demise? Burton had a pretty valuable estate when he died," Sam asked.

"I suppose that's possible. The will leaves her quite a lot of money and property but not anywhere near the hundreds of thousands that Rios could get from drug running–if that's what he's up to."

"Or Burton may have antagonized someone from Ecuador who wanted to stop him from whatever project he's contemplating down there. That country is increasingly getting involved in the drug trade and may not welcome an increase in tourism," Sam said. "But this gets us to the same questions we have about Rios. Why would they go to all that trouble to take him to the rookery, and how would they know all the particulars about the gate and other stuff?"

"A symbolic warning? We're really grasping at straws. It shows how lost we are at this point."

"One thing we haven't done is look closely at local people who were not part of the meeting," Sam said. "There's that guy Tom, there's the volunteers at the rookery, and there's other people employed by the Bird Society. They may all know about the back gate, may know about the availability of the boat, and could have been approached by Burton to take him over to the rookery. However, the people at the meeting seemed surprised to see Burton in town, so who knew that he would be here and how did he know who to ask for help before he arrived? He only had a couple of days to set up his visit to the rookery unless someone else had scouted it out beforehand. Or was he already familiar with the rookery? Had he been there before?"

"Wait," Val said. "Is there any indication that he knew about the meeting before he arrived? Couldn't he have just decided to come down here and then be surprised at seeing these people that he knew? We've been looking at this with the assumption that he came down here *because* of the meeting. What if the two happening at the same time is just a coincidence?"

"What's so irritating about that idea," Sam said, "is that, either before he came or after he arrived, Burton made arrangements with someone to help him with his rookery visit. If after, we may yet figure that out, but if that person is outside our dragnet, we may never find him–or her. If Burton set up his visit before he came down, it might be someone local, but it could also be almost anyone. In that case, we might as well close down this investigation and go back to the cold cases. The only indication we have that something took place that morning that demands we take a close look at it as a possible homicide are the absence of a watercraft and the bullet wound."

"And a dead alligator," Val said.

"Oh, yes, of course. There is *that*," Sam said. "That takes us right back where we started. So, what's next?"

"Let's take a photo of Burton over to the Foghorn Café and see if the Ernie Davis or his cook–whose name escapes me–remember him. Burton may have had others join him or asked questions, or.... I know I'm tilting at windmills, but we haven't talked to Kapoor and if anything did take place there, we should know about it before we talk to him."

"The cook's name is Rolando," Sam said.

"Yes, Rolando. We can then come back and see if the M.E. has responded about the timing of the heart attack after Burton got out of the water. We need to check with the people Ms. Adkins says she had dinner with that Sunday night as soon as she sends us the names. We can then write up our report of today's activities and send them to the chief. We are getting nowhere fast, and he wanted this over by now. Then let's drive over to the businesses near the rookery and see if the people there can give us any leads on Tom. We need to know if he saw anything on Monday morning."

"Are you sure this Tom guy wasn't involved?"

"Yes. Well, yes, I think so. If he was hired by a cartel to do Burton in, he wouldn't still be walking around. It would be easy to get rid of him. And how would Burton, acting on his own, contact a recluse like this Tom? How would he even know he existed and why would he trust him?"

The Foghorn was not very busy when they arrived, but the tantalizing aroma of coffee and grilled food made Val wish she had time to sit there and relax for a while. Ernie came out of the kitchen and saw them standing at the counter. "Detectives," he said, "I hope this is a personal and not a business call."

"I wish it was too," Val said. "Do you have a couple of minutes to look at a photo and tell us if you remember this guy being here a week ago Saturday?"

"You have more faith in my memory than I do, but, sure, glad to help if I can."

Val handed Ernie the photo of Burton and he stared at it, frowning. "Give me some background," he said.

"Well, it would have been around lunch time. He was sitting with another guy that's probably of south Asian heritage, Indian perhaps."

Ernie nodded slowly. "I really don't remember this guy," he said, pointing at the photo. "But I think I remember the other guy. He was really hyper, enthusiastic, talking about taking videos of wild animals..."

"Wild animals?"

"Yes, it was interesting listening to him when I was out here by the cash register. He had an encounter with an elk once that made him climb a tree to get away. And he wanted hot tea. No one ever asks for hot tea here, especially this time of year when it's heating up outside. I thought maybe he wasn't used to iced tea. He looked like he could have been Indian, very good looking, like a Bollywood star, but he talked like a Texan."

"Bollywood? You into Indian movies?" Sam asked.

"My girlfriend likes them," Ernie said. "Her grandmother is from India, and she used to watch them with her when she was a kid."

"Getting back to the subject of our visit," Val said with a little impatience, "did either of them pay by credit card?"

"Not sure. Rolando was waiting on them. We were pretty busy that weekend. I'll check our receipts. You say it was a week ago Saturday?"

"Yes, at lunchtime, whenever that is."

"I'll talk to Rolando when he comes in tomorrow–he's already gone for the day. And I'll check our records. What am I looking for?"

Val tore a page out of her notebook and wrote Burton and Kapoor's name on it, along with her direct phone number and her cell number. "Don't just look for the name Kapoor. We're interested in anyone who might have been here during lunchtime that day who spoke with the gentleman shown in the photo."

When they got back to the car, Val let out a low whistle. "That seems to confirm the story Ms. Aiello gave us, that Kapoor had lunch with Burton on Saturday. And he is the one person who was at the meeting that we haven't yet interviewed."

"Don't get your hopes up," Sam said.

"I know, I know. But it has potential. At this point, I'm looking for any glimmer of light."

"We've already put Kapoor near the bottom of the suspect list because of being at breakfast by 7:30."

"But if it was Kapoor who was with Burton at the Foghorn, and that looks to be the case, we need to find out what their relationship was."

There was a message from the M.E. when they got back to the office. "Cardiac event could have occurred anywhere from a few minutes to an hour after near-drowning," was all it said.

"That's not a lot of help," Val said.

"Well, it was probably not an hour," Sam said. "It's good to know that our timetable seems to agree with the M.E.'s time estimates. Burton had been dead at least an hour when he was discovered a little after 8:00, so that means he landed in the water at 6:00 or after–if our timetable holds."

"While we're waiting for callbacks, let's start with our report to the chief. First, I need to light a fire under Forensics," Val said as she dialed the phone. "We've been fortunate to be able to focus on this case without interruption, but we're pushing our luck in thinking we won't be called out on an emergency assignment in the near future."

She had just about given up as the phone at Forensics rang over a dozen times before it was finally picked up by someone at the CSI reception desk. Sighing, she left another message to have someone in Forensics call her back regarding the camera and cellphone belonging to Lester Burton that were retrieved from the rookery pond the previous Thursday morning.

After hanging up, she immediately placed another call, this time to the Bird Society. It was answered on the second ring. "Egret Bay Bird Society, Adeline Alvarez speaking."

"Ms. Alvarez," Val said, "is Mr. Wallace in by any chance?"

"He's on another line. Can I have him call you back? Shouldn't be long."

Ten minutes later, the call came through.

"This is Vince Wallace. You called?"

"Just some follow-up questions," she said as she put the phone on speaker and motioned to Sam to listen in. "You said that you were with Ms. Alvarez and Mr. Kapoor at breakfast a week ago Monday. You also said that Mr. Kapoor was not a birder but had been hired to videotape the conference."

"Yes, indeed. It had been suggested that we would benefit by having the planning meetings videotaped rather than just an audio recording or appointing someone to take notes. Mr. Kapoor did a fine job and we're very pleased with the results."

"How did you happen to hire him rather than someone else?"

"He was recommended by another nonprofit that we do business with—a turtle restoration group. They hired him to videotape a conference and were not only pleased with his work but were also pleased with the rather generous discount that he gives nonprofits. He videoed the meetings and made sure to capture all the charts, graphs, photographs, and such, so that anyone who missed the meeting or gets involved later on can review and refer to them in the future."

"Thanks. That's all we needed to know. We'll let you get back to work."

She hung up before Wallace had a chance to ask her about the investigation.

"Well, that all makes sense," she said, "but I keep hoping for more. Let's see if we can find the elusive Tom. We've left messages for Forensics and Kapoor to call us. I should have left my cell number with Kapoor. Wasn't thinking. Also wasn't thinking when we were at the Foghorn that we could have ordered lunch and brought it back. Now I'm hungry."

Sam checked his watch. "Let's get a bite to eat and head over towards the rookery. I'm really curious about this Tom guy. He sounds like a character out of a B movie."

"Nah," Val said. "If he was out of a B movie, his name would have been something more dramatic, like...."

"Swamp Monster," Sam said.

Val just looked at him.

They left for the rookery as soon as they finished eating, avoiding a potential delay if they should be seen by the chief if they went back to the station first. They both knew that he was getting inpatient. They needed to put an end to this case, and soon. First stop, the combined gas station and grocery store on the main road going to the rookery. There wasn't much else around except a small café and a dozen or so vacation or fishing cabins on stilts that had survived the last hurricane.

They entered the grocery and were met by the strange combination of odors of fish and fresh brewed coffee. A woman behind a cluttered counter looked up and asked, "gas or groceries?"

"Well, neither really," Val said, showing her badge. "We're looking for information."

"Directions?"

"No, not that either. We are looking for someone known around here as Tom. Just Tom. No last name. We think he may be able to answer a couple of questions about the recent death of a man over at the rookery."

"Tom wouldn't hurt a soul," the woman said.

"That's what we understand. We just think that he may know or have seen something that might help us. He is not a suspect, but he may have been a witness."

The woman looked at them for a few seconds, as though sizing them up. "The people you talked to, have they told you much about him?"

"What we've heard is that he lives alone, has been around for years, keeps to himself, has been absent for a while and is now back, and is kind and helpful to the people who are here to look at the birds."

The woman nodded, "Yes, that's Tom. He's my husband's cousin, second cousin, I think. Never can keep his family line straight. We–my husband and me–have been Tom's support for years. We're his banker, his grocer, his mechanic, and his shelter in a storm. In return, he keeps us supplied with fresh fish, crawfish, crabs, and foraged nuts and berries in season."

"Sounds like a good deal," Sam said.

"It is," the woman said. "It is. We think the world of him."

"We would like to talk to him," Val said. "Can that be arranged?"

"Let me talk to my husband. Help yourself to a cup of coffee and, if you don't mind, watch the store for me for a few minutes. I think I can trust you not to pilfer." Without waiting for a response, she walked to the back of the store and through a door with a sign that said, in capital letters, "PRIVATE."

Sam walked over to the coffee urn, took a clean mug from the shelf above it, and poured himself a cup. He looked over at Val, who nodded. He then grabbed another mug and poured a second cup.

"Smells good," he said as he handed her a mug. She looked at the message on the mug. "Fish Whisperer? What do you whisper to a fish? It doesn't say here what the magic words are." Sam looked at his mug. "I would read what mine says, but I'm in mixed company."

The door marked PRIVATE opened, and a man entered, followed by the woman they had talked to previously. He walked over to Sam and put out his hand. "I'm Fritz Huber, Tom's cousin. Tell me what you want with him and maybe I can help." He then held out his hand to Val. She sighed deeply and Sam was quiet, leaving it open to her to take the lead. She took a sip of coffee and then gave a brief background story of an ambulance worker seeing an individual watching the medical examiner when he was on the island. They were now pretty sure that individual was neither a law enforcement officer nor a rookery visitor. It had been suggested to them by people who frequented the rookery that it may be a person that they knew only as Tom. If it was Huber's cousin Tom, all they want to know is if he saw anything or heard anything prior to the medical examiner's visit, especially from around 6:00 to 8:00 on that morning.

"And that's all you want to know? He doesn't have to go to the police station or anything?"

"Not unless he was somehow involved in the death of the man at the rookery, and everything we've learned to date says that he was not."

"I'm not trying to be difficult," Huber said. "I'm just trying to protect Tom. He's had a hard time since returning from Desert Storm–PTSD and all that. But he would want to help you if he could. Can you talk to him here?"

"Yes," Val said. "When can we meet him?"

"Well, now, I guess. He's over at the house having lunch. I'll go get him. May be a few minutes. Have a seat," motioning toward a bench under the front window.

"That's unexpected good luck," Sam said to Val as they picked up their coffee mugs and moved over to the bench. Huber's wife returned to the checkout counter.

It was almost fifteen minutes later that Huber returned, followed by a sun-bronzed man that he introduced simply as Tom. No last name given. They didn't ask. They would get that later.

"Thanks for talking to us, Tom," Sam said. "As your cousin may have told you, we're investigating the death that occurred recently at the rookery. The EMT who was out there thought he saw you watching them from one of the viewing platforms. We're curious if you were there earlier and saw any other activity out on the island."

Tom remained standing, shifting on his feet a little, then looked at Huber, who nodded at him.

"Yes, I was fishing not far from the rookery pond. Good fishing day. I heard some pistol shots and a lot of distress noises from the birds in that direction, and I was concerned that someone was poaching because the rookery wasn't open yet. But, like I said, the fish were biting, and I didn't hear any more shots and the birds seemed to settle, so I stayed where I was. Then after a while, the birds started up again, just as I was packing up. Their squawking began to bother me, so I put the fish in my ice chest and walked over to the pond, taking a back way I knew, about a half mile or so over. When I got there, I saw a couple of guys and a couple of women in a jon boat looking at a man and a gator lying on the sand where that gator usually goes to bask in the morning."

"How many shots did you hear earlier?" Val asked.

"Four. Two shots rather close together and then about ten or fifteen minutes later, two more in quick secession. Once I got over there, I stayed around for a while watching the boat leave and then come back a little later with four people on it, still two women and two men, but not sure they were the same, except for the woman at the rear. I think she was there both times. My binoculars are pretty old, so I couldn't tell you for sure what they looked like."

"Is it usual to hear shots being fired around the rookery area?"

"Around the rookery, no, not usual at all. But hunting's allowed not far from there, mostly ducks and geese in season. This isn't season, however, which is why it caught my attention. That and the fact it was a pistol. Course you can kill rabbits and hares anytime with anything as long as you have a hunting license. Not many people around here eat rabbit anymore. Squirrel either."

"And you're sure this was a pistol shot, not a rifle?" Sam asked.

"Yes. I know the difference."

"Is there much of a problem with poaching?" Val asked.

"You can only hunt alligator in this county in September, and then only with a special license. It's still open season through June in most counties, so we sometimes have people come to hunt them here because they don't know that open season rules don't apply in Fillmore County. They don't mean to break the law, but they are." He looked back at Huber. "Hell, I shot one once before I knew that. Haven't killed another since. Weird-looking animals, but sort of magnificent. Didn't feel right, shooting them."

"Can you kill an alligator with a handgun?" Sam asked.

"If you're a good enough shot, you can kill one with any firearm. If you can get close enough, you can kill one with a screwdriver, but I wouldn't want to try that."

"With a screwdriver?" Sam asked.

"There's this spot, right near the back of the head, about the size of your big toe, where there's a clear shot into the brain. Or you can go in through the eye if the angle is right. I would prefer being at a distance though. With a handgun, you're taking a real risk unless you're a really good shot. Those gators can sure move fast when they want to."

"This alligator was shot once through the eye and once through that spot on the back of the head," Val said.

"There's not much room on that little sandy area there to get some distance," Tom said. "You'd almost have to straddle the gator to get to that soft spot...or be really lucky."

"Did you see one guy trip when he tried to step over the alligator?" Sam asked.

"Yeah," Tom said with a grin. "Almost fell on his face."

"Did you stick around after that?"

"No, I had to get the fish in the fridge, so I left."

"This has been very helpful," Val said. "If we have more questions, can we contact you through your cousin here?"

"Just let me know and I'll set up a meeting or get your answers for you," Huber said.

"That was very clever of you to get him to describe the M.E.'s misadventure," Val said to Sam after they left. "We now know that he was indeed there and saw what happened, at least at that point in time."

"And if he's correct and there was really a second set of two shots, that reinforces our assumption that someone else fired those shots, not Burton," Sam said. "It might be possible for Burton to, say, drop the gun and have it fire, hitting him. But twice? He picks it up, drops it again, and it fires and misses?"

"We didn't find another bullet, but then again I don't think anyone was looking for one," Val said.

"It's probably in the pond," Sam said. "Burton was lying face down, his feet in the water. That indicates a high probability that he was looking in the direction of the nesting area, not the pond, when he was shot. If someone was shooting at him, one bullet hit and the other would go past him and into the water–or across the pond and into the viewing area."

"If that's the case, it's just as well all this happened before the rookery opened."

"At least so far, our hypothetical scenario seems to be holding up. Someone picks Burton up in the wee hours of the morning and takes him to the rookery via the county road. They go to the gate and either open it or climb over it, get the jon boat out, and head to the front of the rookery, across from the viewing area. When the alligator appeared, we don't know, but the timing suggests that if Burton killed it, it was before he landed in the water. The M.E. is convinced that Burton could not have been that accurate with his shots after he got out. If Tom is correct about his movements, there may be as much as fifteen minutes between those two events. So Burton may have been in the water for part of that time, and then he crawls out or is pulled out, only to be shot. Talk about out of the kettle and into the pan."

"Into the fire," Val said.

"What?"

"The expression, I believe, is out of the kettle and into the fire."

"I stand corrected. But you must admit that the scenario is holding together pretty well."

"With luck we may be able to fill in some more gaps when we hear from Forensics about the camera and the phone and when we talk to Kapoor. The Wrights may be back in civilization today or tomorrow. They left here a week ago Sunday and were going to spend a week or ten days in the Cascades."

"Good Lord," Sam said. "Have we been on this that long?"

"We've been on it–note the emphasis on 'we've'–for a little less than a week. The case preceded us by a few days, remember. But I'm surprised that it's taken this long. I think it's because the initial suspects are so scattered. We've been lucky that another case hasn't turned up in Egret Bay or, given the demands on the sheriff's office, in the county. You know this won't last. If something else comes along, I'm almost positive that the chief will set this aside, especially if the new case has anything to do with public safety. If that happens, I doubt this case will ever be solved. For now, we got what we came for and we can return to the station."

The uniformed sergeant at the desk waved at them as they entered. "You have a message to call Forensics," she said. Val and Sam hurried straight to their office. Val put her phone on speaker as Sam rolled his chair over to her desk.

"This is Detective Forster in Homicide," she said to the woman who answered the phone. "We had a message to call."

"Ah, yes, Detective. Specialist Gottlieb wanted to talk to you. I'll put you through."

The phone only rang twice before it was answered. "Gottlieb."

Val introduced herself and asked if the call was in reference to the immersed electronics at the rookery pond.

"Yes, indeed. That was a challenge. We weren't as successful as we hoped, but we do have a few images for you, all of them from the camera. We've not been successful in accessing the phone. Most of the camera images don't make much sense to us, but they might to you. I can email them over or put them on the internal drive and you can download them from there."

"How many and how large are they?" Val asked.

"All in all, there are fifteen images on the memory card. Only about six, all from the central part of the card, have a readable image on them, but there's not a lot of data on any so they are not very big. Why don't I send those to you now by email, and I'll download all the rest, even the real fuzzy ones, onto the drive and you can look at them later."

"Sounds wonderful. Thank you," she said as she activated her computer.

Val had trouble identifying the first image she opened from the email. However, it only took a few seconds for Sam. "That's the bluff with the viewing platforms." Val looked closer and agreed. The image, which was mostly fuzzy black and white with a touch of color in random spots, was composed of horizontal bands: one band across the bottom was the pond, the next band up was the bluff between the pond and the viewing platforms. A blurry strip of shrubbery at the top of the bluff was broken up by periodic railings of a viewing platform. At the top, the photo showed a dark band, probably the trees and bushes on the far side of the footpath that led from platform to platform.

"Milly and Angela were right on when they said the lens Burton was using would be best used photographing the viewing platforms," Val said.

"But why?" Sam asked.

"I have absolutely no idea," Val said, opening another image. It was similar to the first but showed a more distant view of the bluffs along the far side of the island. The third had a little more color that made it easy to identify the subject as one of the many nesting platforms that had been constructed on the island. The last three were similar, two of the bluffs and one of a constructed nesting platform.

"This is sort of anticlimactic," Sam said.

"There may be some on the other images when we download them, but from what the forensic specialist said, these are the best ones."

Sam went to his computer and opened the internal drive. "He's already uploaded the other images. I can see what he meant by 'not making sense.' We can play around with these to see if we can figure out something they couldn't since we're more familiar with the scene."

"I don't know if it will make things any easier for us, but I feel that at least we have a direction. Burton is reported to have come to Egret Bay to take some photographs at the request–actually I get the idea that it was more of an order than a request–of one of the investors in the project in Ecuador. Burton went to the island and preceded to photograph the rookery and its surroundings. So I think we can safely assume that those photographs are the ones the investor asked for. But why all the sneaking around in the early morning hours instead of just getting permission to visit the island and take some pictures?"

"Maybe he wasn't given permission."

"Yes, that's possible. We can ask Wallace over at the Bird Society about that, but you'd think he'd mention it if Burton had asked for permission to visit. I'll give him a call."

Wallace was just leaving for a meeting, but he said he had about five minutes if that would help. "It won't take very long," Val said. "I only have one or two questions. Did Burton or anyone else approach you over the last, say, month about getting access to the rookery for some reason?"

"No," Wallace said. "They would have to go through me to get permission, and I wouldn't give it unless they had a very pressing reason. This is still nesting season, and we don't want the birds that are there to be unduly disturbed. We're hoping all the activity that has been going on over there doesn't have an impact on nesting next year. Usually we only go over in December or January for repairs."

"What's a 'very pressing reason'?" Val asked.

"Weather cleanup is the primary reason for interfering with nesting season, especially tropical storms or hurricanes. Infestations, like the one we had a couple of years ago, of fire ants. That kind of thing."

"And no one asked you, not even in what seemed to be jest?"

"No, not that I recall. If I think of anything, I'll call you."

Val sat at her desk, doodling on her desk calendar. What could be so important about the design of the rookery that Burton would visit it on the sly before opening time? And who was with him? "We still need to talk to Kapoor," she said. "He may be able to fill in some gaps. And we need to talk to the Wrights. They should be back by now."

To Val's surprise, the call to the Wrights' cellphone number shown on the Bird Society's list of meeting attendees was answered almost immediately. She identified herself and why she was calling and then asked if the two of them were home or still on the road.

"Almost home. We're in Houston traveling south."

"And am I speaking to Eric or to Phil?"

"This is Eric. Phil's driving."

"Would you call me as soon as you get home?"

"I can talk to you now if you wish, unless you want to talk to Phil."

"Actually I want to talk to both of you together."

"It'll be about an hour or so. We're going to stop for lunch shortly before the last stretch home."

"We're here until 5:00 at least. You can swing by the police department on your way, or we can come over to your place after you return."

"Just a sec." Val could hear him talk to Phil and there was a pause and then more conversation.

"Why don't we come by. We're pretty tired and would like to just kick back when we get home."

"That will work. When you get here, ask for either Detective Forster or Pierson in Homicide." After hanging up, she said to Sam, "Let's press our good fortune and try reaching Kapoor again." She dialed and got voicemail. She left the same message as she had previously, but tried to sound like the request to call back had some urgency–which of course, it did.

"Nope, no string of luck," she said. The office phone rang and he picked up. She heard him say, "Wait a second. I'm putting the phone on speaker so that we can both participate in the conversation."

She pulled her chair over to his desk. He opened his notepad and wrote "Kapoor" on it.

"Mr. Kapoor," she said, "thank you for calling back. We've been talking to all of the individuals who attended the birding meeting here in Egret Bay a week and a half ago. We have a few questions that we're asking everyone."

"Sorry I didn't respond sooner. I was checking my messages when you called right now. I've been in Kings Canyon National Park. The cellphone service there is very limited."

"Kings Canyon? In California? It's off the grid?"

"Yes, surprisingly. They recommend visitors use paper maps when they're here. I was hired to film some trees that so far have escaped the terrible forest fires that seem to be everywhere this summer. They want to make sure they have visual records, just in case. Absolutely beautiful country and those sequoias are magnificent. Every once in a while, this job of mine provides some real perks."

"Sounds like it. Next to that, Egret Bay is pretty dull."

"I enjoyed going down to your town. Funny, I've been living in Houston for three years and this was the first time I made it down to the coast."

"When did you arrive here?"

"Friday morning, before the meeting began. Vince–Mr. Wallace–at the Bird Society wanted me to come early and set up so we'd be ready to go when the others arrived."

"You were there to film the entire meeting?"

"Just the group discussions, not the breakout sessions, since they all reported back to the entire group."

"Isn't that a little expensive way to record the meeting's events?"

"It could be, but we've been making a point to provide low-cost services to nonprofits, especially nature-oriented nonprofits. We usually do one or two a month. The Kings Canyon trip was another."

"We?"

"My wife, Lola, and I. She does all the booking, purchasing, publicity, the things that keep us running. I do the videos and the editing."

"Did she come down to Egret Bay with you?"

"No, she seldom accompanies me because of her responsibilities with the business, but she did manage to get out of the office for Kings Canyon. That's why I missed your message. She usually picks up messages for me when I'm off the grid and sends them on or responds to let the caller know I'm out of town."

"So you came down on Friday morning. Did you stay here, or did you go back to Houston every evening?"

"I stayed there. At the Fillmore. Mr. Wallace provided the room."

"Did you meet Lester Burton while you were there?"

"Yes, he introduced himself to me when I was wandering through the lobby at the hotel and invited me to go to lunch with him. He had some questions about video production."

"And you went to lunch?"

"Yes, at a little downtown café. He was full of questions. We must have been there close to an hour because I had to excuse myself and get back to the meeting."

"What kinds of questions?"

"Some of it related to my background, or the appropriate background for someone doing work like mine, videotaping meetings. But he was also curious about short video pieces that could be used for marketing. As you know, he's a photographer–was a photographer–but he said he had never gotten into videos except for instructional pieces, like how to use a tripod or different types of lenses, that kind of thing, for YouTube. He much preferred single frame images. He talked about an ecotourism project that he was working on in Ecuador, one that would attract both native and migrant birds, with birding trails and a rookery, and…"

"He specifically said a rookery?" Sam said, interrupting Kapoor.

"Yes, he spent a couple of minutes talking about the rookery they were developing, one that would attract ecotourists from other countries, especially the U.S. There's apparently many ecolodges in Ecuador, but he was envisioning something greater, with self-led walking trails and experts not only in birds, but also in botany and zoology. Sounded like a challenging project and I half-expected him to ask me if I was good at videotaping birds, but he never did." After a pause, Kapoor said "I wonder what will happen to that project now." He paused again and then resumed, "I asked him if he was concerned about the growing cartel-related crime in Ecuador. I'm very touchy on this point, having had my best camera stolen from me in Mexico and losing my microphone to a sidewalk thief in Cambodia. He said that was something they didn't have to worry about because they had arrangements for protection."

"Did he say what kinds of arrangements?" Val asked.

"No, and I didn't ask him either. I hear the word 'protection,' and I immediately think of what that word means in many second- and third-world countries." He paused, "And here too, I guess, but not as noticeably."

"But he didn't offer you a job?" Sam asked.

"No, but he gave me his card and told me to call him if I was ever in or near Ecuador."

"What did you think of him?" Val asked.

"He was very serious, intense. I made a few side remarks that I thought were funny, but he didn't crack a smile. He listened carefully when I was explaining the advantages of taping meetings and the importance of not only careful planning prior to videotaping anything but also editing afterwards."

"Such as?" Sam asked.

"As an example, one that I gave him, the location of this project that he was talking about is apparently near or in the cloud forest. What do you do if you have planned for weeks to film a–whatever–on its nest and the whole forest is suddenly shrouded in foggy mist? If it were me, I'd film the fog coming in and try and capture the muffled sounds that come from the obscured landscape and add those to the video. But you have to be prepared with that as a fallback, have the right equipment set up in the right place, or you don't have that option."

"And that was the only time you talked to him while you were here?"

"Yes. He wasn't at the meeting. In fact, he wasn't invited, something that surprised me."

"Did you discuss the meeting?"

"No, not directly."

"When did you return home?"

"Right after breakfast on Monday morning. I had a lot of editing to do and wanted to get a start on it because I was leaving again on Wednesday morning and would have limited time to work on it for a few days. I didn't hear about the death at the rookery until later that day and I didn't find out it was Burton until after we had landed in L.A. I tried to get more information, but everyone was in a hurry and I wasn't able to find out much more until we got back in last night. I was hoping you could give me an update."

"We can answer some of your questions in a couple of minutes. Right now, we need a little information from you. Mr. Wallace said that he was late to that breakfast Monday morning."

"Only about ten minutes. That meeting made a lot of demands on him. He looked pretty bushed."

"You say Burton introduced himself to you when you were in the Fillmore lobby. Do you think he was waiting for you?" Sam asked.

"Yes, I got the idea that it was not just serendipity that we bumped into each other. I was a little flattered, to tell the truth. Here's this great photographer wanting to get information from this unknown videographer."

"Is there any particular reason why he wanted to talk to you instead of some other videographer, or do you think he was taking advantage of the fact that he wanted answers to some questions as soon as possible and you were handy?"

"Probably primarily the latter. As I said, he had mentioned bumping into acquaintances and I thought maybe one of them had told him about me. He seemed to know a lot about me and my work. He said he was interested in me because of my experience with both conferences and outdoor nature events, something all meeting participants knew. Or he may have visited my website."

"How would he know to look at your website unless he knew you'd be there?"

"I don't know. I guess he could look at the Bird Society website. It had a list of the people who would be at the meeting."

"Do you think he knew about the Bird Society meeting before he arrived in Egret Bay?"

"I don't know. He didn't seem to have been surprised to see people he knew, as if he was aware they'd be there. But it seems to be pretty coincidental that he was there at the same time."

"That answers most of my questions right now," Val said. She then gave Kapoor a brief summary of the Burton case to date, careful to keep in mind that although he was low on the list of suspects because of the early Monday morning meeting, he had not been officially cleared.

"That is a really sad tale," Kapoor said. "And you have no idea who might have been on the island with him?"

"Not at this point, no," Val said.

"Could it have been an accident?"

"We really don't know."

"I'm back in Houston for the next couple of weeks. Please let me know if you need anything else. I promise I'll be more responsive in the future."

"Thank you," Val said. She gave him her contact information in case he thought of anything more and hung up. "Well, that's interesting."

"He seems to think that Burton might not have just coincidentally come down on a weekend when the Bird Society was having their meeting. But he didn't say anything about Burton wanting to photograph the rookery here," Sam said.

"No, but the fact that he mentioned wanting to develop a rookery in Ecuador supports our theory about why he might want to visit the rookery here."

"But why did someone want him to photograph something so–for want of a better word– unexciting as viewing platforms?"

"...And nesting platforms," Val said. "It would be wonderful if we could tease at least one more image out of the camera's memory card to see if there is any other topic of interest to Burton."

"Or a photo that would help us identify who else was there."

"You are such an optimist," Val said. "But wouldn't that be nice?"

They were still talking about the conversation with Kapoor when Sam's desk phone rang. "That may be the Wrights," he said as he answered it. "Yes, thanks, we were expecting them," he said to the officer at the front desk. "Ask them to have a seat and one of us will be right out."

"Do you want me to check the conference room?" Sam asked.

"Yes, please. I'll take them over there if it's free for a half-hour or so." Val waited until Sam had called administration about the room's availability. He nodded at her as he hung up and she left to meet the Wrights.

During introductions, she noted that both young men looked sunburned and tired. She was sure that they would like to make this meeting as brief as possible so they could get home.

"You've been in the Cascades, I understand," she said as she led them to the conference room. "I hear that is beautiful country."

"It sure is," said the one who had introduced himself as Eric. "We want to return sometime. The wildlife there is phenomenal."

"And both of you are what I think Mr. Wallace called environmental scientists?"

"In a matter of speaking," Eric said. "I'm an ecologist, a title that is so broad that it means almost nothing. Since I met Phil–he's a meteorologist by training, but his work is primarily in the effects of climate change in South Texas–I've been working more as a field ecologist."

"A field ecologist?" Sam said.

"Yes, doing habitat assessments of cross-border birds, those that breed in both Mexico and the U.S., especially the Green Jay and the Great Kiskadee. Both of us are ardent birders, so the overlap in our professional life works out great."

"According to what we've been told, the two of you flew out on Sunday for Washington state," Sam said.

"Yes, we stayed in Seattle until Wednesday morning and then flew out to meet a friend in Stehekin. He's a bird and wildlife guide at a resort there, and we stayed at the resort."

"And did either of you know Lester Burton?"

"Know?" Phil said. "No, not really. We're photographers, but amateurs as far as he's concerned. The few times we've been in the same vicinity, he pretty much ignored us."

"That's a little harsh, Phil," Eric said. "We have some disagreement over Burton, as you can see," he said to the detectives. "I've always gotten along with the guy."

"I just remember what he did to MacPherson," Phil said. "Nicest guy in the business, and he was treated so shamefully."

"We heard about MacPherson," Val said. "Sad story. Did either of you talk to Burton while you were here?"

"I did, briefly," Eric said. "I asked him what he was doing in town when he joined us in the bar on Friday night. He said he was doing some research for a project that he was a consultant on. I asked him if it was related to photography, and he said no, that it had more to do with bird habitat. Beyond that, we chatted about the nice weather, wished each other well, and parted."

"But he didn't describe the project?"

"No, and I didn't ask."

"There are rumors going around among bird photographers that Burton was in the process of retiring from photography and setting up as an ecotourism businessman," Phil said. "He's been asking questions of a lot of people who have ties to the tourism industry."

Val thought of their recent conversation with Kapoor. "Any rumor about where he wants to establish this tourist business?"

"No, but my guess is that it would probably have to be in Ecuador. That's the place that he keeps returning to as both a photographer and, more recently, as a bird guide," Phil said. "Can you tell us a little more about what happened to him? We hadn't heard about it until we talked to a friend at the airport in Seattle just before we flew out to the resort. He told us that Burton had drowned," Phil said. "He also told us that he was surprised at the cause of death. He had heard from a mutual acquaintance that Burton had a phobia about still water and that he always wore a life jacket when he had to get in a small boat."

"Still water?" Sam said. "Just still water, like unrippled water in a pond or a lake?"

"Yes," Eric said. "Maybe it's the small size of the boat that worried him, but he never seemed to be hesitant about getting on a yacht or a merchant ship."

"He did fall in the water," Val said, "but he did not die from drowning. He had a heart attack."

"Was he alone?"

"No, we don't think so. That's why the case has been handed to homicide. But we don't know the exact chain of events that led to his death."

"Do you know of anyone who had such animosity toward him that they might wish him dead," Val asked.

"No, I don't," Phil said.

"Nor I," Eric said. "I mean, you can be mad at a guy, or not like him, but thank heavens that doesn't usually lead to murdering him."

Val handed each of them her business card. "Please call me if anything comes to mind regarding Burton."

"Well, that was another lost hope," Val said. "And speaking of hope, I'm beginning to lose any remnants I've had that we might solve this case."

Sam's desk phone was ringing when they returned to their office and he hurried to answer it. "Ms. Adkins. Hold for just a second. Detective Forster has just returned. I'm putting you on speaker."

"I had a talk with Terrance Easley today," Adkins said, "and I think you may be interested in his response."

"That might be helpful," Val said. "He wasn't a lot of help when I talked to him. If he knows anything, he's not willing to share with us."

"That's Terrance. Don't know why Les put up with him for so long. When we were chatting, Terrance let slip that it was ironic that Les died on a trip that he–Les–thought was a stupid, useless activity. I asked what he meant by that, and he said that one of their investors wouldn't be satisfied until every I was dotted and every T crossed. The investor was concerned about constructing stable viewing areas on an embankment or bluff or something like that. I'm not sure who that person is, but I got the idea that he's an architectural engineer who is footing a lot of the expense of enlarging an existing rookery in Ecuador into one similar to yours."

"'A stupid, useless activity,' that's how Easly described it?" Sam asked.

"Yes. I don't think Les would have been at the rookery except for the demands of that investor. That is so sad, to think that Les died because he was photographing something he thought was a fool's errand."

"I'm so sorry it worked out that way, Ms. Adkins," Val said. "Do you think Easley was being honest in his assessment? Did he know Mr. Burton that well? How long had they been working together?"

"I'm not sure, but at least five years. I'm getting more and more eager to let him go."

"We may need to talk to him again. I will let you know when we have all the information we need," Val said.

"Can't come a minute too soon. Thanks. Now as to the information I said I'd send you." She proceeded to give the detectives the names of the couples she had dinner with that Sunday night. She asked Val if there was anything new in the case that they could tell her. Val said that a few of the camera images had been partially restored, but they were difficult to make out. Val assured her that they would share what they had when they were finished.

"Today is a telephone day," Val said to Sam as he hung up and took his phone off speaker. "Terrance Easley obviously didn't tell me all he knew about Burton's business deal. We may need to talk to him again. For now, shall we continue to try and reach Burton's attorney? It's 5:00 on the east coast, so she may still be around. We can give it one more try and then let's see what other alternatives we have to get in contact with her."

"Audrey? Is that always a girl's name?" Sam asked.

"Can be either, I think. People get it confused with Gene Autry, different spelling, similar pronunciation."

"Who's Gene Autry?"

"I sometimes forget I'm working with a millennial," Val said with a grin, reaching for her phone.

This time their call to the attorney was answered with a curt, "Brennan Legal."

Val introduced herself and asked to speak to Audrey Brennan.

"She's with a client. May I take a message?"

"I called on Saturday and left a message and have tried again since then. As I said, I'm with the Homicide Division of a police department and this call is of some urgency."

"I'm sorry, the office is closed on weekends."

Val felt like asking whether the answering machine was also closed on weekends but refrained.

"This is Wednesday," she said.

"Ms. Brennan has been in court since then."

"Would you please ask her to call today when she is free. We are on central time, so we will be here until at least 7:00 your time. It won't take long, but it is important." She repeated her number and extension.

"I'll give her the message," the receptionist said. With that, she hung up.

Val sighed. "Let's get the paperwork done. My guess is that we won't hear from her, but I really don't want to leave until 6:00, just in case she calls. I don't want to give that receptionist something to complain about if we're not here."

The call did not come through and they left at 6:02.

CHAPTER 10

The Second Tuesday & Wednesday Morning

When Val stepped into the police station's reception area, she saw the chief talking to the desk officer and thought about turning around and heading back outside, but she had been seen. Too late.

"Well, Detective. Where have you been hiding the last two or so days?"

"Busy, sir."

"So I understand. Sort of grasping at straws, aren't you? Trying to find hidden messages in damaged negatives?"

Geez, he's heard about that already, Val says to herself. "We think they may be valuable in helping us understand what went on the day Mr. Burton died."

"You're still pretty certain it wasn't an accident?"

"Almost positive it wasn't an accident in the standard sense of the word."

"Meaning that something accidental could have taken place?"

"It's possible, sir."

"Rising to the level of felony?"

"Yes, sir."

"Do you think whoever had a role in Mr. Burton's death poses a risk to the public at large?"

"No, sir."

"Well, if nothing else comes up, you have 48 hours. If something else comes up, shelve the Burton case for now. Either way, I expect a closing report on my desk by Thursday morning."

"Yes, sir."

Sam was already at his desk when Val walked in.

"You look unhappy," he said.

"We have 48 hours to finish the Burton case or it goes into the archives, never to be seen again."

"You weren't able to avoid the chief?"

"He was waiting for me, I think. Probably enjoyed every minute of the soft scolding he gave me. I felt like a schoolgirl who had been waylaid by the principal."

"Hate that."

"What, feeling like a schoolgirl or being waylaid by the principal?"

"So what do we do now?" Sam said, ignoring her question.

"Have you contacted the people who Ms. Adkins said she had dinner with?"

"Yup. Done that. They all came for dinner and she ended up driving one couple home because they had too much vino."

"So the only outstanding lead is Burton's attorney?"

"Looks that way," Sam said.

"Can we go over this one more time from scratch. See if anything pops up that we've overlooked?"

"Can't hurt."

"OK, here goes. We have a photographer, Lester Burton, who traveled to an island in the middle of a rookery to take some photographs that had been ordered—contracted according to Kapoor's story—by one of the investors in his—Burton's—efforts to building an eco-friendly birding business in Ecuador. Another partner in that endeavor is Salvador, known as Sally, Rios, who is connected in some way with the drug cartels in the greater Houston area. One or more of those cartels is currently under investigation by the DEA. The DEA, in turn, has enlisted the assistance of the Fillmore County sheriff and his office in that investigation."

"Must be true. You couldn't make that up," Sam said.

"It gets better. The good Mr. Burton is found on the island, deceased, having survived a near-drowning and a gunshot wound to the thigh, only to die from a heart attack. At the time he is found, he is lying next to a dead alligator that has been shot, twice, by a very accurate gunman–gunperson–wielding the same handgun that shot Burton.

"The sheriff's office was informed of the discovery of the body and took the initial steps in certifying the death, attempting to locate next of kin, ordering autopsy, and sending CSI deputies to the scene. It was not until two days after the event that the brilliant detectives in the City of Egret Bay Homicide Division were formally handed the case."

"And by that time," Sam added, "the crime scene was a mess and nothing of consequence had been discovered there, including a missing handgun, a camera, and a cellphone, all of which there was reason to believe that Burton had with him when he landed on the island."

"We are convinced," Val continued, "that said Burton did not go out to the island by himself because he couldn't swim and must have gone by boat. That means he needed to go out there by some sort of watercraft, of which none could be found. We are sure, for various reasons, that he arrived on the island before he fell–or was pushed–into the water. We believe he was taken out to the island by an unknown person or persons in the jon boat owned by the Egret Bay Bird Society and housed–kept, moored, whatever you do with a boat–on the mainland at the rear of the island."

"And that boat," Sam added, "was protected from thieves by a gate with a coded lock known by few. It is possible, however, to climb over the gate. But it would be difficult to carry anything heavy, such as another watercraft, over the top of the gate without help of at least two more people. The idea of using a lighter-weight craft, such as a kayak or canoe, is ruled out because of the proximity of alligators. This reinforces the idea that, if there were only two, or maybe three or four, people—Burton and his unknown escort or escorts—they used the jon boat to get to the island."

"I agree," Val said. "More and more, I'm siding with a single companion. I can't figure out any reason there should have been more than one other person and that person drove him out there and probably handled the watercraft."

"Burton could have handled the watercraft."

"But he hates—fears—small boats in still water. I don't think he would choose to handle the boat."

"I agree," Sam said.

"Once on the island," Val continued, "Burton took photographs of the bank across from the island where the bird-viewing platforms are located and also some photos of man-made bird nesting platforms on the island. And when he fell—or was pushed—into the water, he did not have his handgun with him. Possibly dropped it when he fell. Can't figure out why he would have removed it from the holster and left it on the island. Upon making it back up on dry land, he either picked up the gun and accidentally shot himself, or the other person shot him."

"And it's more likely the other person shot him because there were two shots," Sam said, "but only one hit Burton. Burton could not have accidently shot himself twice."

"The other person then left," Val said, "but we don't know if that was before or after Burton died. We also don't know if that person pushed him in the water or tried to help him out, or even if that person left while Burton was still in the water...."

"No," Sam said. "Burton had to have been out of the water before the other person left *if*—and I stress the *if*—the other person was the one who fired the shots. Burton was shot after he got out of the water."

"Ah, yes. So we don't know if Burton was dead when that other person left but we are pretty sure he was no longer in the water. But he was certainly injured or already deceased by then, and no one called for help or notified authorities."

"And that is what we don't know. The most important thing," Sam said. "Who was that person?"

"Well, it was either someone he knew, or it was someone he didn't know or didn't know well. If the latter, we can stop now. The only person on our working list that we haven't talked to is Burton's attorney. I really don't expect anything there because of client-attorney confidentiality and the fact that she does not seem predisposed to even bother to call us and confirm that expectation."

Just then, Val's phone rang. "Ah," Sam said as Val put the phone on speaker, "maybe the answer is at hand."

"Detective, this is Gottlieb in Forensics. I've been fooling around with the nine images that I said were fuzzy and worked out a few more details on five of them. Three are earlier on the memory card than the six that had some details on them that I sent you earlier, and two are from near the end of the card. I'm going to let you take a look since you're more aware of the environment where these were taken than I am. Don't get your hopes up, however. There's no one in the background waving at the camera."

"Thank you. We appreciate your working on this. We were told that Forensics tends to resist giving up on the tasks before them and you've confirmed that."

"Glad to know we have a reputation. I can send them electronically or, if you have an hour or two to wait, I'll have someone bring you prints. No sense in sharing the few remaining. They are still graphic gibberish."

"Can we have both electronic and prints?"

"Sure thing. I'll send the electronic images right now. The pixel density is very low so I'll just attach them to an email."

As soon as the email arrived, Val opened them one after another, but there was little to see but shadows. One of them looked like another version of the viewing platforms, another had what looked like wavy lines." She shrugged. "Maybe the prints will be better," she said.

"Well, they won't be worse," Sam said as he looked over her shoulder at her screen. "What say we take a break and go for donuts and coffee. I feel a sugar low coming on."

"One of us needs to stay here, just in case. Coffee, as you know, black. And a fritter instead of donut."

She was glad she had made that decision to stay and cover the phones when the long-awaited call from Burton's attorney came through–finally. She answered it with the long version of her credentials.

"Detective Valerie Forster, Homicide Division, Egret Bay Department of Public Safety, Law Enforcement Division."

"Please hold while I transfer you to counselor Brennan," the caller said.

There was a half-minute pause before another voice came online, "Audrey Brennan."

"Ms. Brennan, this is Detective Forster. I'm head of the investigation into the death of Lester Burton. I understand that he was a client of yours."

"Yes, and I'm sure you understand the limitations of the information I can give you."

"What I really want to know is if Mr. Burton ever exhibited some fear or deep concern about his personal safely."

"No, never."

Well, that was blunt, Val thought. "And did you have a role in his efforts to develop an ecotourism business in Ecuador?"

"I am the American attorney of note for El Refugio de San Juan."

Well, at least they now had a name for Burton's project. "We understand that Mr. Burton traveled to Egret Bay at the behest of one of his investors, but we do not know the reason for that visit. Did he mention to you why he was coming down here?"

"He told me in passing that he was going to take photographs of a birding site near Houston. He didn't mention Egret Bay."

"But he didn't say what kinds of photographs?"

"No."

"Are you familiar with the name Salvadore Rios?"

"Yes, I know the name."

"Did Mr. Burton mention visiting Mr. Rios when he was in Houston."

"No."

"Can you think of anything that you can tell us that might help us in our investigation?"

"No."

"Thank you. You've been very helpful," Val said as she ended the call. That was a lost cause. Obviously, Brennan thought she was on the witness stand with those terse responses. And they had waited for this conversation? She typed "El Refugio de San Juan" in her search engine and came up with...nothing. They had a day and a half left and were getting nowhere fast.

Sam returned and set a container with two cups of coffee on his desk. He opened the bag and pulled out a rather large pastry and a napkin. "One apple fritter coming up," he said as he handed it to Val. He stopped mid-action and looked at her. "What's wrong?" She told him about her phone call.

"So we're now in possession of the name of a non-existing entity? I guess you can call that progress, however slight. Eat your fritter and then we can talk." He handed her one of the coffees.

There was a knock on their partially open door and a uniformed officer stuck his head in. "We have a delivery from Justice for y'all. Can you sign for it?"

"Sure," Sam said as he initialed the delivery form. "Thanks."

He put the envelope on his desk and they both sat there until they finished eating. It was Sam who broke the silence.

"Do you have the copies of the photos that Deputy Jefferson took during the initial visit to the island?"

"Yes, they're in the file."

"And the ones that the CSI deputy took when the M.E. went out?"

"Yes, also in the file."

"And I've printed the couple of shots I took as I was walking around the pond and put them in the file. Didn't get many because I was too busy looking for snakes."

"And now we have the photos, such as they are, from Burton's camera," Val said. "Why don't we put them all out on the table and see if we can learn anything by comparing and contrasting."

"It sounds like something to do. I think I'm at my wits end, but let's give it a try." Sam cleared off the top of his desk while Val went through the files and pulled out the photos. They then opened the envelope from Forensics and pulled the five photos that had been sent over.

"Let's look at them all carefully," Sam said. "Especially the background, looking for anything we didn't see before. We need to compare them. Is anything different?"

"And then we can use them to fill in some of the blank spots on the images from Burton's camera," Val said. "That might help."

Sam's photos and the two sets of images from Jefferson and the crime scene investigator had time and date stamps and were easy to put in chronological order. While they could put the images from Burton's camera in the order Forensics had identified them as being recorded on the memory card, they had no idea at this point whether any of the earlier ones were taken before the trip to the island or if all were taken while Burton was on the island.

"It would make sense," Sam said, "that Burton, as a professional photographer, would have used a fresh memory card for each project, just like we do when we close a case. If he did, he might have put in a new memory card when he arrived in Egret Bay. Or, I guess, he may have waited until he arrived at the rookery."

"So far, so good," Val said.

"I think," Sam said, holding one of new prints so Val could see it, "that this is another shot of the viewing platforms." She looked at it carefully and agreed.

"We need a magnifying glass," Sam said. "These other four don't seem to match any of the previous ones, but they could have been taken from a different viewpoint."

"Or before he reached the rookery," Val said. "I'll be right back," she said as she left the room. Sam continued to look at the photos, sorting them into subject matter as best he could: viewing platforms, nesting platforms, the bluff between the viewing area and the pond. He compared them within each of the subjects but couldn't see any differences except for the angle of the shot. One of the viewing platform images looked as though it may have been taken on the boat as it came around the end of the island. No matter how hard he tried, he couldn't make out any semblance of a person on the boat. But then he remembered that if there were only two people, the other person would have been at the rear with the motor, not in front.

Val returned brandishing a small magnifying glass on a handle.

"Where on earth did you get that?" Sam asked.

"I noticed last week that Rosie Perez was using this to work a crossword puzzle in the break room. I teased her about growing old and needing glasses. She's still working intake while waiting for her foot to heal, so I tracked her down and borrowed it."

Sam picked up one of the photos from near the end of the memory card from Burton's camera and began scanning it with the magnifier. "This helps some. I can make out some things. The last one looks like a photo of an old log."

"What old log? I don't remember an old log," Val said.

"Good Lord!" Sam said. "It's the alligator!" He passed the photo and the magnifier to Val.

"You're right, it is! I doubt they would have landed if the alligator was already there, so it must have come ashore while he was taking the other photos."

"Are there any photos on the card that were taken after this one?"

"No," Val said, looking at the list from Forensics. "That's the last photo we have from his camera. So he stopped taking pictures when the alligator arrived."

"That makes sense. Would you stand there and continue taking photographs with an alligator just a few feet away from you?"

Sam picked up another print, this one from the beginning of the memory card. "This is the one that confuses me," Sam said, reaching for the magnifier. "It looks like rippling water, but the pond is very still." He scanned it from top to bottom, then side to side, and then put it down and sat back.

"Val."

She looked at him and then picked up the photo and the magnifier and took it to her desk where the light was a little better. She scanned it just as he had.

"Look near the upper left-hand corner," Sam said.

"Not sure, but it looks like a bird's beak."

"Now look over a little to the right of the beak and up a little, what do you see?"

"It looks like a bumpy caterpillar."

"Look closer."

She looked at the beak and at what she had called a caterpillar, and then she saw what he had seen.

"And the ripples," she said, "aren't from the water. They are feathers, layers of feathers. Maybe a wing.... Oh, my God, it looks like...."

"Yes?"

"Well, I'll be damned. He just couldn't keep from taking photos of birds. What I thought was a caterpillar is a comb!"

"Yup. His passion may have solved the case. Couldn't resist taking a shot of a bird, not even one of a chicken," Sam said.

"Oh, my God," Val said. "Ms. Gomez, we are onto you!"

Val sat down. She was at a loss for words.

"Ka-ching," she finally says. "It all falls into place. Burton must have been at her house sometime over that three-day period. She has no alibi for Monday morning except the chickens. Lives close. Knows key code to gate. Knows how to use the jon boat. Listened to all of the chatter around the case from the deputies the day the bodies were found–the EMT, the M.E., people from CSI, and Forensics. Then later, you and me. Conveniently out of town for three days after Burton is found. Time to gather her wits and figure out what to do next. Just one problem."

"Yeah," Sam said. "Who will write us out a warrant based on a fuzzy photo of a chicken?"

"Do we have anything else to go on?" Val asked.

"No photos, no fingerprints that would hold up. Of course her fingerprints are on everything. No witnesses–except the one that was killed and he couldn't relate what went on anyway–no footprints, no pieces of clothing snaggled on twigs. I doubt anyone ever saw them together. She may have driven him out to her house, so no car registered to him in front of her place."

"His fingerprints at her house?"

"I suppose that's possible, but we don't even know where to look. Did he ever go inside? And she's had days to wipe the place down, and her car too. Doubt we could get permission anyway. 'Gee, judge, we have this photo of a chicken and it looks like one of hers....'"

Val interrupted. "That won't work either. What do you bet that chicken tasted pretty good after she cooked it."

"So what do we do now?" Sam asked.

"We write this up and give it to the chief."

"We'll be the laughingstock of the department, you know."

"It's the price we pay for our public service."

"Could we at least go out to lunch first so we can write this all up on a full stomach?" Sam said.

"I just finished a giant fritter."

"Desert before lunch. That works."

They put the photos away and left.

It took them almost two hours upon their return to write up the summary for the chief. They kept writing and rewriting, trying to make it sound technical and professional. They finally gave up and sent it on. The chief must have read it that afternoon because a uniformed officer passed Sam in the hall and congratulated him on catching the serial killer chicken. It was past 4:00 when they were summoned to the chief's office. They were not surprised to see the district attorney there as well. The chief motioned them to take a seat. "Ah," Val thought. "Maybe we're not on the carpet." She wasn't sure what their status was, given the conclusion they had offered in the report.

The chief was the first to speak. "You're trying to tell us that you think you know who was on the island with the deceased and may have been involved in his death, not based on hard evidence, but because you saw a blurry photo of what you think was a chicken?"

"Yes, sir," Val said.

"But you don't know what role this person who owned the chicken played in the death?"

"No, sir, but we are almost certain that she left the deceased–alive, dying, or dead–when she left the island. In addition, she was taking the only means that the deceased would have had to leave if he was still alive."

"You don't know if she shot him or if he accidentally shot himself?"

"No, sir, but we do know there were two shots fired after he got out of the water and that she had to have been responsible for at least one of them."

"And there is a dead alligator. Who shot that?"

"We believe Mr. Burton shot the alligator."

"And did Mr. Burton fall into the water or was he pushed."

"We don't know, sir."

"But you think we should close the case?"

"Not close, no, but put on suspension. We really don't believe anyone else was involved in the events of that day, but we lack evidence to prove that the woman we suspect was the person who may have been responsible for Mr. Burton's death or, at the very least, left the scene of an accident that resulted in injury or death."

"And do you know why he was out there? Something about photographs?"

"Yes, sir. He was asked–no, I think, coerced–to take photos of the rookery and its tourism amenities, viewing platforms and such, so they could be replicated at a rookery being developed in Ecuador."

"Good Lord," was all the chief said.

"Have you talked to this woman?" the DA asked.

"Yes, but only in reference to her actions in taking individuals out to the island for investigative purposes."

"And where does this chicken come in?"

"The woman said that she was tending her chickens at the time of Mr. Burton's death. That's how we knew she had chickens. So we thought of her immediately when we found that Mr. Burton had taken a photograph of a chicken. We knew that he had contacted someone to take him to the island, but all our efforts to find out who that person is led nowhere."

"And you didn't think of her as a suspect earlier?"

"No, sir. She had been extremely helpful with the case and we had no indication that there was any type of relationship between her and Mr. Burton."

"But now you think there is–or was?"

"Must have been if our assessment is correct, because we are almost certain he was at her home within a few days of his death."

"There are other chickens in town," the chief said. "Did I really just say that?" he asked as an aside.

"Yes, sir. Probably quite a few, but Mr. Burton was a wildlife photographer. I don't think he sought out chickens to photograph. But if one was standing right in front of him...he might succumb to the temptation."

"And what else led you to target this person?" the DA asked.

"She fit all the qualifications we had identified for the person who went to the island with Mr. Burton. She knew the code to the lock on the gate, thereby allowing easy access. She was skilled in handling the particular watercraft that was used, she lived nearby and would have time to clean up before meeting with others investigating the scene, and she wasn't on the list we had of prime suspects."

"And those prime suspects were...?" the chief asked.

"People who really disliked the deceased or who had friends who had been hurt by his actions. It just so happened that there was a meeting in town of wildlife scientists, artists, and photographers, most of them acquainted with Mr. Burton and a few who really disliked him and had reasons to. But they all had verifiable alibis."

"You know, of course," the DA said, "that this is going nowhere based on what you have. No judge will approve a warrant. We don't even have enough to be able to call her in for an interview. All she needs to do is show up with her lawyer and that's that."

"There is also the wrinkle," the chief said to the DA, "that the deceased seems to have a business relationship with a suspected cartel member in Houston."

"Did you look into that?" the DA asked Val.

"Yes, but the relationship seems to be as much a friendship as a business relationship. We do not believe that Mr. Burton's death was the result of having crossed the cartel somehow. We were asked to not dig too deeply into that, but really didn't think we needed to after our conversation with the alleged cartel member."

"You talked with him?" the DA asked with some concern.

"With my permission," the chief said to the DA. "And only in relation to the deceased's reasons for being on the island."

All four sat there for a few seconds without saying anything before Val said, "So where do we go from here?"

"My suggestion," the chief looking at the DA, "...and tell me if I'm off-base here...is that you go out and visit her one more time and walk her through everything. See if she slips up somewhere or gives you something you can pursue. If not, suspend the case unless something opens it back up. We have more serious problems we need to attend to in cold cases, and tourism is at its height right now. We're lucky that we haven't had to investigate another homicide for the past week. That won't last."

"That's fine," the DA said. "And while you're there," he said to Val, "ask if you can take a picture of her chickens."

When they got back to their office, Sam plopped into his chair and swung around a few times. "That went better than I anticipated," he said.

"Yes, indeed. Let's give Ms. Gomez a call and set up a time to talk to her once more." She looked for Gomez's number. The phone rang quite a few times, but no answer.

"Maybe she's at the rookery," Sam said.

"That was her cellphone I called. But I guess it's possible she turns it off when she's near the birds."

"You didn't leave a message."

"No, you're right. The voicemail never kicked in and I let it ring at least a dozen times."

"We can try again tomorrow morning," Sam said.

"Let's call it a day and go home. Tomorrow is another day."

"*Gone with the Wind*."

"What?"

"The closing lines of *Gone with the Wind*, 'Tomorrow is another day.'"

"I thought it was 'Frankly, my dear, I don't give a damn.'"

"Nope," Sam said, "but that's closer to my feelings right now."

"And how on earth did you know that line?"

"I saw the movie. I'm not entirely a cultural idiot, you know."

Val was rather surprised when she got a call about 9:00 that evening from Vince Wallace. Why would the Bird Society be calling her this late?

"I hope I'm not bothering you," Wallace said, "but you gave me your cellphone number."

"What's up."

"Lainey Gomez just contacted me from Guayaquil, Ecuador. She's taken a job down there as rookery manager for an ecotourism project now under construction. She's not coming back. She told me to tell you that she's sending you a letter."

Val was stunned. "That was rather precipitous, wasn't it? Did you know about this?"

"No. Thankfully we have a good crew who can help with the rookery here until I can find a new manager, but I think there is more to the story than she told me. Can you fill me in?"

"I don't think I need to fill you in. My guess is you've already guessed why she took off. If it's any consolation, I don't think she intentionally killed Burton."

"But she was there?"

"I think so. Yes."

"Is she safe?"

"You mean from extradition? Probably yes."

"Will you share the letter?"

"If I have permission, yes. It's no doubt a legal document, so I can't promise."

"Thank you," he said, and hung up.

Val called Sam and left a message when he didn't answer. Then she went to the kitchen where Deke was scooping ice cream into a bowl and told him what had happened. She thought about calling the chief, but that could wait until tomorrow. She didn't know if she was angry, relieved, or sad. A bowl of ice cream helped calm her down.

It was fortuitous that the Burton case came to such an abrupt end. Val and Sam were both roused from their sleep at 4:00 on Wednesday morning after a late-night reveler discovered a badly beaten body at the base of a pier overlooking the Gulf. As they headed across the sand in the dark to begin their new investigation, Val realized that Sam had not listened to her message from the previous night. She decided to wait until they were through with their tasks out on the beach to bring him up to speed on Gomez. They were able to leave just as day was breaking, revealing a magnificent gulf sunrise. "Breakfast?" Sam asked. Val nodded.

Val waited until their orders had been placed before bringing Sam up to date on the Burton case. "A letter?" he said, with some bewilderment. "So we were right with our conclusions."

"Yes, no doubt. She must have been planning this move for days, maybe even since the morning Burton died."

"She only had a week."

"She may have had some help."

"Rios?"

"That's my guess. If she knew about him and his relationship to Burton. But I can't think of anyone else. She might give us that detail in the letter."

"I'm of mixed emotions about this."

"So am I. The Bird Society is in a quandary. Wallace seemed to be most concerned about rookery management. I'm sure that this is a problem he didn't need, what with the obligations of their grant and all."

"Well, we can at least show the chief and the DA that we're not a couple of idiots to call the case solved because of a blurry chicken photo."

"Yes, there is that."

The breakfast came and they ate mostly in silence, paid their bill, and went back to work.

CHAPTER 11

Two Weeks Later

To: Detectives Forster and Pierson,
    No doubt you are now aware, if you weren't before, that I played a role in the death of Lester Burton. I was initially pretty sure that I was safe from suspicion, but the uncertainty began to gnaw on me as I drove to the wedding in Louisiana. Could Tom have seen what went on and just decided that he didn't want to get involved? Did someone see me with Burton in my car? Even if I was accused but not convicted, the legal costs would be enough to bankrupt me and I would most certainly lose my job and many of my friends and possibly my home. I became concerned that if I managed to escape capture, someone else might be charged and suffer the consequences that so frightened me. I decided to write this letter to make sure that never happened.

Lester Burton contacted me about a week before he flew down here. He wanted a tour of the rookery and I was glad to oblige. He asked that I keep quiet about his visit so that he would not be bothered by other photographers who wanted to ask him questions about his techniques. I agreed because I knew he was a photographer of some note and I was pleased that he wanted to photograph the rookery. We settled on the Thursday before the Bird Society meeting for the tour. He knew about the Bird Society meeting somehow and was rather upset that he wasn't included, but he had other things more pressing that needed to be done while he was in town.

I picked him up on Thursday morning and took him all around the rookery and the surrounding woods. That included walking the entire *path around the island.* As we were walking, he periodically asked if I knew the Spanish word for this and that. I'm not Hispanic, but my husband and his entire family speak both Spanish and English in the home and I had become good enough to serve as a translator for Spanish-speaking visitors at the rookery. When we finished the tour, I took him to my home for an iced tea and to talk about the trip to the rookery and he said that he and his partners were upgrading a natural rookery in Ecuador and were looking for a manager. The search was turning out to be more difficult than they had thought and he wanted to know if I was interested in applying. I was amazed. I told him I was self-taught in rookery management, but that didn't seem to bother him. He said that he had asked around about the rookery, if people liked it, if there were complaints, etc. He was especially pleased with my bilingual ability and thought that was a real plus. He told me to think it over and he'd contact me the next day.

On Friday morning he called and said that his partners were very happy with the photographs he had taken on the tour, but that they wanted some that showed the viewing platforms and the drop-off to the water under the platforms so that the rookery's architect could study them. He said that he had argued that they were not necessary, that the terrain in Ecuador was different than that at the rookery, but the architect said he wouldn't go any further without that information. I knew that Vince would not approve a visit to the island, but I thought if we went early in the morning, just after sunup, we would not be observed, providing we were finished by 7:00 at the latest. The birds leave soon after dawn to feed, so we might be able to avoid unduly disturbing them. I must admit I really wanted to please him because of the rookery offer, even though I was aware that he might be using me.

I picked him up at his hotel's side entrance and we were at the rookery just after it began to get light. I hadn't been aware of his fear of water until we got to the boat and I motioned for him to get in. I don't know what he was expecting, but thankfully we had life vests there and I gave him one and it seemed to reduce his anxiety. I noticed that he was carrying and *that upset me, but he said that it was a habit where there were poisonous snakes since he had been bitten twice in the past, so I dropped the subject.*

When we got to the island, I jumped out and pulled the boat onto the shore, tying it off on a small bush. Burton, complaining about the humidity, took off his life vest and tossed it in the boat. He was very cautious about getting out, but once on land he began to wander around a little, taking a few photos here and there of the viewing platforms across the water and also of the nesting platforms on the island. We were getting ready to leave when the alligator, El Jefe, the boss, as I called him, slid out of the water onto the island and made himself comfortable on the sandy shelf there, lying about four feet from the side of our boat.

Burton was upset with the alligator's presence. I tried to tell him that I didn't think we were in any danger. It was still mating season and El Jefe had spent the night feeding and mating and was probably exhausted. He had never been at all disturbed by people on the island providing that they didn't move too quickly or make too much noise. To my horror, Burton pulled out his pistol and aimed at the alligator. I said "Don't shoot. It's a wonderful animal and you'll frighten the birds." But he aimed and shot the poor thing right through the eye. El Jefe reared in the air, trying to bellow but nothing came out of his mouth but a faint bark. He shivered all over, reared again, and fell down with another barking sound and laid still.

The birds all around us went crazy and began flying around. I was crying and started hitting Burton with my fists, asking him over and over why he had done that. I don't think I have been more upset about something ever before in my life. But he just pushed me away and said that it was only an alligator, what was I so upset about? Then he said that he had always wanted to shoot an alligator and that he understood that there was this soft spot in back of the head that would kill one instantly. Even though this one was already dead, he thought he'd take a look. He handed his camera to me and told me to take a picture, but I dropped the camera and tried to pull him away from El Jefe. Burton straddled the animal, felt the back of its head until he found the spot he was looking for, raised his pistol and shot it again. El Jefe must not have been dead because he reared again, turned to try and grab Burton, flicking its tail, gave him a swat across his legs, and the next thing I know Burton had thrown his gun in the air, taken a few steps backward, and ended up in the pond, thrashing around.

"I can't swim," I heard him say. He kept going partially under and was swallowing water as he tried to yell. I was still sobbing and shaking with anger and I just let him flounder. If I had been in the water with him, I would have pushed him under. He came up once more, nearer the shore and grabbed onto El Jefe's tail, using it to pull himself gradually onto land. With some effort he stood up and began moving toward me, cursing me and calling me horrible names. I picked up the gun from where it was lying and pointed it at him, telling him to stop, but he kept advancing, although with some effort. I shot once in the air, but that didn't stop him. So I shot him. He looked at me with such hate, and then he fell and, just like El Jefe, tried to get back up and then fell down again. I let him lay there for a few minutes, watching to see if he would get up and attack me again, and then I realized that he was either unconscious or dead.

I looked around. The birds were still flying around and squawking. I looked at my watch and realized that it was almost 7:00 and that people would be on the viewing platforms within a short period. I didn't bother to check Burton. I really didn't care at that time. I thought I was done for, that he would tell the police that I had shot him, I would be arrested, and that was that. I threw the camera and the pistol into the pond, saw Burton's cellphone sticking out of his pocket and pulled it out and threw it in too, got in the boat and left. The birds were beginning to settle as I tied the boat up and just left it there, half in the water, by the boathouse. I grabbed the life jacket and took it with me, drove home, cleaned up, and waited for the police to call. Instead I get a call from Doris, one of the volunteers, telling me that there was a dead man on the island. You know pretty much what happened after that.

At first, I thought I had lucked out. Maybe I was in the clear. If Tom saw Burton and me, he hadn't said anything. I knew how hard it is to *remember lies, so I decided to answer all questions honestly and hope for the best. But guilt does strange things to you. I jumped every time a car door slammed near my home. I tried to eat, but nothing tasted good. I kept thinking about fingerprints and the things I had thrown in the pond. No doubt they would fish them out. I couldn't remember if Burton had taken any pictures of me when he was at my house. I didn't know if they would be destroyed or if the camera was waterproof. I kept going over what had happened. The wedding in Louisiana was a godsend. It gave me a while to think about what had happened and I came back with a determination to see this whole thing through.*

I called you as you had requested and was relieved when I seemed to have passed that first test. No sooner had I hung up when I got another call, this one from a man called Salvadore Rios, one of Burton's partners in the ecotourism venture. He said that Burton had told him about me and given him my phone number so he could talk to me about the rookery job. When I realized that the job offer had been legitimate, I came unglued. I told Rios what had happened at the rookery and that I couldn't take the job because I would probably be arrested. When I was through, he was very quiet and I started getting scared. But then he said that he was very sad about Burton's death because he really liked the guy and loved talking to him about birds. However, my story was consistent with what he knew about Burton. He was known to act without thinking, ignoring the effect of his actions upon other people and the wildlife around him. Mr. Rios said that he had warned Burton about his behavior, but it obviously hadn't done any good. And then he asked how much money I had that was easily accessible. He said that he knew a little about the law and that he doubted that I would face serious charges given the circumstances and Burton's reputation, but that the cost of defending myself if someone wanted to charge me of manslaughter or something worse could reach into the thousands. The other partners in the project wanted to continue, but they needed a rookery manager. He asked if I had a passport and I said I did. He urged me to go to Ecuador, that he would pay for the ticket and would take care of any technicalities that I might need as a temporary res-

ident, or as a permanent one if I wished, and mentioned a salary that was four times what I was making in Egret Bay.

I called my son and he came over and we talked for hours about what to do. The next morning, Saturday, I called my attorney and we met to complete the paperwork to transfer what I had to my son. It wasn't much outside of the house and car. I went home, packed, and left by Sunday afternoon, staying at a hotel in Houston. I flew out Monday night. Mr. Rios has been very helpful and the people here are friendly. The birds are absolutely gorgeous. And, just like the Egret Bay rookery, the pond is patrolled by alligators.

Lainey Gomez

Val read the letter out loud to Sam. They sat in silence for a few moments and then she said, "I guess I need to take this to the chief and then we can begin closing the case."

"What if she comes back, turns out she doesn't like it down there."

"I doubt she'll come back to Egret Bay. What are we going to do, put out a notice to apprehend her if we find out she's back in the U.S.? Forget that."

"It's ironic that the task that led to his death was one that he thought was unnecessary, a foolish request. That brought a rather dismal end to an adventurous career," Sam said.

"That's not quite correct," Val said. "It was not the task that did him in. It was his disregard for the life of an alligator that led to his death. The unnecessary task merely took him to the island. From there, it was all in his hands. I read somewhere that someone said that we drive the car of our life. Burton's car crashed when he shot El Jefe."

ACKNOWLEDGMENTS

Thanks to Suzanne Becker, Peter Deichmann, Susanne Kaboord, Alice Anne O'Donell, and Mary Vinnedge for their time and insights, and for sharing their knowledge, each in their own way.

The front cover photography and design are by the author.

www.ingramcontent.com/pod-product-compliance
Lightning Source LLC
LaVergne TN
LVHW010203070526
838199LV00062B/4474